Middle Time

PRIYA VASUDEVAN

Middle Time

NIYOGI
BOOKS

Published by
NIYOGI BOOKS
Block D, Building No. 77,
Okhla Industrial Area, Phase-I,
New Delhi-110 020, INDIA
Tel: 91-11-26816301, 26818960
Email: niyogibooks@gmail.com
Website: www.niyogibooksindia.com

Editor: Nandita Jaishankar/Niyogi Books
Cover Design: M/s. Seema Design
Layout: Nabanita Das/Niyogi Books

ISBN: 978-81-89738-70-9

Publication: 2011
Reprint: 2018

This is a work of fiction. The names, characters and incidents portrayed in it are a work of the author's imagination. Any resemblance to actual persons, living or dead, events or localities, is entirely coincidental.

Printed at: Niyogi Offset Pvt. Ltd., New Delhi, India.

To Vasu and Billy, for all their patient listening
and to Usha, for being there for me
in all the most important moments of my life

Cast of Characters

Hampi

Achalabbe	A *devadasi* of Virupaksheshwara Temple at Hampi who lives near Alur, at Jogahalli
Ningi	Achale's maid
Bhima	Achalabbe's major-domo
Ajji Roopavathi	Achale's grandmother, a retired *devadasi* of Simhapuri
Puttalakshmi	Achale's mother
Iruneeranbadi Narayana Iyengar	Achale's father and a physician at the King's court
Indra and Kesava	Achale's brothers
Chenna	A Dombra acrobat who knows Bhima and helps in the investigation
Acharyulu	A singing sage
Ajji Jakkini	A Jain nun
Malavva	A gossipy washerwoman
Madhava Shastry	A poet who seeks fame at the court
Virabhadra	A potter and sculptor
Bhadrinatha Shastry	An ambitious Brahmin landlord
Manjunatha	An illegitimate child who becomes a Brahmin saint
Thulasi	A widow who has a son, Manjunatha, out of wedlock

Narayanacharlu	Thulasi's reversioner; also her brother-in-law and a chief suspect in her murder
Amalotpava Devi	A minor queen with major plans
Achyuta Deva Raya	King of Vijayanagara and brother of Krishna Deva Raya
Aliya Rama Raya	A powerful noble and son-in law of Krishna Deva Raya who covets the crown; a plotter inimical to *devadasis*, especially one as powerful as Achale
Kondoja	A barber who rose to nobility and is in Rama Raya's toils
Vajrabahu	A Sangama courtier who wants power
Boriah	A Bedar goatherd
Betappa	A watchman and official chief investigator

CHENNAI

Maya	A lawyer in Chennai
Patricia and Meena	Maya's partners in ALIBAI, their law firm
Tulsi	Maya's client who dies mysteriously
Srinivas Shastry, Shibani	Tulsi's soon to be ex-husband and their daughter
Toni and Anees	Tulsi's partners in Ghungroo, their fusion dance school
Kamala	Maya's clerk
Thomas	Owner of Footloose, a school of modern dance
Harsha and Surilee	Instructors at Footloose
Sunny, Paru and Uma	Dancers at Footloose
Mridula, Aryan and Meghna	Maya's elder sister, her husband and children
Dr. Gopalakrishnan	A helpful History don

PROLOGUE

ALUR, MADHAVASWAMY TEMPLE
WINTER, 1535

Thulasi felt her son's absence before she actually saw it. He must have gone down to the river for his ablutions, she thought, drowsily. It was still dark—that time before dawn when the light was stealing across the sky, but the heavens seemed to be waiting for that first warmth of cosmic breath. The fresh breeze was already carrying the sound of the bells of the Madhavaswamy Temple which dominated the distant horizon. That was what had woken her. She lay awake for some time, letting sleep leave her completely before she got up to another day. She waited for a few moments. No Manju. The first sight that met her sleepy eyes when she went out was Manju's freshly washed loincloth drying on a bush. She felt a faint whisper of unquiet. Where was Manju?

"Manju?" she called. "Manjooooo!" Sleep fled in panic. She began to run towards Alur.

In Alur, the temple drum sounded, its deep bass notes issuing from the portal, presided over by the mark of Vishnu guarded by his conch, the *panchajanya* and his wheel of destruction, the *sudarshana*, symbols of protection and admonition. The early morning ceremony was almost drawing to a close. The sweeper stopped in alarm as Manju ran down the main street, scattering the coins on the cloth spread before a streetside musician who stopped his flute-playing, and gaped. In the Brahmin enclosure, housewives were gathered near the well. They looked curiously at the small boy until Rangi, the chief priest's wife, exclaimed, "Aii! It is that slut Thulasi's son! What has brought him to the village after we banished her? See his audacity, eh!"

Lakshmi, a young woman from a distant village who had recently married a minor priest, looked questioningly at her. "Banished? Why did they do that, *akka*?"

Before Rangi could reply, they heard a shout from the temple. Flinging their pots down, the clatter echoing the shout, they ran into the temple courtyard. The boy had entered the temple and was climbing the sacred pillar in the inner courtyard. A young priest tried to climb up after him but the post was slippery and the child too agile, so he gave up after a few attempts. The boy soon reached the top. By this time, a crowd had gathered around the pillar. The boy hung precariously, a leg braced on the top of the column, hands clinging on to the decorative frieze on the top. "Ranganatha Sastry! Ranganatha Sastry!" The piping voice rang out strong and clear across the courtyard. "When will you arrange my thread ceremony?"

Rangi's husband pushed his way through the crowd. Beads of sweat appeared on his forehead and ran down his neck to his chest. He wiped them with the thin shawl covering his shoulders. "Manju, *putta*, come down. We will arrange it. We will hold a council and decide. Climb down, son."

"No! Tell me now! When will you arrange my thread ceremony?" The answer was loud and definite.

"*Putta*, listen to reason. You know that only the twice-born can wear the sacred thread. We will have to talk it over." He did not say it but everyone present, including the boy, understood the implication. Since his origin was not clear and his mother insisted on her preposterous story, there was little hope of the matter being resolved by mere discussion.

"Don't promise him anything," the village headman who was standing close-by warned. "We don't want to condone immorality and start a trend."

Someone in the crowd said, "Do you think a boy could have come up with this idea? Someone must have put him up to it."

"Maybe his mother," another answered.

Lakshmi poked Lalitha who was standing close to her, "*Akka*, why was his mother banished from the village?"

"Her husband's ashes had long grown cold when she became pregnant. She insisted that…*appappa* I can hardly say it!…that Madhavaswamy himself came down to give her a boon!"

"The cheek of her!" Rangi butted in.

"How daring!" muttered Lakshmi..

"What's that?"

"Nothing, *akka*. I said, how dare she!"

"Hmm…"

"There were riots when our Great King Krishna Deva Maha Raya died. Our King was named as his heir, but some of our nobles did not like it," Lalitha answered Lakshmi, ignoring Rangi. "They spread even to our village: beasts, birds, lives, property, nothing was untouched. Thulasi was caught coming home over the fields where she had gone to gather firewood."

"But *akka*, perhaps it was not her fault. She might have been set upon and forced," Lakshmi protested.

Manju had suddenly slipped down the pole and butted aside a young priest. He ran down the steps of the temple tank slippery with water and algae and slid into the pool. The bystanders gaped in surprise.

"Listen all! I will stay under the water until you tell me when the ceremony will be held," the boy cried, before immersing himself. Ranganatha tried once again to convince the boy to give up his cause, "*Putta*! We will speak to Bhadrinatha Shastri. He will help you. He has always been interested in you."

"Acharya! Don't try to trick me. This is my father's house!" The words exploded in the midst of the crowd.

"Of whom does he speak, *akka*? Does he really mean the deity?" whispered Lakshmi in the shocked silence.

"I will have the ceremony at this place and nowhere else! O, Madhava! I am a boy like you. Help me! Make these people see reason!" The crowd marvelled. Where had this small boy learnt to speak with such clarity? He was certainly a unique child. His face shone with sincerity and strength. Manjunatha immersed himself once more.

Ranganatha Sastry and the village headman moved off and went into a small enclosure at one side that housed the temple treasury and storehouse. They dispatched a young priest to call all the elders, including Bhadrinatha Shastri.

At this moment, Thulasi entered the temple. The crowd parted to make way for her. Rangi's loud murmur protesting an excommunicated person being allowed to enter such hallowed ground fell on deaf ears. Everyone was too disturbed by the situation to act at all.

Thulasi spoke to the nearest person. "Where is my son? Lalitha, we used to be friends. Tell me the truth for old time's sake. Where is he? I asked the people gathered outside. They said he had climbed the sacred column and then he had climbed down. I don't see him. Has anything happened to him?" Lalitha found her voice; with great sorrow, she narrated all that had happened. Thulasi moved towards the temple tank, wringing her hands in agitation.

Rangi's whisper managed to sound ferocious, "He was in a fever to get married, to her, that Brahmin, Srinivasa Shastri! Don't they say he who hurries is a fool? Poor man! Such a great scholar! He dodged marriage for a long time. Then he saw Thulasi, the daughter of a priest of the Chidambaram temple and his fate was sealed. His days were numbered. He enjoyed married life for hardly a year before he died of the dreaded inner sickness."

"She took care of him faithfully, *akka*," put in Lalitha.

By this time Bhadrinatha Shastri had entered the temple. Lalitha saw him. "You know, I saw Bhadrinatha Shastri wandering about on that day. The day of the riots," she slipped in, thoughtfully.

Rangi pushed her. "Then, it's more than your life is worth to say so. Shut your mouth! But, to be sure, he persuaded the elders to allow her to live on her *stridhana*, that piece of land at the end of the village, and they say that he arranged for the boy to attend the village school."

Bhadrinatha did not look at Thulasi but went straight to the tank and entered it. He came out in a short time and announced that he could not find the boy underwater. He addressed the crowd, "People of this beautiful and sacred village of Alur, you are indeed fortunate to witness this miracle. The boy who entered the tank has disappeared. This is a sign. This is not an ordinary child. A great Being has deigned to live amongst us. Let us honour his presence among us by immediately indicating our consent to his thread ceremony." A few in the crowd began to shout "Hai Madhava!" and "Honour to Bhadrinatha".

Someone from the crowd shouted, "Look! Look!" The child Manjunatha was standing on the top step of the tank, a garland of marigold and roses around his neck and a gleaming gold sacred thread slung across one shoulder. Thulasi turned joyfully. She ran to him and gathered him to herself, sobbing with relief.

"*Amma, amma*!" The childish call cut through her tears.

"What, *putta*?"

"A beautiful Being in gorgeous robes met me underwater. He took me to a palace and put this thread on me. Then he told me to go to my mother." Overcome, the child hid his face in his mother's shoulder.

Bhadrinatha Shastri who was nearest, had been listening to all this. He turned and rushed to them. He flung himself at the child's feet in a full body obeisance and then, raising the child to his shoulder, began to dance, singing: "We bow to you, O young Gopala!" The crowd was buzzing with excitement. Disapproving faces filled with wonder at the miracle they had just witnessed.

The entire assembly surged out into the street. Thulasi was the last person to leave the temple. She followed the crowd and reached the gate of the temple. Her son, who until then had no name or home, had now been hoisted on their shoulders to sainthood. They had driven her out when she was pregnant. How soon would they relegate him to memory? Only time would tell whether her son's charisma would last.

Lalitha looked at Thulasi, elated that at last, her childhood friend's troubles were about to end—surely now the village would relent and accept her back into its fold as the little boy-saint's mother? Instead, Lalitha got a shock—why was Thulasi looking so displeased, so....murderous?

Chapter I

February 1996

Maya looked at her watch and frowned. Tulsi should have been here by now. Granted, she was quite laid back about appointments and timings, but Maya had thought she had made it quite clear that her time was not to be wasted. In a few minutes, she would be due in the Additional City Civil Court for a trial which had been dragging on for months. All the lawyers and clerks had gone off on their lawful preoccupations and she had just the typist for company.

Tulsi was a dancer, and Maya really liked her. She was a very strong woman and good fun. They had got together a few times in the early stages of the case and gone out for coffee. However, that did not give Tulsi the license to upset her schedules. She would give her a few minutes and then she would leave for court.

She had just got up to leave, when she heard the high-pitched tones of her typist interspersed with the lower murmur of a man's voice. The typist came in and placed a letter on her desk.

Maya was about to shove it in her desk drawer, when she caught Tulsi's name on the bottom left corner. Maybe she had decided to send a letter instead of calling? That would be strange, but not uncharacteristic, especially as she had been known to miss appointments in the past. Still, she could have called to let her know about her absence.

The envelope felt heavy and had been taped clumsily many times. Maya cut it carefully and pulled out a letter and with it, a key. Puzzled, she twirled it a few times between her finger and thumb, but beyond the fact that it seemed to be a sturdy key, the kind that fits into a small mortise lock, she could tell nothing. Maya frowned. Tulsi was going from merely creative to eccentric and would soon be barking mad if she didn't watch out. She flicked open the letter impatiently. She didn't want to be late for her next case, with all this unnecessary mystery.

The letter was maddeningly brief and didn't tell her anything. *Maya,* it ran, *I'm sending this to you just in case*. In case, what? Maya wondered with mounting irritation. She read on. *I'll tell you more when I see you*. It had been dated five days ago. So much for the postal department! And Tulsi hadn't even showed up!

Maya opened the phonebook at the frequently used contacts' page and called up Tulsi, drumming her fingers as she waited for her to pick up. The phone kept ringing. She slapped her forehead with the flat of her hand in exasperation. She rang Tulsi's flat. It was too late for her to be home. She was more likely at Ghungroo, the dance school she had founded and helped run. She rang the school, her tension mounting as she realized she would be late for the case which would probably start in ten minutes. The phone rang a long time before the engaged tone came on. The receiver's click, as she replaced it, had a final sound to it.

Sighing, her rest period at an end, she left for court, the familiar vagaries of the property trial almost a welcome respite from the unknown trials that lay ahead of her in the Tulsi tangle.

Maya stepped out on the balcony of her flat and watched the quiet tree-shaded road. A breeze was blowing off the river a few streets away and she could hear the bells of the local temple ringing. She could almost imagine herself in a quiet village and ignore the city sprawl beneath. The dark was soothing after the clamour of the day. She turned to answer the demands of her stomach and went in with a sigh.

The flat was on an open plan. The living room, dining and kitchen were divided only by curtains. As she made herself some *dosas* with tomato chutney, she watched the news on the TV, which was on a swivel pedestal. They were interviewing some young kid and a dance class seemed to be in progress in the background. She turned up the volume—it was a young movie star whose latest film had had a good run at the box office. He was dressed in a track suit and was gesturing towards the class in progress behind him. He stopped and called to someone behind him and a pretty girl joined him. She introduced herself as an instructor and spoke about the moves she was teaching her class. The actor and she seemed friendly, though their body language seemed to be saying the opposite, arms and legs tightly locked, knees stiff. Her attention caught, Maya switched off the stove and went out to the living room for a closer look.

After a while, the interviewer turned to speak to another instructor. It turned out that it was his school and he had started it ten years ago, after a stint in New York. With one part of her brain, she noted that he looked quite good. The other part was busy analyzing the tension between the actor and the two instructors. They were all smiling and chatting about different dances and funny stories from shows the actor had danced in, with them. The girl broke in on the actor's lines with, "Hey, I heard that there was a show where no one turned up and Harsha had to do solo after solo. Poor guy! He was brilliant though, I heard." For a moment, the actor looked furious and the proprietor of the school seemed mortified. Unfortunately for him, the show closed on this note, the camera freezing on the proprietor's ghastly smile. She hadn't caught their names but the credits did give the name of the school—Footloose. Maya turned to a news channel and went back into the kitchen. It was time to wrap up her day.

Later her thoughts went back to the show as she lay in bed and took up her latest bedside read. She wondered idly about the undercurrents between the trio who had been interviewed and the story behind their embarrassment. Why would an incident involving an impromptu solo dance make the proprietor look so embarrassed? And the actor had looked like it was a calamity which had affected him badly.

She turned on her side and snuggled into her pillow, switching off the lamp. Time for some rest. If she didn't sleep at this time, she would be good for nothing the next day.

Maya was caught up in a difficult appeal at the High Court the next day, so it was evening by the time she thought of Tulsi again.

It had been a long and tedious day in court and she opened the windows of her office as wide as she could to blow the cobwebs away. Maya's firm was called ' Alibai' an acronym for 'Associates for Liberty Against Injustice'. Her partners K. Meenakshi (Meena) and Patricia Arulchelvam (Pat) were her old friends from law school. More than her flat home, the office was her space. Her desk and chair were Edwardian, solid and venerable, offering instant comfort. Her special favourites were the three coconut-shell monkeys which stood on a shelf. They demonstrated Gandhiji's famous adage 'see no evil, hear no evil, speak no evil,' but were cuddly with it.

She sat down at her desk and waited for Kamala, her clerk, to bring her court diary. Her shoulders were tight and she could feel a headache starting between her eyes. She revived a little when Pandian, the junior office assistant, brought her the spicy, hot and strong tea and the special crispy biscuit, neither too sweet nor too salty with a hint of nutmeg, from the Irani café round the corner.

Kamala, her clerk, was a little late coming, so she had time to finish her tea before a visibly distraught young woman dropped into her seat opposite, clutching her red court diary. "What, Kamala? Why are you looking at me like that? What happened?"

"Madam, I don't know what to say!"

Maya interrupted her, "We had Tulsi's case today. Didn't the junior get there? Was Tulsi there? I told you she didn't show up yesterday. Did you ask her why? Why are you looking so worried?"

"Madam, I went to the court but Tulsi was not there. Her husband, Srinivasa Shastry was there. I waited for Tulsi, but after some time, he came near me. I moved away because I know I'm not supposed to talk to the other side party in a case. But he followed me, so I stopped. I wanted to shout at him, but he asked me if you were coming, madam. Then he told me straight away that Tulsi would not be coming. That she was dead."

Maya went cold. Ever since she had received the strange packet the day before, an unknown dread had eaten away at her. And now her worst imaginings had come true. "How did she die? When did this happen?" she whispered. "Why did no one tell me?"

"Very strange no, madam? That man didn't say anything else. He just walked off. Why did he come when she was dead? Didn't he feel anything? His skin is too thick! Why didn't her parents ring up? Maybe they did not know your number, but her daughter Shibani may have known where to look for the number."

"I must ring them up. Do we have their number?"

"I'll go through the file. We might have it."

Maya's headache had become worse. How had missed the obituary? The client's family was sure to be angry that she had missed the funeral, if it was over. If not, she had a slim chance of forgiveness. Why had Tulsi sent her a key? If it was an accident she had died in, who had helped them with the formalities for releasing the body? She leaned her head in her hands and thought, God, what a day!

She poured herself another cup of tea from the flask. It was hot and strong and she let the warmth steal through her and work its magic. Outside, cars were hooting at a truck which was holding up the traffic with its cargo of long pipes. Just beside the road was the local temple tank, its water still and green. Chaos and calm lay side by side. As in life, she thought.

Just then, Pat walked in. "Maya, you look terrible! Bad day?"

Maya told her, glad to be able to download. Pat listened intently. She frowned when she heard about the key and raised her brows at the death but was quiet. Finally, she said "You don't even know when she died? Let's check last week's papers. That should tell us something." She called Pandian for the papers and they settled down to pick over them. They were soon joined by Meenakshi.

"The papers are a good idea, but I think we should make an effort to get in touch with the parents. It looks bad if we don't send our condolences." Meena looked somber.

"Kamala is searching the file for their number," Maya said, a little defensively.

"What's taking her so long, for heaven's sake? This is exactly why I insisted we should have a separate database of all the clients addresses and numbers and a hard copy, too. See? You said the husband told her didn't you? How on earth did he turn up today? Must be a cool character," Meena commented.

Pat interrupted her, "Maya, do you remember her father's name? Let's just check the phone book."

"I think its Ramasubramaniam. He's no more. There's only the mother."

Meena was already leafing through the directory. "Rama..." she was murmuring. "Do you know the general location of their place?"

"Alwarpet, I think" replied Maya.

"I think this must be it," Meena said, just as Pat cried, "Here it is!"

They crowded around Pat, "The usual, 'We'll miss you,' 'mourned by husband', etc," sighed Maya.

"No joy there, but wait...here's something. 'Woman falls to death from height.'" They all keenly scanned the news item Pat was pointing to, which gave just the bald facts.

"It mentions no names but says she fell from a height from a dance class in Nandanam." Maya leaned back with a sigh.

"From the balcony, I suppose. What a way to die. She had a small daughter too, no? Poor kid! What a tragedy!" Meena shook her head.

"They must have had a lot of trouble getting the body from the police—the inquest, the post-mortem and everything. You'd better ring them up, Maya." Pat gave her a push.

"The police would have contacted the husband. He must have got his lawyer to help," Meena said.

"Yes, that's probably what happened. Poor, poor woman! Just imagine losing a daughter so suddenly. She must be going out of her mind. No wonder she didn't call! She must have expected me to see it in the paper," Maya said over her shoulder as she went to the phone to ring up Tulsi's parents.

The phone kept ringing for some time before it was picked up. The voice at the other end was quiet, a little hesitant. Who could blame her, thought Maya. In all this sudden chaos, every phone call must be dreaded as a possible harbinger of fresh trouble.

"Aunty, I'm sorry for not calling earlier. Today was Tulsi's case and Srinivas told my clerk. That's how I came to know." She sounded lame even to her own ears.

"I thought you would have read about it. We have been busy getting the body released and the funeral."

"Has the body been released, Aunty?"

"The funeral was this Monday. It took a long time and they questioned everybody but they could not find out anything."

"I read the news item just now. It says she fell. Was the balcony very low? Did she overbalance or...?"

"She fell from a window. I'm worried about Shibani. She's staying here now and she's so sad. I don't know what to do. It's very difficult." Maya heard some noise in the background. It sounded like Shibani crying and it seemed to be getting louder. "I have to go to her."

Maya fixed up a time to see her and rang off.

That afternoon Maya went to Tulsi's mother's flat in Alwarpet. A maid let her in and the first thing they saw was an occasional table with a big photograph of Tulsi surrounded by a montage of her dance photos and press cuttings, garlanded by marigolds. Incense sticks gave off fragrant smoke nearby. This, more than anything underscored the reality of Tulsi's death for Maya and she went close to the photo and gazed at it for a long time before bowing her head. The rattling wooden bead curtains heralded the entry of Tulsi's mother and she turned to wordlessly embrace her, while Tulsi's mother returned the embrace and then wiped her teary eyes.

After a few murmurs of condolence Tulsi's mother said, "The police are saying it was suicide but I don't know... She seemed quite happy to me. She told me she was working on a new dance and writing something."

Just then, Tulsi's ten- year- old daughter, Shibani scurried into the room. Maya got up to hug her, but she pulled away and said, "You didn't come, aunty. Why?"

"Oh my God, I didn't know about it, Shibani. I'm so sorry. I would have seen you as soon as it happened, if I had known," she tried to explain.

"Aunty, I thought you would care. She liked you. You are *her* lawyer." Maya felt awful. Her platitudes had not convinced the child. She tried again, "I'm sorry. I only saw the item in the paper, when your Dad told my clerk this morning."

The child sobbed some more while Maya patted her back, feeling helpless."I don't think my mother jumped from the window. They are just saying that. She must have been pushed," Shibani blurted out suddenly. Maya didn't know what to say.

"How do you know all this, Shibani?" her grandmother broke in, looking perturbed.

"Daddy was talking to you, *Patti*. I heard everything," Shibani went on, her voice rising. "The police are saying she suicided. She didn't want to die. I know. I would have told them if they had asked me but no one asked me anything." Her words ended in an aggrieved sob.

Maya hugged her and patted her head. "What do you know, Shibani?" she asked as over her head she grimaced to show Tulsi's mother that it was best to humour the child.

"Aunty, Mummy was going to bake a cake for dessert. She had all the flour and butter and everything ready in the kitchen. How could this happen? She loved me." The child began weeping again.

"Shibani, your Mummy loved you. She did not want to leave you. You can be sure of that."

"Aunty, can you find out who pushed my Mummy?" she asked, raising tear-filled eyes trustingly to Maya. Maya was caught. She was not a detective or even a criminal lawyer. She doubted she had the skills. But the child was so upset and she felt it was the least she could do in the circumstances. Maybe she could just look through the police investigation and see if everything was in order. "Shibani, I'll try my best," she said, feeling inadequate.

Tulsi's mother broke in, stroking Shibani's back. "You don't worry about that, Shibani. Your Daddy will see that everything is OK. I will talk to Maya aunty and tell her everything. She will help. You go in and ask *Thayi* to give you that buttermilk we made this morning, OK?" As she spoke, she propelled the little girl towards the other room and thrusting her inside, firmly shut the door.

She turned to Maya, "I'm sorry, but she is a little overwrought. It's been very difficult to console her and since I feel shocked myself, anything I say sounds hollow.I feel sure she did not jump. But what other explanation can there be? There was no one else at the dance class. Class had ended."

"What dance class, Aunty? Are you talking about Ghungroo, the school she ran? "

"No. This is another one. They dance to western music. Tulsi called it something...er, jazz, I think. I didn't want to ask you on the phone, but can you go over to her flat and look? See if you can find anything? She turned and rummaged around in one of the drawers in a table against the wall.

"This is Shibani's key. She used to get into the flat when she came home from school if Tulsi wasn't at home. Her Daddy doesn't know she has it. Don't tell him. He will be angry that sometimes Tulsi wasn't home when Shibani came back from school. Tulsi trusted her Shibani. She knew she would not do anything naughty but just have something from the fridge and watch TV."

"Aunty, I am not a criminal lawyer but I will go to the flat and check the police investigation. I'll let you know if I find anything." She tried to sound more confident than she felt. At least she could do this much for Tulsi.

Maya reported this conversation to the others over tea and biscuits the next day.

"Maya, you can talk while you eat. Don't keep us in suspense. What, you think you're the next Sherlock? You're turning Alibai into a detective agency?" Pat had a worried frown.

"A suspicious death, Maya? Suppose the murderer finishes *you* off?" chipped in Meenakshi.

"Why all this worry? We've done suspicious deaths before. Remember that case, the girl who was supposed to have jumped with her baby daughter into the well and it turned out the husband had tripped her up with a well placed string so he could marry again for dowry? You and I did it, Meena. How different is this one?"

"We knew that it was a murder for dowry, so it was easy. All we had to do was prove there was a case for reopening the investigation. Here, the husband may have a good alibi. The killer, whoever he or she is, seems clever and there is no shadow of a motive. Why are you complicating your life now?" She didn't say it, but her manner also implied *and dragging the firm in*.

"I promised Tulsi's mother, Meena. She was so upset about it. Tulsi's daughter Shibani also didn't want to feel her mother had abandoned her. I only promised to check out the records."

Maya tried a number of times to go round to the flat, as she had promised Tulsi's mother, but something or the other got in her way, usually a last minute change in the court docket. This was the thing she both hated and loved about litigation—you could always expect the unexpected. At last, a few days later, she stood outside an unimposing flat door with the number 12 in black plastic lettering on it. Getting in had been easy, the bored watchman had asked no questions. The key slipped in smoothly and she was through. Hearing the click of the door locking itself, Maya felt a thrill of nervousness run through her: where to start looking? She decided on the bedroom, though it felt a little creepy to be all alone in the flat, knowing its owner was dead and if Shibani's suspicions were true, not of her own volition. She had taken the key that Tulsi had sent her, just in case, but it was hard to see what it could unlock in the minimalist flat.

The bed had been tidied: by whom? And when? There was no dust to be seen so it had been cared for. Maybe a maid still came in to clean up. There was a double bed, probably for Tulsi and Shibani, a desk and chair, a fitted wardrobe and that was it.

For want of a better idea, she went to the desk and half-heartedly tugged at the drawer. One part of her did not want it to open at all. It would be a violation of Tulsi's privacy and voyeuristic in the extreme. Expensive runners had been used, for it slid out at the first touch and noiselessly gave up its contents for inspection. There didn't seem to be anything here to excite a sleuth. Just the ordinary detritus of daily life—a cheque book, some pens, clips, stationery, a pink plastic box of visiting cards, some receipts for bills. She lifted them out, one by one. Rifling through the cheque book, she found most of the leaves were unused, and those used tallied with the receipts. There was one for the dancing school: pretty cheap at two hundred and fifty rupees a month, but it must have been fun. Just to be thorough, she lifted out the bills and stationery. Tulsi had been neat—the bills clipped together, spare clips in a box of their own, the ends of the various items squared off. There was a black book, about an inch thick, smaller than a note book but larger than a pocket size diary. She felt uneasy touching it, but steeled herself to go through it. It was a diary but Tulsi seemed to have treated it like a cross between an appointment book and a journal. Even her expenses were totted up at the end of the week—quite organized for such a creative, free spirited woman. Maya lifted it out and put it into her bag. She could go through it later. She pushed back the drawer and stood up.

She moved near the bed. Was it worth checking under the pillow? It felt a bit eerie, sitting on a dead woman's bed. She lifted the pillow. Nothing there. She felt around the edges of the bed. Everything seemed normal. A glance at her watch showed her that it was nearly 5 o'clock. Time to go back to the office, dispose of waiting clients and head home. She was about to get off her knees, when her hand felt something hard. She lifted the mattress. A small enameled metal box with a lock nestled there. She decided to take it with her.

Maya put down the mattress and stood up. She heard a small click as a key turned in the lock of the front door. In a terrible moment of panic, she rushed into the adjoining toilet and gently shut the door, just as she heard the door stop grate on the floor as the door swung open. She waited, sitting on the toilet seat and praying that the visitor would not have to use the toilet. She heard him or her moving around, the wardrobe doors being pulled open and shut, the drawer sliding open, a sound of papers being rifled through. A cold sweat broke out on her upper lip and forehead and her heart began pounding. She felt exactly as she used to feel as a child, playing hide and seek. Would the intruder know that she had gone through the papers? Was it obvious? After what seemed like hours but was only fifteen minutes by her watch, she heard the footsteps retreating from the room. It sounded like the person was wearing shoes, but if it was a police officer, surely he or she would not have come alone. She waited another fifteen minutes before cautiously opening the bathroom door and stood still, listening, straining her ears for sounds from the kitchen or living room. The house seemed to be quiet. She girded herself up and made a dash for the front door, grabbed the handle and let herself out. She clicked the door shut and hurried to press the lift button. There was no sign of the other and she could now breathe and smoothe her hair and look less flustered.

As she lay in bed later that night, she suddenly remembered the TV show about the dance school. Maya wondered if there could be any connection between this class and Tulsi. After all, how many schools teaching modern dance could there be in such a conservative city? Probably not even a handful. Perhaps it was just a coincidence—two stories in the same week about a dance school. She wished she had asked Tulsi's mother the name of the school earlier. She went back to the front room to her desk and got the diary and the box she had picked up in the flat. She rippled the pages of the diary again.

Acting on a hunch, she tried the key Tulsi sent her on the lock on the box. It turned as she had known it would. What valuable thing had Tulsi secreted there with such intent? The box opened and she felt a stab of disappointment. There was just a cheap, old paperback in Tamil, the pages coming loose and the cover, a discoloured monochrome. White-fish holes dotted the pages. Worse, she could see that it was not even complete. What had ailed Tulsi at the end, to make a mystery of such mundane stuff?

She began to read the book. After all that drama, it had to count for something.

CHAPTER II

FEBRUARY 1536

Ningi shook off her weariness. She was late already, even though it was still dark. It was the sixth period after dusk. Achale had to be dressed and in the temple by the first period of the first part of day. As the *rudraganika* she would sing the rising hymn for the Lord and later, dance in the first religious service of the morning. The temple was on the other bank. *Ajji* would already be up and supervising the cleaning of the stove. It did not pay to invite her anger. After all, she was in charge of the kitchen and the servant's daily ration. She should not have spent so much time last night with her crone Malavva, the washerwoman. That toddy had been too potent.

She hurried down the path to the rough hewn rock steps, which led down to the general bathing ghat at Anegundi. Good! It was deserted. She could bathe and perform her ablutions in peace. The river whispered darkly in the pre-dawn calm. She pulled loose the knot at her waist, spilling the neem twig and rice-husk ash, the turmeric tuber and the soap nuts, in her haste.

Flicks of the neem twig on her teeth and a rub of the turmeric tube on her body were all she had time for today. The village council had posted guards all along the bathing ghat. They would soon be out, checking on all those who did not decently inter their refuse. She had better be quick and clean if she did not want to get caught. For those such as she, who did not have the privilege of toilets in their own mansions, the dark was their only refuge.

As she reached the water's edge she realized that she was not alone. The curve in the path had hidden the other bather from view. She seemed to have immersed only her head in the water. It struck her that it was a curious way to bathe but she had no time to waste looking at oddities when there was so much to do and so little time to do it in. When she had finished her bath, she glanced again at the other woman. Strange! The bather had not come up for air but was in the same position. Was she perhaps a water-nymph or some kind of fish-goddess that she could stay under water for so long? Or was it just a woman who had gone to sleep on the bank and rolled down. She decided to risk a call, even though by talking loudly at night she might awake some evil spirit waiting for just such an invitation. "Who is there? Do you need anything?" There was no response.

She finished wringing out her sari and then went over to the other woman. The woman was lying with her head in the water. Her body lay out of the water, on the step of the bathing ghat. Her sari had come loose and was flowing with the gentle currant. Her hair was loosely knotted and was escaping its constraints. She seemed to be asleep. There was a strong smell of vomit and something else. Ningi sniffed the air. Had this woman also had too much toddy? She looked closely at the sleeper. She started back in shock. She knew this woman. This was the disgraced Brahmin widow Thulasi whom Bhadrinatha Shastri, the landlord of all the villages east of Achale's lands, was keeping. It had been the scandal of the season, a long time ago, before Thulasi's son had been born. People had talked of nothing else for many months. "*Amma*, please get up," she shook her by the shoulder. After she had shaken her for some time, she realized that the body was cold and that Thulasi was dead.

Now what should she do? She could not pretend that she had seen nothing. That would be too sinful. If she called the guards, it would make her too late and *Ajji* would be angry. She exhaled loudly. She would have to hurry and not let that old fool Betappa waste her time with questions.

As she hurried out of the bathing *ghat*, she met a young woman she knew. The woman agreed to stand guard over the body while she ran to alert the guard. Anyway, the water was befouled and they would all have to bathe a little further on. She met the guard on the road leading to Jogahalli, not far from the bathing *ghat*. He greeted her kindly knowing that she belonged to the famous Achale's household. As soon as she told him about the incident, he began to question her closely: what exactly had she seen, where was the body, what was its position, did she notice anyone else there, did she know the dead woman well (a preposterous question as he well knew, for what could a Brahmin widow, outcaste or not and she, a serving maid of a *devadasi*, have in common?), and finally, what was she doing there at this hour? At this she lost her temper.

"Enough! It is too much! Is this how you reward me for reporting a death? I went there to bathe. What else does one go to the bathing *ghat* for? Don't you have women in your house? I get up early, go about my duties, report a death, like a good citizen and I am rewarded by your insulting questions! Go do your duty and find out why she died. I am not going to fly away. You know where I stay. You ask me your questions later. I have to go. I am late already. Don't bar my way or I'll tell *Ajji* you made me late!" Betappa fell back hastily, unmanned by the flood of angry words and Ningi ran stumbling, glad to get away.

Maya woke up with a start. It was morning and the clock showed her that she had barely an hour to make the early morning appointment she had given a new client. What a strange start to Tulsi's secret book! She felt goosebumps: was it a coincidence that the dead woman in the book was named Thulasi? But it seemed to have happened centuries ago. It had seemed so real too! Had Tulsi been spooked in the same way, when she read it? She pushed the thought away. Come on, Maya, grow up—all work and no play is making you jump at shadows.

Chapter III

February 1996

Maya ran up the stairs to her office. The traffic was getting worse all the time. She had taken the beach road to avoid the snarls on Mount Road but huge truckloads of people from the country had taken over the road, probably on their way to some demonstration or convention and she had had to crawl all the way. Her mood, never at its best in the morning with the tension of getting the urgent stuff out of the way, had considerably darkened. Luckily, all the clients would probably have also been delayed by the procession. As she had hoped, the waiting room was empty, giving her time to cool down before the morning madness had its way with her day.

In ten minutes, she was smiling. Kamala greeted her brightly. "Good morning! Only the admission in the list. I met the other side's lawyer in the title suit; he's going to mention to the court that he wants an adjournment—something about more instructions..."

All Maya said was, "Ha! He must be waiting for more fees," but her heart was singing. Ah, an unexpectedly free day—the admission would not take long as it was on top of the court's list. The juniors would take care of the other cases.

As she took off her gown at 11:30, something had already started nagging at her: she had to get hold of Tulsi's post mortem report and the first information report of the death, maybe even the closure report and other statements of witnesses if she could. But how to do so without alerting Srinivas Shastry's lawyer was the question. After all, for all she knew, Srinivas Shastry may be a suspect.

She rejected the idea of approaching the local inspector who had conducted the investigation. She would have no joy there. She had no history with them. Besides, he might have an inside line with the husband's lawyer. She flicked through the names in her address book and card file. There, triumphantly exposed, lay the card of a Deputy Inspector General of Police, who had served with her on the panel of a seminar they had attended together. She would have to go and see her but first, she needed to know if she was still in the same post.

An hour later, she was back on the beach road. The DIG had sounded delighted to hear from her. She had landed a soft option—she was in charge of the Police Training College and she needed to pick Maya's brain for her thesis on women's rights. As the breeze ruffled her hair, her mood lifted along with the tendrils escaping from her plait, which were dancing gleefully. The local beach salesmen were lining up to serve them, their day made.

It generally came down to the beach, if you thought about it. Life ended here, as ashes mingled with the waters, the fisher folk eked out a living from it, people bathed here and walked on the sand and what would the beach be without all the *bhajji* shop-carts and rides? Water, salty or not, sustained all life. It took her back to the body in the river in the book she had read last night—Tulsi's secret book. In the bright light of day, her feelings of unease about the book had evaporated.

She hoped she had remembered to put it away safely. You never know, it could be an important clue, though it seemed too old to be the key to Tulsi's death. Maya's pensive mood didn't last, all the colour and bustle was weaving its usual magic and she was tempted to give the interview the go-by and run down to the beach. She accelerated until she had reached a busy Mount Road and was forced to slow down. The college was hard to miss, wedged next to the post office at the corner, the usual squat, sprawling government building washed in the colour of dirty clotted cream. It was a pity to be indoors on a day like today. Luckily, Sarala, the DIG, had her office on the topmost floor, and had a view of the neem and laburnum tree tops. Maya was admiring the lush foliage when the secretary ushered her in.

The DIG was all smiles, preening in her cushy elevation. After the necessary preliminaries, the enquiries about fellow members on the committee they had been in together, they turned to the important topic of the day—the great magnum opus she was about to embark on.

"So what is the focus? You said you were writing about womens' rights—that's a huge topic."

The DIG smiled. "I thought I would start with existing laws, then touch briefly on the status of womens' rights in the country and focus on the implementation of those laws in Tamil Nadu. I want to help women, you know. But my IG, he is already worried."

"Yes, he must be a very modest man. He does not want you to reveal all his 'help', no doubt."

The DIG darted a quick look at Maya. She did not know whether Maya was pulling her leg or not, but Maya had on her straightest face, so she contented herself with saying, "Something like that, yes."

"I have some papers and books which you may want to see. I'd like to see it when you're done. It would make interesting reading, seeing things from the eyes of someone on the inside."

"Madam, I hope you are not expecting me to reveal anything startling. This is a self-development exercise and as you know, I can't tell all."

Maya smiled. She knew what the DGP meant—she'd blame the law, the courts, anything to keep the searchlight from the force's own shortcomings or face career suicide. "Yes, that is what is needed at the moment. People want to know the great work that is happening here." She promised to send the material with her office assistant. They talked technical points about the book and the laws she would be covering.

The DIG relaxed a bit, having got what she wanted and then asked, "You mentioned some matter—a suicide?"

Maya told her about Tulsi and watched as the DIG made a call to the police station concerned and asked the writer to have the copies of the First Information Report, witness statements, post mortem and Investigation reports in Tulsi's case ready for Maya immediately.

"He's a bit worried. Are you planning to get the investigation reopened? If so, madam, he will get into deep trouble."

"I can't assure you that I won't but as of now, it seems impossible, as my client is dead and her family hasn't contacted me. I'm just curious as she was a personal friend."

The DIG relaxed. "The police writer says that the postmortem confirms that she fell from a height and there was nothing to show foul play."

"In that case, he and you have nothing to worry about from me," said Maya, smiling serenely. They left it at that and within the hour, Maya had the information she wanted.

The writer at the police station had seemed sincere when he had assured her that they had spared no effort to investigate the death but had found nothing suspicious—no injuries which were inconsistent with the theory of a fall and no suspicious person lurking near the crime scene. They had questioned everyone they thought important but that had yielded nothing.

Maya decided that the day had advanced quite enough for her to go home and read through the reports. Once she was back in her flat, she went straight to the kitchen to get her tea and chocolate biscuits before sitting down to scrutinize the details of the death.

The post mortem seemed straightforward, as the writer had claimed; the cause was fall from height, death due to shock. So the heart must have stopped before she reached the ground, which was a blessing as she would have felt no pain. There were injuries as well—a long linear fracture of the left parietal bone and there was an underlying extradural hematoma. She seemed to have fallen from the third floor, just after a practice class. The security guard and about ten others, who had just come out or were going into the building which had several offices had not seen anything since they were all at the front of the building.

The crime scene inspection report elaborated that the building faced a side street and since it was past 8, it was not very busy, so there had been no spectators outside the building. It was the last class of the day and the students had all left, the instructors had also exited the practice room for the outer office. The windows were big, and unbarred in the new style, protected by large glass screens. There was a foot-wide ledge outside, which had only her footprints. Tulsi had been less than 5′5″ in height but she must have weighed at least a good sixty kilograms, most of it muscle from her dancing. She wouldn't have been easy to lift over the parapet of the window—how could the murderer have hoisted her onto the ledge?

She closed the file containing all the police documents and took up the diary again. She flipped through it, looking for clues to Tulsi's movements on the day and the week before her death. Tulsi used to speak of her friend Tanuja at Ghungroo. She would have to speak to her, find out her state of mind. She put aside the diary and took up the book. It was proving to be quite absorbing....

Chapter IV

February

Mahashivarathri 1536

The kitchen was still cold. The firewood must have been damp. The fire was smoking and hissing instead of roaring into life. The pale pre-dawn light struggled in between the brick fretwork on the one big window. *Ajji* cursed under her breath and pushed aside the maid tending the fire. Taking a stout stick, she prodded the wood. She added a few more dried cakes of cow-dung, muttering to herself. Suddenly, the fire roared to life, illuminating her still-dark hair and turning the few gray hairs to gold. Sitting on her haunches, blowing at the kitchen fire through a long iron pipe, dressed simply in a coarse cotton sari, her hair carelessly knotted, no one could yet fail to mistake her for what she was—the once celebrated courtesan of Simhapuri, the peerless Roopavathi.

Ajji's daughter, Puttalakshmi was still not reconciled to her only daughter opting to give herself as a *bhakta*—a devout *devadasi,* dedicated by vocation, to the Virupaksheshwara Temple. She had refused to take charge of her daughter's affairs and *Ajji* who doted on her granddaughter Achale and considered her daughter a weak fool, had stepped in and stayed ever since.

The maid, who had been tending the fire, now helped her mistress up and resumed her duty. *Ajji* sat sipping a herbal drink.

Ningi stopped running when she reached the gates of Achale's mansion. Achale had only been dancing for four years after the completion of her training. Already, she was the favourite of the King and had been granted this land and mansion by him.

Ningi passed the female guards and hurried inside. She had to pass through three courtyards to reach the kitchen. It would have been quicker to just go in through the back door but as Achale's maid, she was entitled to the front entry and she did not want to give up that privilege even to save time.

At the second quadrangle, a buffalo snorted as she passed and the cowman said, "What, Ningi, even Jana knows you are late today."

"You just wait until you are late!" warned Ningi.

The third quadrangle was tastefully decorated with samples of Achale's artistry and refinement, by *Ajji*'s orders, much to Achale's embarrassment. A pet peacock suddenly came from the rose-garden and let out a piercing screech. Ningi picked up a fallen leaf and shied it at the bird. "Shoo!"

"Aii," *Ajji* called out, from the kitchen. "Hasn't *Chikkamma* been woken up yet? It is almost dawn. Where's Ningi?"

"She hasn't come back..."

"Here I am, *amma,*" Ningi tumbled through the doorway before the other servant could finish her sentence. She busied herself, pouring water on her feet and hands, snatching up small copper vessels to carry the unguents, dipping into various pots, assembling the paraphernalia of Achale's bath.

Ajji was not to be so put off. "Where were you? Why are you so late?"

"*Amma,* that Betappa! How troublesome he was! Would not let me go. Would not take no for an answer. Why did I go there? What did I do? Didn't I tell him that I had to have another bath?

That I would be late. That I would have to get back here early, that I was already late?"

Ajji was an inspired interrogator. She went straight to the heart of this speech. "Yes, why were you already late? And why did he accost you so early in the morning? He must be getting really past his duties if he can't contain himself at the sight of a young woman."

"That is...I saw a body at the bathing *ghat*. I had to tell him. Otherwise if someone had seen me, he would think I...Then I had to have another bath."

"Whose body did you see, girl?"

"That Brahmin widow, *amma*. Thulasi. It was she. Bhadrinatha Shastry's..." Ningi said hesitantly.

"You have said enough. Be quiet! Go wake up your mistress and help her get ready. It's nearly dawn." She muttered under her breath, "Have I not told that girl a hundred times that she should live in the dancer's street at least when she has the dawn duties? Just arrogance that's all! Stuck here so far away and so much trouble for everyone!" Ningi quickly made herself scarce.

The distilled blue stain of light in which dust motes sparkled like stars spread slowly through the room. It mingled with gold the bronze shoulders visible over the coverlet of coarse black and red striped cotton, and the thick, black braid of hair tied up with banana fiber. A slight rose-tint crept over the sleeping face, half-covered by a supple, tautly muscled arm. The golden flush spread over to the feet, slim and well arched, delicate gold anklets encircling a neat pair of ankles. The sleeper turned and the early morning light illuminated a high cheek-boned, strong-featured face: the large eyes fringed with long, curling and luxuriant lashes; the shapely eyebrows flying in a long arch towards blue-veined temples; the nose well-formed with small, pinched nostrils and the lips finely-chiseled with a generous curve.

The sleeper stirred just as the door creaked stealthily open. Ningi slipped in, her hair still wet, her *saree* clinging damply, exuding the clean, scrubbed smell of turmeric and the holy ash on her forehead. Ningi began to press Achale's legs. Humming like bees at a honey pot, Achale stretched, looked at her open palms and sat up, rubbing her eyes. She looked at the light streaming into the room from the window. "Aii! Why did you wake me so late? It will be nearly dawn. The trustees will be angry. That Bhadrinatha is waiting for just such a chance to poison their ears. And if I am dismissed where will you be, eh? I'll tell you: without your ration of rice, pickles and buttermilk."

"*Chikkamma*," Ningi began but Achale cut her short, "You tell me as I bathe. Come!"

They went down a flight of stone stairs. Achale ran to the privy outside, placed far back near the boundary wall and then came back to bathe. In the bathroom, the water had been heated, and Ningi was waiting patiently. Achale sat on the waiting stool and disrobed until a strip of flimsy white muslin covered only her loins. Ningi rubbed a scented herbal oil into her body while another maid massaged a different one into her hair.

Every time Ningi looked at her, she was struck anew by her exquisiteness. Atukuri Molla, that amazing woman of the potter's caste who had taken only three days to master the Ramayana,had said of Sita's eyes that they were like Manmatha's arrows or perhaps like lotuses. What would she have said of Achale's eyes? Poets had described each one of her physical attributes, usually using hackneyed phrases plagiarized from the classics. Her gait, encumbered slightly by the weight of her pale saffron, round breasts pressing against each other so that even a lotus-fiber would not find room between them, was like that of a swan and so on. She seemed born to challenge all existing standards of beauty and elevate them to new heights. No one, thought Ningi, had caught her essence which lay in her sparkling glance, brimming with intelligence and laughter, and her forthright manner. "I should not have asked for this special bath today," Achale grumbled. "I feel so sleepy again!"

"Naturally. You must be very tired after the *Vasanthahabba* dances," said Ningi, soothingly.

"Decorate my hair simply. We have no time for an elaborate costume."

Ningi's fingers were deft and quick, twisting and plaiting Achale's hair becomingly. While she was adorning Achale's forehead with a mark, using yellow and red ointment and anointing it with sacred ash, Ningi said, "Why did you agree to the rising hymn this fortnight, *Chikkamma*? You could have done it next fortnight and let Sundari do it this week. After all, you danced all week at the spring festival while she gave only one performance."

"I didn't want to ask her any favours. It would have been a big favour and she would have made much of it." Achale said of her arch rival Sundari, the other *rudraganika* belonging to the temple. Just when the last gold bangle had slid onto her wrist, a servant came up, "*Chikkamma*, *Ajji* has called you for the morning prayer. The priest is waiting."

Bhima was waiting in the hallway at the foot of the stairs. A high slit on the curve of the stair wall spotlit the landing with a clear blue glow. Bhima saw her first, irradiated by the blue light, the gold of the torchlight picking out the luster of the tissue and roses on her garments and the brilliance of her jewels. He had been squatting on the floor, leaning against the wall, but now he stood up, his hands joined in respectful greeting, his mouth open to say, '*Chikkamma*,' but the words were snatched away by her sheer loveliness, his brain drumming, is she Goddess Amba or is she Achale?

"Bhimanna," Achale laughed, "Not awake yet? Wake up! It's time to go." Rubbing his eyes, pretending to be sleepy, Bhima smiled sheepishly and muttered, "*Chikkamma*". After the morning prayer, Ningi came up with Achale's millet gruel and when she finished it, they set off.

Ajji was waiting with turmeric and saffron powder on a silver salver and Achale bent down to touch her feet and was anointed with the orpiment before she got into the palanquin which was to bear her to the riverside.

The cock had just climbed to the top of the hut near the river and given a rousing crow. Achale and Ningi were gliding over the water of the Tungabhadra River from Anegundi on its north bank to the Pampapati temple at Hampi a week after Ningi had found Thulasi's body. Shukra, the silver planet was rising and the bards had begun to strum their lutes to sweeten the auspicious moment when night flees before the dawn. The boat with its round shape and leather covering rode the waters like the tortoise, journeying to the Ocean of Milk to help churn it. Behind Achale's boat, swirled that of Bhima and the palanquin bearers.

Pillared temple pavilions flung into view as the boat slewed its way across the river. As daily commuters, Achale and Ningi were used to the river's ways. "How long it takes! *Ajji* is right.

You would have been much better placed if you had stayed in the Soolai Bazaar," Ningi grumbled.

Achale smiled, "And then I would miss this beautiful morning ride! Remember, we are going to serve God and it is better to suffer a little and win peace of mind at the end than to constantly suffer the gossiping and dealing that would surely accompany us every morning in that street."

"If you had accepted the King's offer, by now, this long daily journey would not be necessary at all, *Chikkamma*," Ningi looked at Achale slyly, from the corner of her eyes, a smile hidden under her hand. The King, Achyuta Deva Maharaya, he of the illustrious house of the Tuluvas, had sent several messengers, not least his brother-in-law, Salakaraju Tirumala. He had even offered to make her his Queen. Not his chief queen, of course. That right was reserved for Tirumaladevi and Varadadevi.

"Ah, and you would, perhaps, have me dressed up as a sandalwood doll, awaiting his Majesty's pleasure which may well be never, given his five hundred wives. I did not know you had an ambition to serve in the palace. I'll speak to Bhima to get you a place there."

"Forgive me, *Chikkamma*. Do you know what Malavva told me?" Ningi had a friend, a washerwoman who had the free run of the palace. "The minor queens dress up every night and stand in the courtyard outside their rooms, calling to the King as he goes past. It's so funny." Malavva had seen this scene and repeated it with much merriment.

"Rascal girl! I have not escaped from the *devadasis'* quarter only to be part of just such a situation. At least, the *devadasi*s have servants who bring their customers to them. I will confine my royal services to dancing for the Assembly when commanded."

"As you did yesterday. *Chikkamma*, why don't you listen to your mother and marry? As chaste and pure as you are, and a Brahmin's daughter, learned, beautiful and good, who would not want to marry you? You don't lack offers."

"Yes, I have received all sorts of offers, everyone desires the dancer Achale, but who wants Achale the woman?"

"*Chikkamma*, I sometimes wonder if you understand yourself? If you keep asking your husband such questions, he will tear his hair out in confusion."

The river had another name and a story. She was Pampa, a daughter of Brahma, who served the *rishis* on the Hemakutam hill. In return, they taught her penance and austerities to win Shiva as Virupaksha, who took the name of Pampapati after he had espoused her. It was to this temple, built to honour this manifestation of Shiva, that they were going.

"Did you meet Betappa after that morning? I wonder what happened to poor Manjunatha."

"O *Chikkamma*, didn't I tell you? I thought I had. Manju is living in Bhadrinatha Shastry's house. Bhadrinatha is ecstatic. He is a great Vishnu *bhakta,* so they say, and he has always wanted Vishnu *bhakti* and his guru's teachings to spread. He is saying that Manju is a saint. I can't believe it. That small boy who only recently was stealing our clothes as we bathed, so he could laugh at us!"

"If Krishna could hide the village girls' clothes so might a boy-saint."

"Oh, who knows the ways of gods?" sighed Ningi.

The river rushed along, suddenly dipping into a ravine and the small craft was swept ruthlessly along but the boatman was skilled and managed it with ease. A gateway, unfinished but imposing, came into view and Ningi clutched Achale's arm.

"*Chikamma*, they say the sculptor who is building this gateway is very good. And also very handsome, like his idols." Achale gently put aside Ningi's arm. "Who could be more handsome than Virupaksheshwara? My heart is not in me but with the lord."

"*Chikamma*, If you saw a man you could truly desire, then your heart will come back to you. Is it not possible to love a man *and* God?" Achale only swatted her and said, "Foolish girl!"

The huge stone beam supported by two pillars that formed a balance then appeared. "Poor King! He performed the *talapurusha dana* ceremony on the first new moon of his reign by weighing himself against pearls. Did he then expect that he would face so many problems?" Achale sighed.

At last, the Hampi bazaar glided into view. Achale took a deep breath. "Ah, I can smell the bazaar!" The air became redolent with the smells of spices, incense, musk, perfumes, roses, jasmine, the jaggery of sweetmeats, sandal paste, sweet limes and garden produce. Everything was overlaid with the smell of horse-dung and cows. Merchants were setting up their stalls, in front of the magnificent, two storey houses that were lined up in rows, wall to wall, on either side of the street leading to the temple, and women and men were milling round.

The spring festival had just ended in the preceding fortnight. For ten days, people had celebrated the birth of spring by feasting, dancing, wearing flower garlands, watching plays, swinging and praying to Shiva and Kama. This had set the joyful mood for the ensuing spring season. However, the recent mysterious death had shocked all. Here and there, snatches of conversation could be heard.

"Have you heard that Thulasi, that notorious widow was found dead?"

"Why should she have killed herself just as her son was gaining prominence? It's very puzzling."

"Do you think she killed herself or was she done to death?"

"By whom? That is the question."

The air was thick with the smoke rising from the sacrificial site. "Can you hear the chanting? The priests must have started the sacrifice, ordered by the King. He must be hoping that at least now, he will be allowed by Rama Raya to rule in peace," said Achale.

"If he was good enough to be picked as successor by our great King Krishna Deva Maharaya, he is good enough for me," Ningi replied.

The landing spot was bustling with activity. Boatloads of firewood and sandalwood were being off-loaded for the *yaga*. Brahmins were hurrying to and fro, their tonsured heads gleaming, their topknots swinging with every step. The *yaga* had already begun and one could hear the priests chanting the *yaga mantras* loudly and sonorously.

Achale tripped on the sides of the boat, her sandal caught on a loose piece of leather and she would have fallen headlong into the water but for the hands which gripped her forearms and held her tight. For a moment, Achale could see nothing but a brown chest covered in fine white muslin, could feel nothing but the warmth and strength in those hands, could smell nothing but the scent of sandal, clean skin and freshly washed cloth.

Her eyes stung a little with the smoke but she could not rub it. The collyrium would smudge, so she dabbed it with her upper garment and looked up. A giant stood there, his muscular torso disappearing into a plain white cotton loin-cloth, his feet shod in wooden sandals, he was smiling at her discomfiture but made no comment, except to say, "Go carefully, *devi*!"

"O Agni!"

The words resonated from the *yaga* site, Achale only heard the lines from the *Mahabharata* describing the great Kings gathered at Damayanti's *swayamwara*. Her mind and eyes were filled with images of arms as thick as iron bars, shining locks of hair, and nose, eyes and brows sculpted out of stone.

The priests finished the invocation and Achale came back with a jolt. It was time to move on. The priests at the temple would be waiting. While they were waiting for the palanquin, Ningi pointed. "*Chikkamma,* look at those pots. I've never seen such colours or designs!"

"You are right! I wonder where the potter learned to glaze them like that?" said Achale. "From China, *devi*." The voice came from the man who had saved her from falling. Achale picked up a pot.

"Aha! The pot is well paid for the kneading and pummeling it underwent! It came through the Hades of the kiln, only to be cradled against the lovely lady's breast! The poet Dharmakirti has spoken well!"

Ningi darted a sharp look at Achale's face, snatched the pot from Achale's hands, which had suddenly gone nerveless and banged it down in its place among its fellows. "Potter! My mistress does not required bandy words with the likes of you. Bhimanna settle with him for that pot." Ningi clapped her hands. "Aii, you! Hurry! Gently! Now lift it up!" The palanquin, gaily bedecked with flowers and hung with curtains of sheer embroidered muslin, ornamented with silver, was off in the direction of the temple, with Ningi running alongside.

Bhimanna stood watching, until he recalled that the potter was waiting for him. Then he said, "I apologize for Ningi's rudeness, master. She has been with *Chikkamma* since she was found abandoned as a small girl near her grandmother's house. She is very protective of her mistress's honour."

"Who is your mistress?"

"She is the celebrated dancer and handmaiden of Virupaksheshwara, Achalabbe."

"All this parade of honour for a temple-dancer! I thought she must be a nobleman's daughter at least. Tell her that Janakachari Virabhadra, the sculptor will spend tonight with her."

"Master! You mistake the matter. My mistress is dedicated to God. She does not receive anyone in her chambers. She is as chaste as she is good. Do you know the well that is located on the road from Anantasayanangudi to Kamalapura? My mistress built that for travelers. "

"A dancing girl and chaste! Please present her the pot with my compliments. Does she give public performances?"

"Yes, she will be dancing in the temple on Mahashivarathri day."

"I will meet her then."

"Achari! You said just now that you are descended from Janakachari. Did you mean *he* who is known as Kai Dala, the architect of the Ishwara temples at Belur and Halebidu? If so, our house is honoured by your notice. I shall tell my mistress."

"Yes I am his great-grandson. You may tell her with my goodwill." With that, Bhimanna was dismissed.

Chapter V

February 1996

Maya awoke feeling every one one of her thirty years. She felt as if she had come back from a long journey. Her limbs and back were aching, even though she had overslept and the clock showed the time as eight in the morning. She was lucky this was a Saturday and she had no early consultations, only the office meeting at 10:30. There was plenty of time for that. She'd read the book till quite late. But it had been worth it. So absorbing! Strange, how close she had felt to the characters. In her mind's eye, the characters had taken on a presence; she could see them clearly, like a moving picture. They felt like family.

In this chapter, the woman she had first read about had turned out to be the maid of a dancer—a *devadasi*. First she had noticed the similarity in the victims' names and now there was the repeated pattern of dance binding the two. She felt distinctly odd, disoriented. Had Tulsi seen the book as somehow connected with her life? If so, how? More important, was it related to her death? What had she meant to tell her when they met, when she sent her the key? She got up with a jerk. No, she had no time to follow up on these conjectures. Besides, living alone as she did, if she kept on like this, she would be spooking herself to madness.

She'd better tell Pat and Meena about it at the office and see what they said.

For the moment, she needed to bathe and dress, but more importantly, she needed coffee. As the rich smell of the brew, a special mixture of pea berry and chicory hit her senses, she began to feel more like Maya of the twentieth century, not Ningi, maid to *devadasi* Achale in the declining years of the empire centered around Hampi.

She dressed with her usual Saturday morning abandon: a pair of bright indigo harem pants with a white-tie-and-dye pattern, a hot pink tunic with a mirror-work yoke and an indigo tie and dye wrap; anything to counteract her habitual white and black weekday uniform. Maybe after the meeting she could go and meet Tanuja, Tulsi's friend who had once before accompanied her to an interview in her office. After that, she had nothing more exciting planned for the day, other than dinner with her sister.

Being a Saturday, there was plenty of space to park her car at the court complex. Maya drove a Maruti 800. It was gleaming red—it brightened her mood every time she looked at it.

There were some clients in the waiting room, but none she knew. The office assistant, Selvi who doubled as receptionist merely smiled her good morning. It looked like none were for her, and no messages either, which meant she could push off after the meeting.

It was a ritual every Saturday to review the week and update the diary with Kamala. She sat down at her desk and waited for Kamala, her clerk to bring her court diary. Kamala was a perky young woman, much younger than Maya's thirty years and she was always on the ball, quick and sharp like a green chilli. She was, as usual, dressed in bright colours: today's sari was a bright orange with a short *choli*. The effect was like a tonic and she grinned in response to Kamala's bright smile and shining eyes.

"Sit down, Kamala," she invited. "Is there something urgent this morning or can the juniors take care of it?"

"No, nothing urgent, madam, just routine work. I'll just give the lists to Selvi, ready for the juniors as they come in, okay? I've given them cases in courts close to each other, as usual, for Monday, so they'll manage. Don't worry madam." They had nearly finished when Pandian brought the fragrant, spicy tea. Maya remembered that she'd had no breakfast and asked Pandian to get her a stuffed *dosai* from the local Meals Ready restaurant. She felt like a big breakfast and could carry it into the meeting.

She finished up with Kamala. The property case would be continuing and a motor accident case was coming up for trial. Some old client wanted information on a case which had ended in 1988. She wondered where the records were. Kamala, seeing her anxious frown, said, "Don't worry, madam, I'll find it, or I'll search our bills' file. If we still don't find it, then we can apply for another copy of the order, right?"

Maya smiled at her. "Thanks, Kamala."

Maya carried her tea and diary to the meeting. Meena and Pat were waiting for her. The library was well stocked and comfortable. The meeting usually was at two levels. Level one had all associates, clerks, and typists. Level two was exclusively for the partners when confidential, financial and administrative issues could be hammered out, without constraint. .

Maya had told Pandian not to bring her the *dosai* till level two, so she sat sipping her tea as Kamala filled the others in with their work. Slowly, the agenda was completed and when the last clerk had filed out with her instructions for the week, the partners relaxed.

Patricia stretched out her arms, "What a week! One negotiation, where the company would give Shylock a run for his money, a strike averted and an injunction against the company lifting goods from the factory during another strike obtained after hard bargaining. Glad to get that over."

Meenakshi instantly retorted, "No one can cap my week—a brief against a rapist, then murder and gang robbery defenses!" She turned to Maya and smiled. "You're looking really colourful today. What's up?"

For some moments, Maya was too busy tucking into her *dosai* to reply. While she chewed she rehearsed what she was going to say. She decided to run the repeating patterns in the two Tulsi/Thulasi murders by them and see what they could make of it.

Her friends were looking quite relaxed, so she said, "I don't remember if in that entire ruckus over her death last week, I remembered to tell you that Tulsi had sent me a key, just a day before she died. She stood me up, you know. We were supposed to meet at the chambers to discuss the next step in her case, a petition for interim maintenance. I was worried when she didn't show so I rang her at home and Ghungroo. No response. I didn't know it then, but she was already dead." Pat shivered.

"When I went over to her flat later on," Maya continued, "I found a diary and a tiny metal box under her bed. The key opened the box, but you know what, she had an old Tamil paperback in there, all moth-eaten and crumbling. It's funny you know, but in the old book, a woman called Thulasi was murdered long ago in Hampi, and a maid found the body. She told her mistress, a temple dancer and it's all so strange ..."

She stopped for their reactions but they merely looked interested, so she went on. "I didn't know temple dancers were such powerful people," she hurried on. "Their lives are just like that of modern working girls but their days start at 3 am. She seemed rich and it's all from her earnings. And she doesn't have any lover—not kept by anyone, it looks like. *And* she has a mother who bugs her about getting married, just like mine! Strange isn't it?" She wondered if it sounded like she was babbling.

Characteristically, it was Pat who made the connection first. "You mean, the similarities between the two dead women—their names and both Tulsi and the *devadasi* are dancers?"

"Those sound like ordinary coincidences. But why should Tulsi hide the book?" Meena was matter-of-fact.

"Maybe there is more that we don't know. Who knows, there may be important clues in Tulsi's book, though they don't seem apparent now." Patricia sounded a little doubtful.

"What are you going to do about Tulsi's death?" asked Meena, sounding concerned.

"I don't know. I'm investigating it. I've gone through the police reports and I will be interviewing her friend Tanuja. I'm going to join her other dance class, sort of an insider view."

"You should be careful," Meena said. "*You* could fall from a window next!"

Maya recrossed her legs, trying not to dwell on what Meena had said. "Meena, the post mortem report says extradural hematoma and parietal fracture. Why did she die of shock when she should have died of injury from the fall?"

"Oh, so that was quick. They've closed the case without much investigation. The husband must have insisted. Those injuries may be post-mortem. Shock can kill. It was about 30 feet to the ground, no? Falling from such a height suddenly could kill anyone. Don't read too much into that, there is a good case for the defense in it.

You'll have to prove both motive and opportunity. The question is, who locked up? Chances are, the murderer did, or, if someone else did, could the murderer have slipped in and out and without being seen? Motive would be the most important though. Remember old Kuppusamy and how he used to go on about intent being the foundation of the crime, in college?"

"As if anyone could forget! He must have gone on about it a hundred times. Oh, I almost forgot, your mother called," Maya told Patr, changing the subject. "She wanted me to address a meeting on March 8th." Pat's mother ran a women's group.

"I know. Meena and I have been roped in by Karunalaya and Stri," Patricia answered, naming two other women's groups, regular clients of theirs.

Maya went over this conversation as she drove towards Ghungroo, the dance group which Tulsi had been a part of. Tanuja, Tulsi's friend, whom she was to meet there, had agreed to a post tea interview. Patricia and Meena had reflected her own doubts, back in the meeting. Maybe she could try the coincidence question out on her sister Mridula later and see what she had to say about it. On second thought, however, that would not be such a good idea. Mridula might start fussing. She'd play it by ear. Snap out of it Maya, she could hear Meena's voice in her head. Imagine letting a book spook you and run your investigation! Her mind switched to her present problem, as if by association—suicide or murder? She wished she could be sure. Meena had sounded doubtful… could it be suicide after all? But the child, Shibani had been so sure…

Tanuja had sounded friendly on the phone. Maya pictured her in her early thirties, the same age as Tulsi had been. Ghungroo was in Kilpauk, and the road there was crowded with traffic. She had to pass the Ega theatre and drive down, taking a turning to the school which was in a big, old house. An artistic sort of board in wood and wrought iron announced its name transliterated in English and Tamil—a statutory requirement, though the word *ghungroo* meant bells or anklets in Hindi.

The dance rooms seemed to be located downstairs and the school offices and reception, upstairs, or so the sign up front said. Bright posters advertised classes—beginners, advanced etc. There was a show coming up—the theme was the lotus. Maya heard some music and some kind of chanting from one of the rooms. Doors opened off the lobby but all were closed. On impulse, Maya peeped into the first room in front of her. The music seemed to be coming from there. A practice or perhaps a class was in progress. Students were going through some complicated series of steps, and they ended the sequence with a pose which was supposed to have them standing on crosses marked on the floor, but turned into a huddle around the middle. The instructor stopped the music and seemed about to remonstrate, when a student drew her attention to Maya. She turned to tell Maya to go to the office upstairs before turning back to her class with an air which promised some plain speaking to come.

Maya climbed the stairs and was told by the smiling girl at the reception counter to go through into the verandah. This turned out to be a sit-out, located off the upstairs lobby. A woman was sitting on the stone seat running along the parapet wall, wearing a kurta and tights, legs tucked up underneath, a mug of steaming tea perched precariously on the parapet. As Maya approached, she came out of her trance and jumped up, almost sending the cup flying. "You're Maya, aren't you? I'm Tanuja, but everyone calls me Toni. Come, sit. It's a hot day but breezy out here so I thought we'd sit here unless you want to go into my office. I love that tree," she said, dreamily, pointing to a white jacaranda, which covered one side of the balcony, strewing its flowers on the seat. Maya made the appropriate noises and settled down, having agreed to her offer of tea. Even if nothing came of this interview, she could at least enjoy the peace of this lovely old house in the February sunshine.

Toni looked at Maya with an amused expression and asked, "What does a lotus mean to you?"

"A flower which grows in a pond?" Maya was mystified, but went along with it.

"And?"

"Many tightly closed petals which have to be peeled open or open in water. There are different ones for each Goddess—white for Saraswathi, green for Parvathi and pink for Lakshmi. Lotus Sutra."

"Ah! What do you know about the sutra?"

"Not a lot, its just something the Buddha is supposed to have said and he is depicted on a lotus isn't he? I saw it in Nepal. Isis. I don't know how but the blue lotus is connected with her. I read it somewhere," she said apologetically as Toni raised her eyebrows in exaggerated surprise.

"OK, for a lawyer, you know quite a bit."

Maya shrugged, "What is this, some test? Do you do this to all those poor things who want to join your classes? Do they survive? Have I passed?"

Toni smiled, "Touché! I was just trying out on you what the reaction of the public would be to our show, how much people know or relate to the lotus, etc. Sorry, I'm babbling. The thing is,

Tulsi's death has made us all a bit mad. It was so sudden. One minute, she was here, finishing up a practice session. Then she left for that class and the next thing we know, she's dead."

"So you didn't think it was suicide?"

"If it was suicide, it must have been a very spur of the moment thing. You said something about Shibani earlier?"

"Shibani feels it wasn't suicide. She says Tulsi was going to bake a cake and had kept all the ingredients out, ready, in the kitchen."

"Tulsi thought the sun shone out of that kid's bum. I can't imagine her deliberately leaving the kid to Srinivas's ministrations. She thought he was such a cold fish."

"Did Tulsi talk about anyone from her dance class?"

"She seemed friendly with all of them. She used to demonstrate the moves, that's all. She didn't mention anyone special."

"What did Tulsi do here?"

"Tulsi was our instructor and she and I choreographed the dances. You know, this dance we will be doing was Tulsi's brainchild. She was really into it—went to the archives for research and all. I don't know who came up with the idea of the lotus theme, but I think one evening we were throwing around ideas and we decided on this as it had so much promise."

"So what was her position exactly, in Ghungroo?"

"She was a partner like me and Anees. We studied dance together and had similar ideas, so we started this school. I know quite a bit of Odissi. Tulsi was trained in Bharatanatyam."

"Did you see the suicide coming?"

"Both Anees and I were shocked. Tulsi was gung-ho about this dance. She seemed OK, though I had felt for some time now that she was keeping something from us. She seemed worried about something. But definitely not enough to kill herself. That was not like Tulsi at all."

"Do you know anything about her research? Did she talk about it? I'm sure she must have. You were close and you had to come up with a kind of storyboard for the dance."

"It's so difficult doing it without Tulsi. She and I had discussed the dance and at first we were going to do an abstract presentation. Then she seemed to change. Suddenly one day, she announced that it was going to be a dance drama—you know, a full-fledged play with a script. She claimed she had written a drama script and was going to surprise me with it. I found it in her desk. It's so good." Her eyes filled, so the next words were almost muffled as if caught in her throat, "We will be doing it soon. Tulsi scribbled down anything she came across, in her research. I have the file here, in my office. I'll bring it now; just wait a while, OK?"

She returned after some minutes, her eyes a little red, but otherwise composed.

"Thanks. That is nice of you. We'll have to get together again after I've read it and we'll talk. Is that OK?" Maya was eager to leave. This interview was clearly over.

"Fine." As Maya turned to go, she said, "And Maya—thanks. All of us need some closure on this. Look, why don't you come to the dance? I'll call you and leave your tickets at the reception, when we're ready to roll. Will you be coming alone or with someone? We'll leave it open and I'll tell them two tickets on me, OK?" Maya couldn't refuse.

As she drove to her parents' house, Maya reflected on the meeting with Toni. So, Tulsi had been doing research. This seemed to be a clue. Maybe she had found the story of Thulasi's murder or Achale's story in the archives—how easily the names came to mind, it was almost as if she really knew them well. In a way she did; they had spent the night with her, quite often, since she'd been to the flat. Toni had seemed reluctant to discuss the dance drama's script. Had Tulsi reproduced something she had found in her research? Some instinct had warned her not to mention the book. Had Tulsi been killed because she had stumbled on something? What bearing could a centuries' old story have on modern secrets?

She would spend the rest of the day with her mother and take her parents along to her sister's for dinner. She looked forward to spending time with her normal, noisy and opinionated family. Maybe she could put all this away for the time being. She gave herself a little mental shake. She was doing it again! This mystery could be solved by logic and deduction. Why bring intuition and the sixth sense into it?

CHAPTER VI

MARCH 1536

MAHASHIVARATHRI

Bhimanna was waiting for the cart to be unloaded. *Ajji*, Ningi and Achale had already gone on ahead by boat. They had all gone to Nagalapur the evening before and were just returning home. Bhimanna would have to stable the cart and oxen at the stables they rented in the city, close by, and then make his way home with the baggage. He looked around for someone reliable to wait with the baggage, while he made arrangements with the stable owner. Some courtesans, unconnected with the temple, walked past, giggling as they saw him watching them. Bhima felt a pleasant heat rise in his loins as he watched their tightly encased hips, rising out of loose drapes covering their upper bodies, only partially concealing their full breasts. He pulled himself up. This was not the time to minister to his desire. There was other work to do. Out of the corner of his eye, he saw a caravan pass. It looked like some Dombras had come. Mahashivarathri celebrations were at the end of the week. Perhaps they had come to take part in the juggling acrobatics that usually accompanied such celebrations. Suddenly he noticed that one of them, a youth barely out of his teens, had stopped and was staring at him. The youth came forward, dressed in the traditional Dombra garb of a short cotton loin-cloth and *bijuri,* a padded waistcoat. "*Anna*?" said the youth. Recognition dawned. "Aii, Chenna, well met! Like finding the river flowing elsewhere, flowing at my feet. How are you?" Chenna had often passed through his own village; when he was a young man and he had taken trouble to be patient with the toddler's devotion. Their paths had not crossed for some time but some remembered characteristics had jogged his memory.

"*Anna,* I've joined an acrobatic troupe as a juggler. You know how I always loved animals. I've taught an elephant to juggle balls. I've named him after you!"

"Have you come for the Mahashivarathri celebrations?"

"Yes, *anna*."

"Chenna, just inform someone in the troupe that you will join them later and come back. We have some catching up to do and I need you to guard this baggage for me while I stable these oxen."

"Agreed, *anna*. I'll just be back." And Chenna loped off to join his troupe.

He was soon back. After the oxen had been stabled, he went up to a vendor selling buttermilk and roast gram. Carrying the leaf-cups, they settled themselves in the shade. For a time, neither spoke. Both had travelled some distance and needed replenishment. Chenna began to grind areca nut, preparatory to enclosing it in betel-leaf for a good chew. Bhima sat companionably on his haunches, waiting for him to finish. When both were chewing with enjoyment, Bhima spoke, "Come a long way, have you?"

"Yes, *anna*, we were at Madurai at the last full moon for a festival at the big temple. Ah, she was beautiful, the goddess. We stopped at a few villages on the way. I will be going back home to Raichuru after this festival. It is nearly a year since I saw my mother. I last saw her at the last Sankranti festival and she looked well then. Do you want me to carry some message to your people, at home?"

"This is my home. These are my people." There was a brief, awkward silence.

Bhima was of a higher caste, almost a Kshatriya but his family had fallen on evil days and his father had sold him to the pawn broker. When the pawn broker had shut shop and left for his native land up north, Bhima's mother, who was dying, had begged, cajoled and pleaded and got him resold to Achalabbe's grandmother who had need of a high caste slave to take care of her household. Bhima had embraced Virasaivism. Caste distinctions and rules had no meaning for him—Basava's 'Heaven for the worker' he had taken to heart.

"I needn't ask about you, I suppose. All your needs must be satisfied," said Chenna, smiling slyly. Bhima smiled sheepishly, thinking of his thoughts earlier and realized that the foolish fellow was talking about the household of the Lady Achalabbe. "The Lady is as virtuous as she is wise. She is dedicated to the worship of Virupaksha and you had better mind your filthy tongue,". Bhima said with mock severity.

"Sorry, I thought you had found paradise but I see that your feet are still on this ground." Chenna grinned unrepentantly.

Bhima laughed, "Aii Chenna, I'll take you to heaven on Earth. It's only a few streets away."

"*Anna*, I haven't seen the city before. You will have to take me around. Show me the sights. I want to see the cave where Sita's jewels fell, Vali's pyre and all the beautiful temples I've heard about."

"Done."

"*Anna*, I heard a very strange thing as we came into the city. They say that a Brahmin woman was found dead at the bathing *ghat*. Her son, it seems, is a saint. Bhadrinatha has him live in his house and is telling everyone the boy is a saint. They say he is landlord of Alur and Jogahalli. *Anna*, isn't your mistress's house near Jogahalli? Then you must know Bhadrinatha."

Bhima, thinking of the many times that he had had to deny Achale to Bhadrinatha said, "Yes, yes we know him."

The youth was almost sizzling with excitement, "*Anna*, please tell me what you know."

"Our maid Ningi found the body. I don't know any more." Bhima had an idea that the murder would somehow change their lives. For some days now, the omens had not been propitious. His left eye had twitched. His left arm had throbbed. Something infelicitous was sure to happen.

"*Anna*, I was talking to a guard as we came up to town. They say that the boy Manju petitioned the King."

"The King? Why did he come here? Normally we would have heard about it. But we were in Nagalapur."

"They say he came to supervise arrangements for the festival himself." Chenna seemed smug that he knew more than Bhima.

"How strange! Then the rumor is true. They say the King has been uneasy about his rule, ever since last year when Rama Raya imprisoned him. Even though he was able to bribe the guard with promises of Chief Ministership, and escape. He must be trying to propitiate the tutelary deity. Only when there is a problem, then one says 'God Venkataramana'."

"A drunken priest for a drugged God! They say our King is no saint."

"Yes, but the rivalry between the King's faction and Rama Raya's is now talked about even in the marketplace. The cow pulls towards the shore and the ox towards the water."

"Holding the tail of a winning ox, success has many fathers but failure is an orphan. All those who surround the King are mere sycophants and shifters. They'll shift to the other side in no time."

"All except Salakaraju Tirumala, Queen Varada Devi's brother-in-law. He was the one who put to death the ambitious guard. As long as he remains close to the King, the throne will be safe. However he is unscrupulous and ambitious."

"Like giving power to the scorpion! And what did the boy Manju say?"

"They say the words were so wonderful, listeners could never forget them. Maybe he really is a saint—a six-year-old boy. Where did he learn the words? His mother's milk must have been potent indeed. It could scarcely have dried on his lips. A scribe wrote them down and I can hear them in my head as if I really was there. That rascally Moor Afzal is actually employing a scribe to make copies on palm leaves and is selling them."

Bhima laughed. "You cannot get the better of a Moor in either effrontery or enterprise. Can you really read?"

"*Anna* it was you who taught me the alphabet and I can string them together to read words. I hope one day to join a drama troupe."

"Ah, ah, that is ambitious indeed!"

"*Hogi, Anna*. Don't make fun of this poor youth."

"What did the boy say?"

Chenna struck an attitude, and recited.

"O King, may the days of your life expand like your vast treasury,

Which like the akshaya patra of legend has no beginning and no ending.

Your writ no man can gainsay; your reknown brooks no boundaries,

But like the swiftly flowing Pampa River, deluges your enemies' lands, while it enriches your own,
Long may you reign, and long may your kingdom prosper!
When the King asked him to approach, he said,
'My mother, the unfortunate Thulasi, who lived in isolation,
shunned by all, for a sin committed before my birth, has died,
leaving me alone, without any succour except Madhavaswamy.
O King! Whatever she may have been in life to others,
she was a good mother to me.
Our dharma teaches that mothers, whatever their faults
should be revered by their children.
So I am bereft, my King and demand reparation.
My mother's death was strange in manner and point of time
O King!
You who are the fount of justice!
Surely you know that there should be no mystery about death and only then, can those who have shed their bodies find peace.
So also can those who are left behind, grief-stricken,
find their balance and continue their journey through life.
O King! I beseech you,
Your writ no man can gainsay; your renown brooks no boundaries
Let the murky waters surrounding my mother's death
be cleansed.
Let the murky waters surrounding my mother's death
be cleansed.'

The King ordered Peddanayak to enquire into the death. They also say that Peddanayak is going to consult the astrologer and soothsayer. It was so funny, *Anna,* the way the guard told it. The small boy lying face down on the ground with his hair streaming down his back, unknotted."

"I wonder who told him the King would be coming?"

"Who knows? As soon as the guards called out, 'Make way for the King,' he pulled out a spear he had by his side, tied a stick to it and began to cry out as if in great pain, *ayyo, ayyo*. Naturally the guards had to stop and grant him audience with the King."

Bhima stood up. "I have to go. My duties are waiting for me, up at the house. We will be coming down for the festival. We'll meet then."

"*Anna*, you promised to show me paradise!" the boy cried, his face falling.

Bhima smiled. "After the festival. Be good until then." He gathered the bags and left.

They had reached the outer city gates. From here, the road lay straight down to Kamalapura and then northwest to Hampi bazaar. The guard at the gate had stopped them. Ningi had stuck her head out of the curtained portion of the brightly-hued cart and said, "*Anna*, why do we stop?"

"What, were you asleep? For payment of the toll, of course," Bhima had retorted. The cart driver had been glad of a rest while Bhima had haggled amiably with the guard about the amount five persons and two oxen were expected to pay. Having reached an agreement, Bhima had paid up and had been about to swing himself up beside the driver, when there had been a shout. The clouds of dust had signaled a rider. The driver had not dismounted but had delivered his message from horseback.

"Peddanayak's orders. All travelers from Anegundi and surrounding villages are to be questioned about their movements."

"But this is so far from Anegundi. What question will you be asking us?" Bhima had been irritated at this hitch in their morning schedule.

"Peddanayak wants to know the movements of all Anegundi residents for the last fortnight."

"Then perhaps you can verify from the King. The Lady Achalabbe and her retinue were at the Virupaksheshwara Temple daily and last Monday, she was invited to perform for the King."

"The Lady Achalabbe! Why didn't you speak sooner?" The guard had dismounted and approached the carriage. Ningi had pushed back the curtain revealing *Ajji* and a veiled Achale.

"*Amma*, please excuse this son of an accursed mother for having kept your honour waiting. Please continue on your journey," he had said and bowed low, both hands pressed together in a respectful salute. The guard at the gate had hurried up. He had plucked the sleeve of the royal guard, "Sir, the lady's maid found the body. We have to question her." The royal guard had already been standing back, letting the cart move forward. "We'll inform the local guard to question her. No sense in upsetting the lady." He had kept his hands joined until the cart had moved quite a distance away and mounting again, he had ridden off to the next gate.

Achale had been very tired. She had been quiet up to then, but that incident had loosened her tongue. Perhaps that was what made her snap at her grandmother. "I don't know why you agreed to our staying at that house! When I want to become a lowly Maledavalu *basavi* dancing only at marriages and not in the temple, I'll let you know."

"What arrogance! As a *devadasi* it is your duty to please your public. You did not dance. You merely sang. Indifferently too. I was in turmoil whether they would be offended. Your credit is good enough to withstand the occasional public performance at great houses. Who would dare to question you now? Besides, that man has powerful connections. Don't you want to end the importunities of those such as Bhadrinatha? Remember what happened to Amrapali when she could not please all 7700 of the Lichchavi nobles!"

"She was threatened with treason, on the pretext of her having loved Bimbisara. But she survived to minister to Buddha and became a great nun. *Ajji* you can't be taking Bhadrinatha seriously. He is a vain and ambitious man, but even he would not take me against my will."

Achale had been taken aback by *Ajji*'s sudden warning. The old one was deep. Did she fear something? Doubtless it was related to Ningi finding the body and her enemy Bhadrinatha's rising star, now a miracle had gilded the temple of which he was an elder, in the lands he administered and called home. She was irked by the old one's ceaseless striving to find her a suitable patron. If she gave herself to a man, it would be out of desire and need, not to satisfy material ambition. Her body was a temple, dedicated to God.

Ajji had protected her during the dedication ceremony. Young as she was, she had seen the desire in the priest's eyes as he had chosen the candidates for his ministrations, but *Ajji* had stood guard and in the end, he had only pretended to "initiate" her, in the name of Virupaksheshwara and she remained inviolate. Now of course, as the King's favourite, no one dared to touch her. Perhaps there was truth in *Ajji*'s assertion that when the time came, even he, barely hanging on to his throne, would not be able to protect her. Until now, she had not felt desire for any man. Mere looks had never attracted her. She needed something more. The potter at the landing stage however, had awakened longings she had not even known existed. Even as the thought had slipped into her consciousness, she had pushed it away.

"My bodice is too tight. Ningi, just loosen it a little," said Achale.

"*Chikamma*, it's that rascal, the new tailor. I'll tell him to loosen it."

"You shouldn't have changed your tailor just after training the old one to your satisfaction," *Ajji* said.

"I found out that he was working for that Sundari too. I didn't want him to carry tales from here to there."

"Did you give him the new bustier with the hanging gold ornaments that you want to wear for the Mahashivarathri dance?"

"No, no. As if I would! I gave it to the new tailor. He had approached me, before."

"Be careful. One bribe and all the dancers will be wearing the same design on the day."

"I'll send Bhima to caution him."

The cart had lurched against a stone as it passed the Queen's Bath. The ladies did not bother to look out. The building was an uninteresting square, though it had some pretty stucco work. "They do say Amalotpava Devi has recently become addicted to this place," Achale had commented idly, yawning. *Ajji* had just snorted.

The cart had crossed the Turrutu channel, swift in name and nature, built in the fourteenth century by Bukka II. As they enjoyed the cool little breeze ruffling the waters, *Ajji* had asked, "Has

Bhadrinatha asked you for the prostitutes' tax yet? He has recently been appointed collector."

"But the previous collector knew that I don't have any other source of income except my earnings as *rudraganika*. I am not a common *basavi* to take lovers and coax gifts from them. I don't have a lover, have never had one. I even refused the King!"

"Be careful, he is a clever man, almost as clever as Tenali Rama. Once he forces you to pay the tax, you will be branded a common prostitute and then there is nothing to stop him having you. Remember Tenali Rama and my mother?"

Achale had shivered and covered her ears. Encounters with Bhadri always made her feel as if a lizard had run over her skin.

Ajji's mother Ranga Sani, dedicated by her Brahmin father when he could not pay certain temple tithes, had been famous for her logic and had been humbled only by Tenali Rama, the great court jester of Krishna Deva Raya. It had happened thus. Ranga Sani had offered to give half her wealth to anyone who would defeat her in logic. Tenali Rama had sent his disciple to help her haul a load of firewood into her house.The disciple had kept demanding "more" jiggery as payment for his services. Ranga had found that she could not satisfy his craving for "more". She had accepted her defeat with good grace and Tenali had offered the boy two lumps of jaggery, one larger than the other, asked him to take "more" and solved the puzzle. Ranga had had to give him half her wealth. She had then settled down in Simhapuri, where she had recouped her losses and had given birth to a daughter. She had later trained her daughter to be the most sought after courtesan in Vijayanagara.

They had passed the walled enclosure housing the huge idol of Narasimha the man-lion avatar of Vishnu. "See the Lord

Narasimha, smiling with his lady. Everyone needs security. That is why I keep telling you to take a permanent lover. Bhadri will stop his constant pinpricks if your lover is important enough and you will be safe, even if you have to pay the tax. You will not lose status but instead will gain from your lover's status. Did you notice one Vajrabahu, a noble newly arrived at the court? He is from Anegundi, a descendant of the Sangamas, who were the first rulers of Vijayanagara," *Ajji* had remarked.

"You and my mother are one and the same. 'A reputation lost for a betel nut, cannot be retrieved even by donating an elephant'. You both want me to consort with a man when all I want is to serve my God with purity. Only, my mother wants me to get married and lead the life of a housewife and you want me to take a lover. Each of you wants me to walk in your footsteps." Achale had been annoyed.

Their entire route thereon, for some miles, had been dotted with temples. As *Ajji* folded her hands in obeisance to the temple of Balagopala at Krishnapuram, she had snorted, "Hunh! If it does not bend as a sapling, will it bend as a tree? You were always a stubborn child. I well remember your teacher scolding you for questioning Rama's treatment of Sita when he sent her to the forest. Perhaps it is my fault. Seduced by your intelligence, I gave you more license than is generally permitted for women and see the result!"

When the road had suddenly climbed until it reached a hilltop near the Kadalaikalu Ganesha temple, Bhima had gotten down and stood for a moment, breathing in the cool air and drinking in the scene below. The argument had continued behind him.

"My lover rides a bull, his shoulders wide as the Himalayas his throat blue, his gaze like the lotus, his lingam the primeval seed-giver..." Achale had been smiling.

"His body smeared with ashes, covered with bark and animal skins living in the graveyard, head of a host of fearful demons..." *Ajji* was grim but her eyes had twinkled.

"He is my lord. He kicks at Death and imprisons the moon and Mother Ganga in his topknot. He is worshipped as the conqueror of the three worlds, *Ajji* where can you find a lord more powerful? As Mahadeviakka said, only the true devotee understands, not mosquitoes on a buffalo's back!"

Achale's eyes had brimmed with laughter, and she forgot all her tiredness.

Ningi had been quiet throughout this exchange. Here, she had joined in, "*Ajji, Chikamma* has taken great interest in pottery. She will now forget her God and worship only pots," she smiled slyly.

"What rubbish are you mumbling now, girl?"

"*Ajji*," Achale had broken in hastily, "Look! We have reached the boat-landing!" She had shot a warning look at Ningi.

"It's a good thing we don't have to worry about the early morning ritual for the next fortnight. How did you manage to get off the night and afternoon rituals today?"

"I requested Sundari to do it. She agreed. Haven't I done the same for her many times when she is too tired from her exertions with a lover to take on the night duty?"

They had then got down and got into the boat, leaving Bhima behind to deal with the cart and come up later.

Chapter VII
February 1996

As Maya drove to court on Monday, she reflected on what she had read in the old book on Saturday and Sunday. The boy-saint Manju, Thulasi's son had accosted the King, demanding justice. The High Court had recently installed the statue of Manu Needhi Chozhan in front of the judges' entrance; no doubt to inspire the litigant public with suitable awe. But it had only inspired sly digs at the system. The Chozha's response to what had after all been a case of dangerous driving—a cow had demanded justice when his son's chariot wheels had trampled her calf—seemed to them extreme. He had ordered the son to be killed in the same manner. The modern response, they said, would have been more appropriate. He might have been let off with a fine and a warning that his license would be revoked the second time he was hauled up.

What would the Vijayanagara King do? There did not seem to be any motive. The grandmother, a shrewd old madam, seemed to think that Achale may be blamed anyway. And the state collected a professional tax from prostitutes! How interesting and how much less corrupt than the present day system. Now the police looked the other way for a price and prostitution, an "illegal" profession went on hydra-headed! Ningi seemed a character after her own heart. Intelligent, resourceful, loyal, a lot like Kamala and with a sense of humour to boot! The more she read, the more involved she got. Had Tulsi felt the same? Maya wished Tulsi had confided in her. She sighed as she parked her car.

Maya had a free period in her day. She had brought the file and diary with her, and she sat down with them to work on Tulsi's case.

She went through the file first. Tulsi seemed to have done quite a bit of research. There was a page on Manju's thread-ceremony incident. It seemed it was hailed as a miracle. There were bits from articles on *devadasi*s and on temple culture and rituals.

What would a real detective do under the circumstances? Motive and opportunity—these were the key words Meena had used. She remembered that Hercule Poirot would first assemble a portrait of the dead woman. She had to concentrate on finding the motive.

Maybe a picture of her final week would throw up something. She flipped the diary open to 6th February, the date of her death. The next page, the 10th had 'Maya's chamber,' penciled in for 11:00 a.m. This was the appointment she had missed. If this was a book, the victim would have left a detailed journal at least. All she had to go on was a cryptic appointment diary!

The 9th had merely 'Footloose' penciled in for the evening. Where had she heard that name before? She flipped back the pages. Footloose occurred again, quite often. She searched further back. Ah, here was a name—Thomas! This was again in the evening. Toni occurred a few times and sometimes it was T & A, referring probably, to a meeting of the partners. There were no other names save the Archives and one Dr. Gopalakrishnan. There was one other name that might amount to something. This was Alamelu Maami, some time in January. She decided to ring up Toni and discuss these names with her.

The phone arrested her exit from the office, late that evening. What a day it had been, she thought, as she picked up.

"Maya, I am glad I was able to catch you. It seems you had rung up." It was Tulsi's mother. Maya had kept in touch with her and brought her up to date with the investigation, or as much of it as she thought wise to reveal.

"Aunty, I just wanted to know, did the police find the key to Tulsi's flat in her purse?"

"Now that you mention it, she was grumbling just the day she died that her key which she kept in her purse was missing. Why?"

"Nothing, Aunty. I just thought perhaps there should be another key and I wanted to check. Did Srinivas Shastry have a key to the flat?"

"No, no. This was Tulsi's flat which she had taken on rent. How would he have the key?"

"Oh, OK, just tightening loose ends, Aunty." She rang off after some polite conversation.

Toni had invited Maya to her flat. It was in Kilpauk, one of the older, spacious complexes, set in a neat garden, with discreet car parks. As it was past six o'clock, she saw that Toni was prepared for her visit: a wooden tray with tall glasses and nuts and spicy snacks was already on the low coffee table and a covered glass pitcher stood sweating nearby. The flat was like Toni, bursting with colour.

There was a fuchsia wall with gold calligraphy; the seating was mostly low and at the centre of it all was Toni, inquisitive, warm and casual in an off-white kurta and jeans. An evening *raga* was playing softly. They soon got on to the topic of Tulsi's research.

"Tulsi seems to have gone to the government archives and read up old manuscripts. She's made notes on an incident about the creation of a boy-saint and his later life. Have you read it? It seems he was ordained as a full fledged sage, a holy man, and established a *math* at Anegundi. It exists even today. Why did you think she took such an interest in this bit of history?"

"I think Manju's story was something she just stumbled on, in the course of the research. I don't know if she wanted to do a thesis or something on dance. She didn't talk about it at all. She did say something about sculptures of dancers but maybe that was for the costumes for the dance."

"What was the name of the other dance class she was going to? I am going to enroll as a member. Maybe I can pick up something. But I can't understand why a classical dancer would want to learn jazz ballet."

"Tulsi was big on interpretation of dance and flexibility. She wanted to do some fusion. This was before she decided to turn the lotus dance into a dance drama, like I told you. She abandoned the idea of fusion dance but kept going to Footloose because she was having fun. She said something about helping them with a show. She was running around a lot—taking care of the kid, juggling classes here with her research and those jazz classes. I think her social life also picked up."

Maya raised her eyebrows and Toni shrugged. "Don't ask me, she was very closed-mouth towards the end. Just kept to business and out the door!"

"I got the file photocopied for you. You should have a copy. Something tells me it's safer that way."

"Why? You're really spooked about this, aren't you? You think she was pushed? You'll have to watch your step, Maya."

"Yes." Maya made haste to change the subject. "Can you tell me about her last few days, what she did, whom she met?" Just as she had been reluctant to speak of the book in their last interview, she did not think it would be a good idea to mention the diary, this time. The fewer facts she gave away, the safer she was. After all, for all she knew this fun-loving Toni may be a suspect!

"Oh God, I know it's only a few weeks ago, but I swear, I can't remember!" Toni pushed her hair off her forehead. "I don't even remember my own schedule and no, I don't keep a diary. Tulsi was a do-gooder type you know, always getting into something she thought needed to be right. I thought in the last few weeks that she was once again in the middle of something. But she was so secretive about it."

"Tulsi once mentioned she was meeting some person called Dr. Gopalakrishnan, or so her mother said," Maya said mendaciously. "Do you know him?"

"That sounds like the Professor of History she said she was meeting to get into the Archives and know what to look for. I think he works at a college in Porur. Again, don't ask me. All I know is what she told me. I still don't know much, though I read her file after her death for the dance."

"So what's the dance about?"

"No, no, we aren't going there. It's totally different. That's all I can tell you. And beautiful. It's our memorial and tribute to Tulsi and you *have* to see it," she broke off because her eyes had filled, but this time she let the tears flow and Maya went over and hugged her. Her own eyes were brimming by the time they broke apart.

They listened to the background music for some time, until Toni said, "I suppose it would be no good talking to the husband?"

"You're joking! He hates me. You can try but considering they weren't speaking in court, you think she'd have told him anything? Besides he would have to be our no.1 suspect. Friends, they were not."

Driving back home, she debated her next move. She would have to join the dance school, Footloose, Toni had said. Anyway, it would be interesting and a little frightening to put her body through unfamiliar positions and all in the presence of a possibly critical, certainly teeny bopper crowd. Saturday would see her there.

The next day, Maya's sister Mridula was going shopping for her daughter's birthday and Maya had decided to tag along. She rolled her eyes in relief when she finally managed to convince her sister that her niece would love the jeans and T-shirt that were dressy and practical rather than a frilly frock, which she was sure to reject as babyish. After buying two more outfits, they went on to another shop and spent a satisfying half hour trying out and rejecting half a dozen clothes each, before finally choosing the very outfits that they had first rejected.

It was not until they had sat down at a fast-food joint for some finger-licking treats including melt-in-the-mouth spinach leaves fried in batter, that Mridula wanted to know what Maya had been doing. Mridula had a post graduate degree in History and had taught for some time at a school before her kids had come along. She still talked of getting a doctorate but that dream seemed to be receding of late. Maya was undecided whether to talk about the book and Tulsi's death. She didn't want Mridula to run to their mother with the tale of Maya's dangerous involvement with a murder mystery. At last, she shrugged and launched into the book's story, merely mentioning that she had come across it in a second hand bookshop. Even before she had finished, she could see that Mridula was interested. Her eyes shone with the excitement of a historian.

"It was like me getting ready to go to work in the morning, you know, Achale getting ready. Except that she kept spouting stuff about God and serving Him—Virupaksheshwara. I think she was a virgin! Her mother kept telling her to get married, just like *Amma* and me and her grandmother wanted her to get a lover. She was a courtesan, but retired. And they had media! A scribe wrote down Manju's appeal and circulated the palm leaves for a price!"

"I thought you said she was a courtesan—they had paid sex for a living, no?" Mridula said, tongue-in-cheek.

"Not this one. Maybe they could choose. Not like now. You know, I think it was like a regular job for her," said Maya.

"But a glamorous one. Sounds fascinating,no?"

"It is! I really think so. Anyway, Achale considers herself married to her God. It seems she refused the King, who, get this, had thousands of wives and concubines and spent the night in rotation with them but even then, not all got their turns."

"Words fail me! Did you find out which King it was?"

"I think Achale said something about it being Achyuta Deva Raya. Some thing about Rama Raya coveting the throne."

"I think I remember vaguely that Achyuta became King after Krishna Deva Raya. Rama Raya was a son-in-law and wanted the throne for himself. I'll see if I can find it in my books. I haven't thrown them away. Insurance! If they are there, I might return to teaching one day," Mridula smiled ruefully.

"All I remember is that they and the Bamanis were constantly at odds," said Maya.

"Yes and I think the Bamani kingdom had split up by then into Bijapur, Golconda and I forget what else."

"So in all this confusion, war, etc, normal life went on. People fell in love, got married, had babies, and died. Fantastic!"

"Not so different is it, from now? People still fall in love and get married. I guess you concentrate on the small things as the big are too big."

The next minute, Mridula looked at her watch and jumped up with an exclamation. Maya knew that the moment had passed and her affairs would have to wait another day.

"Oops! It's almost time for Meghna to come home from school! I must run."

Maya parked the car and came out to the front of the building where Footloose was located. She stopped and looked out at the approach road which was a street off the main road and the spot where she imagined Tulsi must have fallen from the third floor. She did not really know the body's exact location. Scorning the lift, she walked up, though she saw a number of people in exercise gear waiting for it. There was no traffic on the stairs even though it was only six in the evening, when offices probably continued working. There were no residences on the third floor. She was outside a glass door with fancy writing in wrought iron and a white signboard with a painted, bearded face, eyes closed. Well, if she gave in to her nervousness, she might just run down again, so it was better to go in.

She pushed open the door. There was a small reception area—this was mostly a residential area and the business spaces available were offices. The studio was probably a few rooms knocked into one. She smiled at the young girl behind the desk as she showed her the driving license as ID and the girl noted down her name and address. As she paid the fee, she handed over a business card, for her contact details. She watched the class in progress through the glass doors. She was glad she had dressed in a T-shirt and sweats, as most of them wore the same. The girl asked her to wait outside and she settled down on a chair, watching as the class went through the complicated salsa moves, smiling in sympathy at the laughing and giggling that went on as quite a few lost their footing or stumbled. The doors muffled the music, so she could hear nothing. Finally, the class ended and the students spilled out. Maya was relieved to see that not all were teenagers. There seemed to be few older men and women.

The chairs around her began to fill up as the instructor came out and took the place of the girl at the reception. After some minutes, the others went in and Maya reluctantly followed.

The girl who had been the receptionist now took charge. Obviously, the instructors took classes in shifts and helped out at the reception in-between. Maya took a good look as the girl raised her hand for silence and called, "Are we all ready?" The girl was pretty in a sharp-faced, kittenish way, and she seemed to be in the habit of taking charge. She looked familiar and Maya realized with a start that this was the girl she had seen on TV. No wonder the name Footloose had rung a bell. The instructor had introduced herself as Surilee. Maya wondered if the name was real, or if it assumed; certainly she had never heard of it before.

There were about eleven students. Most were young college kids, but in front of her was an older man: tall, balding slightly and already damp as if he was nervous. A few students on was another man, slim and spry, with salt and pepper hair. And wonder of wonders, there was an older woman! She wore her hair in a long braid, a black-beaded chain peeped out of her T-shirt, and a bindi on her forehead. Another young woman also looked like she was in her twenties, so Maya needn't feel she was the odd one out. She relaxed.

To Toni Braxton's *Unbreak My Heart* which segued into *Macarena* and then finally, Ricki Martin's *Maria,* they began to exercise—a little bit of aerobics, followed by stretching, then a lot of movement and finally, some yoga moves to unwind. Muscles quivering, legs like jelly, sweat pouring into her eyes, Maya leaned out of the big window for a breath of air. Her knee hit the window sill and she drew her legs up as the window seat was really low. She watched the other dancers. Some of them, including the ultra-conservative one, seemed less burnt out, which meant they must be regulars. Maya smiled at a girl nearby and made small talk—she had to get friendly with a few if she wanted to do any questioning—but there was hardly any time because at this rate she would probably be dead of a heart attack before the month was up and then what would happen to poor little Shibani and her mystery? But the girl proved to be of little help; like Maya, she had joined recently.

Surilee was calling to them; they were about to begin the dance. She explained that this would be a partnering exercise. The ladies got to choose first. Maya chose the grey haired man she had noticed earlier and he smiled at her. They had to break off as Surilee had started up again, telling them that they were going to jive and she went over to the hi-tech machine in the corner to play a Grease remix. Maya's partner and she had barely time to hold hands before they were off, mostly getting the steps right on the third try. It was hot work. Just keeping their eyes on their feet required all their concentration. Who cared about how close partners were or *anything* except the dance? They hadn't even exchanged names yet. Finally, the hour ended and the dance was only half way over. Surilee began the winding down exercises; another set of yoga moves. Maya hadn't even known she had all those muscles!

As she walked out, she wished the class was closer to her flat. A walk would have relaxed her. She felt revved up from the lesson. After her partner had thanked her, he had told her he was Sunny, short for Sunil. He was an accountant with one of the companies in the building. He had seemed impressed when she told him she was a lawyer and they exchanged cards. She decided to take the stairs, rather than wait for the lift which seemed, again, to have quite a good sized queue in front of it.

As she ran down the stairs, two at a time, she heard another pair of feet hurrying down. She made way for a young man, well built, and much taller than her 5'6", to come abreast.

"Hi, I'm Harsha, I haven't seen you here before," he said.

Maya introduced herself.

"So, you like dancing?" Harsha asked.

"Ummmm… I thought it was a good way to lose weight."

He gave her a sidelong look and with a gleam in his eye said, "There's nothing to lose. It's all fine as it is." Maya found that she was blushing and picked up her pace to cover her embarrassment.

"I just joined today. I was worried that everyone would be much younger and I was happy to see some older people."

"What does age matter?" He grinned.

Since there were only three floors, they split up as they had reached the lower level. It seemed to Maya that Harsh had rather reluctantly said goodnight. It was with a spring in her step that she got into her car and drove off.

Chapter VIII

March 1536
Mahashivarathri

Achale reached her mother's house. Once she stepped into the outer courtyard, she shrugged off one robe and put on another. Here she was Achale, the daughter, the elder sister; not Achalabbegaru, dancer to the King, by appointment; *Rudraganika* of Virupaksheshwara Temple.

Achale walked into the inner courtyard where she knew her mother would be, among her herbs, her hair in a careless knot, busy pounding, mixing, sifting, her face streaked with the colours of whatever she was currently concocting. She was right. Her mother was making a digestive. She was sifting the translucent brown crystals of *induppu* with turmeric stained fingers. "Achale!" Her mother accepted her greeting, lifting her before she completed her obeisance to hug her tight. The smell of turmeric and sandalwood mingled and encircled them.

"Where is Indra?"

"Where else? With his tutor, getting ready for the initiation."

"He must be finding it so strange."

"Didn't you when they took you away to the temple and you married the Lord? You were only six."

"Still, a boy of six is younger than a girl of the same age."

"Achale, everyone has to grow up sometime. The time has come for Indra."

"*Amma*, won't you miss him? Your last one, gone to the *gurukula* at Belur?"

"Yes, I will," Achale's mother acknowledged with a sigh.

"It's not too late for you to have another, *amma*."

"When it is time for my daughter to be thinking of starting her own family, it is time for me to stop increasing mine," said her mother. Ignoring this opening move in a game they had been playing for some time, Achale got up. "I need to go in and settle my things. I still have to rehearse some pieces for the entertainment tomorrow."

But she remained on the swing, gently beating time with each creak of the brass chains that held up the old teakwood swing in her mother's courtyard.

Her mother's house was nowhere as grand as her own house. It was built of stone and wood with simple brick *jalis* for windows set amid modest gardens. Achale's father Iruneerambadi Narayanachari, an Iyengar from Mandya was a *vaidya,* a doctor, who was also a skilled *jyoshya,* an astrologer.

"Whom have you invited to the ceremony?"

"Naturally, your father's entire family."

"But not the only representative on your side." The old hurt still rankled.

"Your *Ajji* knows that I would find any disrespect to her, even if unintended, painful. Besides, if they are not privileged to hear the greatest singer on this side of the Kaveri, it is their loss, not hers."

Ah, what you say is true." Achale was heroically biting her tongue. There was no point going over old ground.

When her father Iruneerambadi Narayanachari had been taken by his friends to the famous Roopavathi's house, he had no inkling that a sensitive face, peeping out of the curtain veiling the inner apartments would be his destiny, but he had soon fallen deeply in love. When he married Puttalakshmi, his family had been devastated. He had refused to marry a distant cousin they arranged for him.

"Oh, I forgot..." said Puttalakshmi.

Achale raised her eyebrow and waited. Her mother was trying to appear too casual, therefore she was going to say something which was bound to make her lash her tail.

"You know that Thulasi? The one whose body Ningi says she found? Her husband, Narayana Shastri was a good friend of your father's. They had attended the same *gurukula* together. Her mother's brother's son, Ranganatha will be coming here today. He has some knowledge of medicine, but not of astrology and wants to learn more of both from your father. I invited him to the ceremony. He has another brother, Madhava, a poet. He is translating the 4000 *divyaprabandham* into Telugu. The family is a little worried about him. He wants to enter court circles. You know how difficult that is. One must have the wit of Tenali Rama or the ear of the Dindima family. I don't know what is to become of him. Ranganatha wanted to talk to you about his brother."

"*Amma*, is that all he wants?"

"It is all that *he* wants but I want more. I want my daughter to be happy; secure in a happy marriage with her children and grandchildren around her, " Puttalakshmi said with dignity.

"*Amma*, when will you realize that I don't want to be married? I *am* happy. I can come and go as I please. I can pick any lover. I can immerse myself in my music without fear of neglecting my household duties. I don't have to share myself with anyone. I don't want to give up all this freedom."

Her mother shook her head. "Achale, when you are young, all this will seem like freedom. Don't forget, you are a public woman and cannot keep refusing the advances of all the powerful nobles. Spurned, they will turn on you like frustrated elephants in *musth* and conspire to bring about your downfall. Crazy girl, who needs official permission to take water from a stream? It is better to be the *kamadevi* of your husband than to tread the dangerous path of your choice."

Puttalakshmi called out, "Ningi! Get Achale some *panaka*."

Achale was in no mood to be cosseted. "*Amma* what about you? Don't you ever wish you had been able to devote more time to healing? You are so good at it. Did not *Akka* Mahadevi say that her God, Chennamallikarjuna was her husband?"

"Those times were different, Achale. King Kaushika, her husband, accepted her conditions that he could not force himself on her, that he should be devout and not disturb her prayers. When he could restrain himself no longer and tried to share her bed, she left him. Can you imagine such a thing happening now? Even princesses are held cheap. A King would pursue a beauty into enemy territory even though she has refused him, as our own Devaraya did that Pentala."

"*Amma*, why should I fear those nobles? They are all too busy plotting each other's ruin to worry about me."

Ningi came in then, "*Ammanauru*, the washerwoman has come. She wants to know which clothes she should take."

"*Ayyo!*" Puttalakshmi exclaimed. "She'll touch the clothes I have washed and hung out for tomorrow's ceremony. I have hung out a saree for you too Achale. I'll have to see to the *sandige*."

Achale's brothers ran in just as she left. Before she turned to exit the room she made eyes at Achale and pointed her chin at her elder son. Achale made no sign that she had seen but her heart sank. What now? She said to herself. The elder was nearly eighteen and had just finished his stint at the ashram to which Indra was being sent. They touched Achale's feet and then Indra settled down on her lap. Achale tugged Indra's topknot. "Run and get me a comb, *putta*. I'll plait your hair for the last time before it is tonsured and then I'll fix some flower chaplets in it." She cuddled him and wondered how Indra, this gap-toothed scamp who had just left off wetting the bedclothes, would bear the separation from his mother. The child scurried off, his mind unclouded by any thought other than his lunch.

"*Akka*," Kesava, her other brother was tugging at her upper cloth to get her attention. "What do you think of my joining the University at Kanchi? I want to study astrology."

"Why astrology? What does *appanauru* say?"

"You think I would ask him straight out and live? He wants me to study law and become an *acharya*. Can you see me do that?"

He screwed his eyes half shut and spoke out of the side of his mouth. "Verse 1012, line 4 says...you should behave like a monkey to appease your ancestors. Where is my *dakshina*?" He stretched out his hand and executed an elaborate bow. Achale began to laugh and Indra who had come back, joined in. After a time, Kesava added his chuckles to theirs, but his heart was not in it and he turned serious again. "Astrology is just a ruse to get out from under my father's nose. Actually, *akka*, I want you to talk to our father. He thinks you can apprentice me to some learned *acharya*. But I want to learn to sing and dance and act."

"Act?" Achale was startled. No Brahmin boy ever acted. He could sing. He had a very good, even tenor and could hit high notes along with her. In fact, they sounded very good together. Dancing and acting…she didn't see her way to fulfilling that ambition in the near future. It wasn't just her father. They had a whole community to convince. Maybe she could do something about the singing and dancing.

She winked at Kesava to say no more. They couldn't trust in Indra's discretion. She busied herself combing and adorning Indra's hair. Over the little boy's head, she signed to Kesava with her eyes to meet her in the garden.

She met her father at mid-day. Iruneerambadi Narayanachari came in from his office at the front of the house. She was struck anew by his resemblance to Kesava but knew that it was superficial. Kesava's fire, his love of music and dance, *that* had come from his mother and grandmother and she quaked inside at the thought of old wounds reopened, bile regurgitated.

His greeting was characteristic. "Achale, child, have you eaten?" he asked, smiling.

"What, before you *appa*?" she chided gently as she bent to touch his feet. He touched her head in blessing and smiled his acknowledgement of the exchange. After that, he gave himself up to the enjoyment of the food. Her mother had prepared Achale's favourite *holige* and *pathrode* and these deserved his undivided attention.

After his lunch, while Achale waited for her mother, he chewed the betel-nut thoughtfully, "Has your mother spoken to you?"

"She is busy with the preparations for tomorrow," said Achale, wondering which of the many difficult topics he was going to bring up.

"One Madhava will approach you tomorrow for an introduction to the court. See that you do what you can. I know his family."

"Yes *appa.*"

"It was Ningi who found that Thulasi woman's body, was it not? You had better be prepared for questions. Bhadrinatha is going to make trouble. You know what she was to him. And the boy has been pressing for results. How long do you think before they connect you to Ningi and your enmity with Bhadrinatha? Even though your father is a Vaishnavite, you dance in the Virupaksheshwara Temple and have followed your grandmother's faith. Bhadri wants to promote Srivaishnavism against the dualists, the *dwaitas*. Bhadri respects me, but he can never forget that your mother is born of a Saivite. Your mother wants you to marry this Madhava. He is a bright fellow and will not shame you, especially, if, as he desires, he gets an appointment at court. You need someone to administer your estates. It is not fitting for a woman to do it."

"I have Bhimanna to help me."

"Are you saying that it is enough protection against Bhadri? You were never wanting for sense, girl!"

Achale cast down her eyes.

"*Appa*, Kesava tells me you are going to apprentice him to an *acharya*?"

"Oho, he has got round you has he? Understand me, Achale! I don't want to hear any more foolish talk of *astrology*."

If you only knew what he is actually up to, thought Achale.

"You are my children. I know what is best for my family and what is due to the family honour."

And what happened, then, to you, all those years ago, when you married my mother? Achale didn't dare voice the question out loud and lowered her eyes, lest they reflect it.

Achale bowed her head and, touching his feet, allowed him to precede her into their house. They went their own way, he to rest and she to practice for the ceremony.

Achale was sitting again on the swing in her mother's inner courtyard. Her mother sat beside her, resting her back on the swing's copper chains, her legs drawn up to her chest, her chin on her knees. Her eyes were dreamy and she was humming to herself, the song sung by Achale, the evening before.

"Did you like it?" Achale asked. "Actually, Ningi told me of it. They are singing it on the streets. The poet sang it at the Great Temple on the Seven Hills. I learnt it from a *dasa* who visits me from time to time. I learn songs and he gets a place to rest for some time. He calls himself Acharyulu. Have you heard of him?"

"Uhhhm? So many questions! I have not heard the song but I like it very much. Talapakka Annamaya wrote so many songs before, but all with feeling! Ahaha!" she hummed the tune again. "Acharyulu was your father's friend. He gambled away his wealth, his wife and children."

Achale was startled. "That serene hermit, capable of such fickleness? What happened to his family, then? Oh, how can he bear it so calmly?"

"His wife repudiated him and began to live under the protection of and serve the winner. The children, a son and daughter have grown up. The daughter is Sundari. You know her. Her brother lives with her and manages her affairs."

"You mean pimps for her!"

"Achale, she earns in the only way she knows. She does not have Simhapuri Roopavathi daughter of Rangasani as her grandmother.

She is not as skilled as you in song and dance, nor is her training and knowledge as rigorous or vast. Acharyulu is atoning for it in the only way left to him—as a mendicant, living on alms, wandering aimlessly. They say he helps the poor all he can and also works as a spy for the anointed King. Who knows?"

Achale set the swing in motion with her foot, digesting this.

"Achale, what you did for Kesava today was very good. Ranganatha's family is well connected in the world of music and poetry. His uncle is Guru Ramabhadran who, as you know, trains almost all the minor dancers. He can take Kesava as an apprentice. How well his steps blended with yours and how melodious the two of you sounded! That was very clever of you, to make him part of the programme."

"Do you think *appa* looked thoughtful? At first he was a thundercloud, but later his expression changed to thoughtfulness, especially when everyone complimented him and Ranganatha Sastry even asked who his guru was. Maybe he will tell you something tonight, *amma*."

"I doubt it. Your father takes a very long time to change his opinion but the seeds have been sown. Your father was impulsive in his youth. Responsibility has made him cautious, but Srinivasa Shastry was born like that. He took one whole day to be born. They said he was deciding whether to be born or not, Thulasi's husband. And she was the most alive, wild creature, like a kitten. Always curious, impulsive, saying whatever came into her head. Once, she heard that Muralidhara, her neighbour's father had caught a peacock and had tied it to the pillar of his house. She was dying to release it. She crept up to it at night and cut its rope. It nipped her hand and she bled. Muralidhara's father made a big noise and wanted to summon the village council, but she did not care. Her father managed to smooth the matter over with a gift."

"Aaaaaah!" Achale let out a long sigh. It was good to be able to wash off the sweat and dust of the day's exertions. The night before, they had returned to Achale's house at Jogahalli, near Anegundi. The morning had begun with the usual frantic rush to get ready and commute to the temple of Pampapati. The day's duty done, they had repaired to the beautiful and cool Dancing Girl's Bath, with its backdrop of the craggy Matanga Parvatha.

Ningi was waiting with her clothes on the pavilion in the centre, cooling herself off by dipping the end of her sari and dribbling water on herself. Achale was impatient for her to return. She got out of the water, dripping and laughing at Ningi who had to wade through the pool to the rocks. So much for her attempts to keep dry! Ningi disappeared inside the changing rooms but Achale decided to dry under the sun and then wrap herself with a stole till they reached home. She sat down on a rock.

I labour in vain,
Sacrifcing my soul
With service for bread
Waiting for a crumb
From the table
Of a hollow prince
Were it not for
The round breasts
Of dancing girls,
Rivaling the moon,
How would I revive?

The voice came from behind her, an attractive voice deep yet sweet. But how impudent! She must punish him.

"Oh, 'a man of intellect' who passes off the great classical poet Harsha's verses as his own! Poverty of both morals and intellect! And what effrontery! Don't you know men are not allowed here? I'll call my maid to get the guard."

"*Devi*!" The rogue bowed deeply, his eyes laughing. He made a graceful picture as he stood there. Clean-shaven, his head tonsured in front but luxurious and knotted at the back. His fair chest and shoulders rose from the *kacche*.The silver and gold thread slung around his chest glinted with every movement.

"Please excuse an ignorant poet, a newcomer to the district. I was standing at the far end of the street, selling verses to the lovelorn and lovesick, but it is too hot now and business has dropped. I thought I could try my luck here, as women were sure to come here to bathe. I was merely trying to attract business but did not realize that I was in the company of one more learned than I!"

"What is a Brahmin like you doing selling mongrel verse in the dancing-girl's quarter? Should you not be at your studies... *acharare*? Why do you risk losing your caste hobnobbing with riffraff like us?"

The Brahmin held his ears with opposite hands in a gesture of humility, as mocking as her tone. "The company of one so great as you, likened to hobnobbing with riffraff? Besides, my charges are high. I don't get riffraff as my customers. If you had noticed, as you were bathing, Queen Amalotpava Devi's maid had come here. It seems she wants to be sure to catch the king's attention at least tonight. She has been making do with maids and even the eunuchs for about fourteen moons, waiting for her turn and is sick of it. I almost offered my services but thought better of it, I don't want to sample any sight unseen, nor do I want to ruin my chance of getting a position at court."

"Shiva, Shiva!" Achale shut her ears but her eyes were laughing. "Nice courtier a man as indiscreet as you will make!"

"Ah, I can always tell whether a person is trustworthy or not. May I know whom I am addressing?"

"I am called Achale."

He bowed, "I have seen evidence of your virtue, lady, as I had reason to partake of your consideration and generosity on my way here. Every traveler who used your well blessed you fervently. It is most conveniently located. I am Madhava Shastri at your service."

"You are a strange Brahmin not to observe the caste rules! At the service of a dancing girl!"

"*Devi*, I am always at the service of beauty. There can be nothing more divine. The great Lord Himself placed her at his heart. Who am I to quibble at his decision?"

"Madhava Shastry! My mother mentioned you. Your brother Ranganatha Shastri*garu* is spending some time with my father as his pupil. He wants you to join the court. I remember now."

"Yes, I was coming to see you this evening during your visiting hour, when I was to meet with your servant. It was she who found the body of my cousin Thulasi, was it not? Poor girl, shunned in life, at least her death should not go unnoticed! I would like to question your maid about what she observed."

"Betappa is trying his best. I am sure he will find out the truth."

"You mean the watchman? He may or may not. He is under the local *poligar* who is completely under the thumb of Bhadrinatha. Do you think Bhadri wants the truth to come out? It would tarnish the shining image of the miracle wrought by Manju which he is now milking to the full. I don't know why, but I will discover that.

There is some ambition of his connected to the whole incident. I mean to remove Manju from his care and look after him. Even if he is a saint, he needs someone to look after him with love, not to poison him with ambition."

"Your own ambition to enter court circles being somehow more laudable?"

"Oh, may I not pass through the doorway opened by poets of renown? Where they have ventured, why should I be thought a fool? Or will I win only ridicule, not fame? Time will tell. You have not answered my question, *Devi*. May I come to see you?"

Achale smiled to show her appreciation of his allusion to Kalidasa'a famous verse. "You may, but please do it discreetly after all the other guests have left."

"That is easy enough to arrange. The usual betel leaf and garland of flowers should do it."

"Not if I have to protect my reputation for chastity, but I will think of a way. Come, Ningi!"

They walked away but Achale could feel the poet's eyes boring into her. No matter, the past moon had given her much to think of. She had no time to waste on dalliance.

Chapter IX

March, 1996

They had just finished another class. Maya was about to leave, when she noticed a man sitting at the counter. He looked familiar and she realized he was the man from the news the other day, the one who owned Footloose. OK, this was an opportunity to talk to him. She wanted to ask him about the TV incident, but maybe that could wait until she knew him better. Anyway, apart from being a person who should be interviewed about Tulsi, he was worth knowing better. He was one of the best looking men she had seen so far—tall, wiry and well muscled. He was dark, with a French beard and glasses, a combination which worked really well for him. He looked like Shahrukh Khan crossed with Amitabh Bachchan, not a bad combination. Maya decided to come across as interested, but not too pushy, lest she set off any alarm bells.

"Hi! I saw you on TV the other day. You and Surilee were being interviewed?" she began.

He was busy entering some data on the computer and took a moment to finish, before he answered, though he glanced at her and smiled. "Oh, that show!"

"With the actor, yes."

"I'm Thomas. I haven't seen you before. You're new here?" He turned back to the computer and called up some data. She saw her contact details appear on the screen.

"Yes, that's me. I joined up after watching the program."

His answer was so low, she had to strain a bit to catch it, "At least some good came of that one." He made as if to get up, but she stalled him. She had wanted to catch up with the other girls and try to get some information from them. Maya glanced at her watch so he got the message, gave him a bright smile and said goodnight. He looked disappointed that she didn't want to chat, but let her go after saying goodnight.

As she reached the lift, she saw to her relief that the usual heavy traffic had worked in her favour and about three of her classmates, young coeds by the looks of them, were hanging about, giggling. She joined them. She didn't have to wait long before the subject of Tulsi came up. They were interested in why someone as old as she was had joined. They wanted to dance in college competitions and at parties (more giggles). This subject naturally led to how long they had been coming and since the time was right, Maya could slip in that a friend had mentioned it. They all seemed to know Tulsi.

"Oh she was such fun. She danced so well and kept us in splits, making fun of some of the tougher moves."

"She even made Surilee laugh! One time, she helped me with a turn which I just couldn't get in salsa."

"Very *friendly*," One of the other girls sniggered. What was that? Maya wondered. But the lift had stopped and there was a general rush to leave, so that would have to be followed up later.

Had Tulsi got caught up with something happening in the school? It all looked so ordinary, she couldn't imagine anything sinister enough going on to result in murder. Maybe it was something to do with her divorce.

Maya had not spoken to her sister for a long time. Mridula and she had not caught up at all after their shopping expedition together. When she called, Mridula sounded rushed.

"Is this a bad time?" Maya asked; after all, it was past 10 pm. Her little terrors—seven-year-old Meghna and five-year-old Aryan—must be in bed and Shreyas, her brother-in-law was probably plonked in front of the TV, tuned out to the world.

"No, it's been such a day, don't ask. I just… for a moment there, I felt you were going to ask me for some favour and I'm so exhausted, I couldn't bear the thought!"

"No, *akka*," Maya was soothing, "No favours, just a sisterly chat. Do you want to hear more about the book, the next installment?"

"Yeah, yeah, anything to distract me from party preparations and squabbling siblings and unresponsive husbands."

"So, Achale went to her mother's house. She's got a father as different from ours as can be—intense, unyielding, disciplinarian and I suspect, misogynistic."

"Why on earth did he marry her mother, for heaven's sake? Oh, it must have been arranged."

"Oh, he fell in love with the mother, a *devadasi's* daughter if you can believe it. He seemed ashamed of it, but was proud of Achale, the famous one. She danced at her brother's initiation ceremony. And get this! Her brother didn't want to pursue Vedic studies as an astrologer as the father wanted, but to dance!"

"Were there male dancers then?"

"No, but he could act and sing and teach, I guess, or so they seemed to feel."

"Umm. Even then careers for kids were a problem, huh?"

"This one seemed very chaste—she talks about God all the time. Oh, by the way, speaking of dancing...I've joined a modern dance class."

Mridula was curious. "Why this sudden interest?"

"I want to get fit. I thought this was a fun way to do it."

"You never worried about fitness before. So, how's it coming along?"

"I just got introduced to a guy who's an accountant but I was too busy minding my steps."

"You'd better mind where he puts his hands, OK?"

"Oh please, *akka*! If I meet someone, you'll be the first to know."

"Oh, I looked up the historical period for you and I've taken notes: see, here it is. I kept it here, next to the phone to tell you, but things were so mad here that I forgot. This must be around 1536. Immediately after Achyuta became king. There were a lot of problems—rebellions in the Tamil country, and invasions by his neighbours, the Bahmanis. There were riots at Vijayanagara which had to be quelled."

"You sound like a textbook!" Maya was all admiration.

"That's where I got this from."

"Were there different types of *devadasis*? What's a '*maledavalu basavi*'?" Maya asked curiously.

"Ummm...what I remember is... the chief temple dancer was the *rudraganika* and the *basavi*, one of the lowliest, who sang at weddings and private ceremonies."

"Oh, so complicated!"

"It was a career for women, then. They had better rights than wives." Mridula laughed wryly.

"Yeah?"

"You're the lawyer. You know that they had no rights in marriage under ancient Hindu law—Manu's law."

"Not that much has changed, even now for women. Our laws are all on paper and matrimonial property still a wish. "

"OK, enough of the history lesson. Don't forget your niece's birthday on Saturday. She'll never forgive you if you do."

"Oh, God I've got dance class then. OK, OK, I'll be there to help with the games. Good night." They signed off.

Maya had a nice time at the party. Quite to her surprise, Mridula was very organized and all Maya had to do was to follow instructions. So, rather relaxed and replete with Mridula's good cooking, Maya went to the dance class to work off some of the cake.

The instructor had changed. It was Harsha, the good-looking young man who had accosted her on the stairs the other night. As the class progressed, she found that she was expected to partner with someone new, a good way of everyone getting to know everyone else, the instructor explained. Maya ended up partnering with Paru, short for Parvathi, the girl who had made snide remarks about Tulsi.

"We've got Harsha today," Paru informed her, with a sniff. Maya waited for the meaning of the sniff to become clear, as she knew it would.

"We couldn't please him if we tried, so don't bother," Paru growled, as she missed her footing.

"No, no pleasing anyone, let's just enjoy ourselves," Maya soothed her partner.

"I thought after Tulsi went, he'd be forced to notice others and appreciate what's under his nose, but no, he hasn't changed."

"After Tulsi?" Maya prompted.

"Yes, he was going around with her, you know."

"Umm..." Maya pretended to be watching her feet, though she had got the hang of the steps. Her excitement was mounting, but to show interest now might be fatal to her chances to know more. The dance however ended just then and so did the girl's confidences.

As she was walking to the door, Harsha accosted her. "Hi, there! Remember me? We met on the stairs?"

Maya smiled. All the better to question him. It was providential, this meeting. Surprisingly, he brought up the topic himself, before Maya, who was wondering how to start, could say anything.

"Paru told me you were Tulsi's friend."

"Did you know her well?"

"She was a looker and loved to dance. She really knew how to live. She was a riot. I miss her."

"Were you surprised by her suicide?"

"I wasn't expecting it. She was such a happy person."

"It must be tough on you."

"It must be hard for you too."

"I can't believe it myself."

He sighed. Maya saw Thomas at the counter again. This was as good a time as any to get whatever information he may have. She quickly wished Harsha good night and asked Thomas if he wanted to join her for a cup of coffee.

They went to a coffee shop right opposite, where they seemed to know Thomas quite well. She had seen Paru giving her a sardonic glance from the space near the lift and knew that she would be the subject of her choice remarks as soon as they were out of earshot. Oh well, you can't please everyone, so might as well please yourself! She was intrigued by Footloose, so she decided to draw him out; not that he needed much prompting—it was clear he was keen on dance.

"You won't believe it, but I began learning to dance as a joke. Some guys dared me to try but you felt it too, no, it was fun. I stayed with the dancing. I made some money, and it was a good way to meet girls." His eyes twinkled, and Maya warmed to him. He continued. "So what do you do? Other than watch TV shows on dance groups?"

"I'm a lawyer."

"Ah, a liar!"

"Excuse me!"

"Did I say liar? Sorry, I should have said, add-wick-ed."

"OK, I get it. In your spare time, you go around making atrocious puns!"

The waiter came up, so they ordered their coffees.

"What do you think of what you did just now in class?" He leaned forward, eager for her input. His face was close to hers. His eyes were so dark there was no distinguishing the pupil; it was like falling into a bottomless pit.

"Just shaking a leg," she blurted out, with a sheepish smile.

"Have you watched any of our shows?"

Maya shook her head.

"You think Bharatnatyam, Kathakali, all that is dance and the rest is just 'shaking a leg?' You're dead wrong, man! We can interpret stories and emotions with our dance and it is better, as we don't follow any set format. We can do any move, any time, depending on the the theme. So which is purer, tell me?" Maya had to apologize profusely before she could get him to calm down.

"We'll be doing a show this year. Tulsi, one of our dancers was doing some research for a dance for another dance school called Ghungroo and she came up with this idea for us—something different which would make the old cows sit up and take notice. It was really coming along well. We were planning it together and we would have started the practice a long while back. But she... just... died. I have been working on it, but it's not the same without her input."

Maya didn't want to appear too inquisitive, but clearly she was called on to say something and what the hell, she was dying to know, so she asked, "She died?"

"Yeah, I don't know what happened; she just jumped from the window." He looked down, his hands fumbling with his keys.

"How did this happen? Was she leaning over or what?"

He pushed his hand through his hair. "She...it was just after the last class, I went in to lock up, you know. I do it every night-just checking, making sure everything's locked up and...I don't know, I found a window open. I reached out to pull it shut, you know we have these long metal door stops to keep them open, with several holes. Well, the pane was swinging in the breeze, I was worried it would bang shut and the glass would shatter. I looked down I don't know why, some instinct, and there she was, lying below. I didn't lock up, just rushed down. Everyone had left. I had to call the police. I still don't know why she jumped. Nor do the police." His hand went through his hair again. Maya felt sorry for him; he really looked distressed.

"Why do you think she jumped?"

"She was divorcing her husband, she said. She used to come home when her kid was with her husband and we would talk of the dance till late at night."

Maya felt an irrational tug of jealousy and thought, what else did you do? Though it seemed a foregone conclusion.

"Maybe she did not want the divorce. Maybe her husband was threatening to contest the custody for the child, make it ugly." He was unconsciously echoing what Maya had thought earlier. "I've been off my head, trying to figure it out. Talking with you today has helped. Thank you."

"It must have been terrible for you."

"I really miss Tulsi. The police had a lot of questions for me the next day. I got really worried, you know. They had me down to the station and I had to wait around until the husband came. I went with him to the morgue the next day and the day after, when they released the body. The police questioned me for a long time. I just told them the same thing I told you. They kept asking me about the other students and what I talked to her about, outside class. But I don't think anyone has said anything about her coming home."

Why was he telling her all this? Because he needed to unburden himself or was he just being clever? Did he know she knew Tulsi? Had one of the students talked? The police at least, had followed other avenues to suicide, but had given up too fast and closed the case. So Tulsi had begun to live—her life had been fun. She had been doing what she liked. Another reason for her death not to be suicide. And Thomas; surely, such a passionate lover of art and beauty would not kill? And even if he had, why? Tulsi was more valuable to him alive than dead. The questioning so far had not yielded much. Should she just abandon the whole thing?

Saturday had come around again, and as Maya sat, scoffing *dosai* once more, she suddenly shivered when a strong feeling of déjà vu washed over her. Just to get her partners' reactions, she said, "I joined Tulsi's dance class. Footloose."

"Ooh," hooted Pat, "We'll soon have you making sexy moves on someone."

Maya made big eyes at her, as she said, "And I spoke to Thomas, the owner."

Meena high-fived Pat, "One sizzler coming up!"

Maya rolled her eyes, "God, you two never grew up. He may be a suspect remember? I think Tulsi was having an affair with him. And he was the last one on the premises. He told me."

"How on earth did you get him to reveal that? Magic? Does he know you were her lawyer?" Pat wanted to know.

"I pretended not to know her. He brought it up. He seemed to think she jumped because of her husband making the custody for Shibani tough."

"What about the other students? Did they see something?" Meena asked.

At the same time, Pat came out with, "Was he? Making it tough for her?"

"I don't know. We had only started the preliminaries and he was getting his reply ready but hadn't yet filed it. She had temporary custody and Shibani used to visit him. He's a cold fish—can't make him out at all."

"Hmmm... There are some people like that." Pat conceded.

"I've only managed to speak to some girls, Meena. One of them, Paru, said that Tulsi was seeing Harsha. He's another instructor and quite peppy. He followed me after one class and said he wanted to get to know me. He said age doesn't matter."

Pat raised her eyebrows at Meena. "Ummm… things are getting hotter!"

"Oh cool it, you guys. This is not about my love life and I'm not going to do a Tulsi, no way. You know, she was having fun, seeing two guys, helping put together two shows, wanting to bake a cake for her daughter. It doesn't seem likely that she would have just jumped with all those things going on at the same time. But I can't get my hands on any motive. Maybe I should just dump it."

"That's what we told you in the beginning," said Pat, folding her arms.

"Wrong move, Pat. Just tell Maya something and she'll want to do the opposite. Let's encourage her instead," said Meena as she dodged the pen Maya threw at her. "But seriously, Maya, I've been thinking, isn't it a little odd that Thomas told you so much, so soon?"

"Odd, as in?"

"I really don't know. Just doesn't feel right."

"Maybe that book is trying to tell me something. I've just discovered the book will be ending soon. A chunk of pages is missing." They wanted to know the latest. Maya told them what she had told Mridula.

"How will you exist, Maya, you poor thing? Just living like ordinary people will seem so tame after this," Pat clucked, her eyes twinkling.

Maya said, seriously, "I really don't know, Pat. I'll just have to solve both the mysteries, I guess." Pat and Meena raised their eyebrows at each other and rolled their eyes.

"Look, it's nothing serious. I always get bothered by mysteries, remember? I like neat endings. Always have, you know." Maya smiled brightly.

Meena had been silent until she finished. Now she said,"Maya have you considered what this will do to the kid and even the husband if it comes out?"

Maya winced. "I didn't think of that! Maybe we could suppress that part?" Curse Meena! Now all her doubts had returned doublefold.

CHAPTER X

MARCH 1536

MAHASHIVARATHRI

The music assailed them just as they neared the temple. The immense bulk of the temple's tower was outlined against the sky in gold and crimson. The lamps lit right up to the topmost level, flickering defiantly against the brightening day.

Achale shifted restlessly, and felt the familiar tightening of her gut, the prelude to any performance of hers. More so on this day because the King was supposed to stay on after the prayer and watch. She had ordered a special decoration around the platform. Instead of the usual gauzy cloth curtain, there would be screens of flowers, flirting with her form—daring, innovative, sure to tickle the jaded palate of that old debauch, the King. The thought of her performance reminded her of a new poet who had not revealed his name or his lineage. He had merely sent her some verses through an urchin, wrapped in a jasmine garland, begging her to run her eye over them. He had ended the letter, promising to meet her after the performance. Her senses fluttered in anticipation.

A chain of elephants came near. One of the keepers who was leading some of them, turned at that moment. "Hey Bhimanna!" he called. Bhima, who was standing nearby, turned. "Chenna, how goes it? I will meet you later." After the preliminary morning worship, the procession would begin, but Achale had decided to give it a miss to conserve her own energy for the solo performance.

Achale hurried over to the priests in the sanctum. Even the critical glances of the other dancers could find no fault with her person or raiment. They turned their eyes elsewhere for amusement. "Look," whispered one, nudging her companion. "That's the steward of Rama Raya's household. A steward from the king's household was also overseeing arrangements for seating his Master's retinue."

A commotion was heard at the gates. Rama Raya's steward rushed over, as if he had been given his cue. A moment later, the hated and feared Aliya Ram Raya swept into the enclosure succeeded by a group of women, children and their hangers on.

Bhima, who had been watching from the shadows, now ducked out into the outer courtyard. He needed to make arrangements for Achale's refreshment after the dance.The outer courtyard was crammed with people. The Brahmins and chief nobles were all inside. He went out into the crowded market.

Chenna was sitting in the shade of a stone apple tree in the sacred grove when Bhimanna, after he had finished his task, squatted for a chew of betel. The elephant, also named Bhima, swayed nearby, tended by a young boy so puffed up with the confidence reposed in him that he was afraid to smile.

"They say that Bhadrinatha has been trying to make the Madhavaswamy temple at Alur popular for a long time, since he is the trustee. The Vaishnavites must be overjoyed. First, a great saint like Vyasatirtha, then I hear talk of a *dasa* who they say sings as if Saraswathi had given birth to him, and now this boy saint." He lifted his voice in song,

Raagi thandiro bhikshake raagi thandiro!

Give this beggar raagi.

Bhimanna, covered his ears with his hands. "Enough! Goddess Saraswathi might have given birth to Purandara *dasaru* but one of your ancestors had four legs and a tail!"

"Take care, *anna,* that I don't tell Bhima there to punish this Bhima. Do you know, he refuses to sleep if I don't sing a lullaby?"

"Oh, four-legged brother Bhima, I don't have your great musical sensibility. Forgive me! To the crow, no doubt, a baby crow looks adorable and a baby donkey must charm a she-donkey. You were talking about the saints, Vyasathirtha and Purandara *dasa*. Bhadrinatha is a *visishtsadvaithin*. They also worship Vishnu but they have different saints and different ways. They are from the Tamil country."

They were interrupted by the sound of trumpets. The gatekeepers began to chant, "Victory to the King! Victory to the King!" The heralds ran hither and thither, shouting, "Stand back! Stand back! The Great Emperor of the realm from the Vindhya mountains to the Ocean, the annihilator of the Gangas and the Plague of the infidels is here! He Himself, the King of Kings, the Greatest of all Emperors, King Unparalleled Achyuta Rayagaru of the illustrious house of Tuluva!" The bodyguard clattered in on their horses. In the centre was the King and his chief officers including his important supporter and brother-in-law, Salakaaraju Tirumala.

"Look," whispered Bhima, "That is Salakaaraju Tirumalayadeva, his brother-in-law who helped the King in his Tamil campaigns against that traitor Saluva Nayaka and also in his campaign in Bijapur. They saved the entire Raichur from the Turkoolu. We now hold the entire land up to the Krishna River."

"Where was he when the Aliya imprisoned the king last year and set up that weakling child Sadashiva, then?"

"He had gone to the Cholanadu to oversee the collections to the Tirupati temple there, when it happened. Didn't he come back and kill the jester who had released the king only to set himself up as Prime Minister to loot the treasury?"

"I heard talk of it. A servant to dream of kingship! What next?"

"When Bapanoollu can become commanders of forts, leaving their hymn texts for the sword, why can't the servant seize an opportunity to exchange his broom for the crown?"

"Anyway, *anna*, the king has got back his crown and the Aliya seems to be keeping his ambition in check."

"A thief will always think like a thief, a noble person will always display nobility. You mark my words. The King has not had an easy time of it. First imprisoned by his elder brother and made to live at Chandragiri with the untrustworthy Sadashiva, then all these troubles. It is a good thing our neighbours have troubles of their own."

"*That* was a good move, forging ties with Mallu who has enough trouble already keeping Asad Khan Lari from stirring up the other nobles."

"Ah, you seem to know a good deal of these military matters."

"We fell in with some temporary recruits returning to Jaramali on our way here."

Chenna craned his neck but the crowd was pressing him on all sides, so he clicked his tongue at Bhima, and the elephant lifted him easily until he was as high as his ear. Aha! The King's turban was almost as big as four-legged Bhima's head! *Apapa*! How did he bear it? And the jewels on his person! How many mines at Golconda must have been excavated to form just one necklace! All the jewels could not make his face more handsome, though.

This was a dark King, almost as dark as Chenna himself. To top it off, he was short and fat.

When Chenna was young, he had heard his parents talk about this King's elder brother, the great Krishna Deva Rayudu. Fair and tall, of beautiful mien, strong as a wrestler, which he was; *he* was a King. A courtier Chenna did not know came out from the temple and joined the King. The others in the cavalcade immediately made way for him though the King nodded reluctantly. He had a haughty air and looked straight ahead. At that moment, Bhima, perhaps troubled by a fly, flapped his ears and the haughty courtier looked up, straight at Chenna. He bent down and seemed to be saying something to a dark thin man, running alongside. Chenna, who had been struggling to maintain his balance on Bhima's trunk gave up and lowered himself to the ground. As he craned his head over those of the two men in front, the crowd came to a halt.

Chenna however, was not interested in watching whatever had caused the standstill.

He was too busy ogling the bevy of *raja dasis* who were behind the guard, framing the doorway of the temple their garments of cloth of gold, their arms studded with ornaments so heavy that each could hardly hold up the lighted gold pot lamp she carried in front of her. *Isvara*! Were these women or *apsaras*? No wonder these women, it was said, could do what they pleased with kings and queens; even eat betel in their presence! Kings were mere mortals but these women were divine!

His eyes strayed to the head of the welcome committee. Aah! Had Pampadevi herself walked out of the sanctum to garland the king? An embodiment of grace! She took the *kumbhaarthi* from a waiting maid and began to dance. Could this be Urvashi? The priest sprinkled the rose water in blessing, and the procession then began to move forward. Chenna reluctantly settled down. He could not follow them into the inner courtyard reserved for the twice born. He turned to Bhima, who was waiting for the throng to subside before he followed the procession inside.

"Who was that *anna*? Was I dreaming or did I see Urvashi?"

"Even Urvashi would have felt envious if she had seen her. That was my Lady." He ducked his head to hide the pleasure that praise of Achale always gave him.

"And you serve her! The Gods have placed you in paradise! I did not know I was hobnobbing with such an exalted being!" Chenna was lost in superlatives.

"To gaze on such beauty, knowing it is far, far out of your reach may not be so exalting for some!" Bhima said dryly. They chewed betel for a while in silence.

"Who was that riding from inside, *anna*? The glistening one, who looked like he has been in a fight with an oil-man?"

Bhima laughed "Ho, son-of–a-donkey, don't you know him? Where have you been hiding? That was the great Aliya himself, king-maker and king-breaker. The one beside him was Kondoja, the barber-turned noble."

"*Anna*, when you travel a lot, you often miss that which others take for granted."

"Yes and they say the Aliya never gives up once he has started something. Did you notice the other one?"

"Which one?"

"The other riding the white steed with the brown star on its forehead? One would see the horse before the man. So excellent a creature is it."

"*Anna,* I was watching the King and the Raya."

"That was the Salakaraju Tirumalayadeva. Krishnappa Nayaka from Madurai, Sivappa Nayaka of Tanjavur, Tubaki Krishnappa of Gingee and Venkatappa Nayaka of Rayadrug were also close to the King."

"Ah, so many nobles all at once. They must suspect something!" said Chenna excitedly.

Bhimanna got up. "I must be going," he said, brushing the seat of his *kacchha*. He entered the crowd and was lost.

Chenna settled back against a tree, pondering what he had heard and seen. Bhimanna was not impervious to his mistress's beauty. On the contrary, he was trying to resist it. So many important men! What was up? He had no time to react when two hands jerked him roughly to his feet and dragged him off, outside the temple precinct.

Bhimanna slipped in just as the King's cortège reached the sanctum. He ran round to the hundred-pillared hall next to the main sanctum. He had to push his way through the waiting *devadasis* but since he was Achalabbe's man, the crowd parted easily and no one challenged him.

The ceremony wound to a close. The deity was now ready to be sent out. The deity's consort, whose own rituals had been completed simultaneously, was brought out to be with Him while He rode in state in the palanquin to grant his devotees their seasonal audience. Her hands joined in an obeisance, Achale, who had just ended her final dance of the morning ritual, walked backwards to join the crowd. Bhima walked towards her, intent on finding out milady's desire.

CHAPTER XI

SPRING, 1536

Achale, Ningi and Bhima came out into the main gate. The deity had left the temple. "Let us go on, *Chikkamma,* it seems a Dombra is going to make his big elephant climb a rope, high in the air, as high as the *dwhaja stambha,*" Ningi said, as they stopped to watch the acrobats set up their feats.

Smoke from the fires of the various camps for the preparation of their morning meal still clung to the air, making breathing slightly difficult. Achale inhaled deeply the smell of the nosegay around her wrist. They covered the immediate environs quickly, until they came out to the riverbank. Here, an enterprising troupe of daylight actors had marked out their rude stage and were getting ready for their performance. As the drummer drummed up an audience, the three sat down to be entertained.

The story-teller and his assistant, dressed as a lady came up, to begin the performance. As they began their usual song and dance routine, Achale, closed her eyes and let the music flow around her. The temple procession would not be back for an hour, so they could watch for some time. The crowd laughed, jerking Achale back to the play. "Aye Thimmi, what have you there?" the male player made as if to pluck something from the hands of the other.

"Nothing, it is nothing," the female impersonator hid it behind his back.

"I heard that your mistress wants a baby really badly and is prepared to buy it!"

"Eh! Where did you hear that?"

"Oh, it is common knowledge."

"No, no, you are mistaken, this is a letter to a midwife."

"Oh, strange things are happening—babies are spawned in a day and bundles of cloth can become babies."

"Oh, shoo! Don't say that." So saying, the female impersonator ran offstage. The crowd was abuzz, trying to guess the meaning of the play. In the distance, the sound of the returning procession could be heard. Achale, Ningi and Bhima hurried off, their heads in a whirl as they mechanically got ready for the deity's return. Achale had to perform the rite of the removal of the evil eye, the dance with the pot lamp and then get ready for her performance.

Bhima, watching the performance, was amazed at the complete concentration shown by his lady. Not a step out of time, not a note faltered as she sang each stanza, before the musicians played for her as she danced. She had already danced, as a token of respect to the King, a small piece from Sri Krishna Deva Raya's *Amuktamalyada*, where, the Goddess is described. The composition of a new poet had then followed. He watched the assembled faces as she danced the *Kumarasambhava* that she had set to music. The crowd was rapt, as well they should be, since the King was present but he thought the emotion was not assumed. Her mother and father had joined the crowd and he was relieved to see that her father seemed to be as pleased as the rest.

Bhima looked around. The music was extremely tuneful, the flute's notes swooping there, the stream sometimes widening full-bodied and powerful, then mellowing gently, dipping to a low cooing, then soaring and looping above all the other instruments, rivaling the cymbals in crispness and clarity. There seemed to be a new flautist. The regular man sat outside the circle of musicians, a bemused look on his face. Bhima slipped through the crowd, until he was circling the outer corridor which would take him to the old flautist.

"Aii, what's up? Why the change?" The flautist looked up, and hastened to his feet. Slighting Achale's man would not be to his advantage.

"The man insisted and he was playing so well, I could not refuse. He is a Brahmin. Maybe he wants to catch the King's eye," his smile slipped to a leer, "or my lady's."

"Continue to bandy my lady's name and yours will no longer be in the temple's list." The flautist looked down sheepishly and Bhima stayed where he was. The mystery had to be cleared up. Achale had seen the man. He was sure of that. Her glance strayed to the musicians more often than was usual in a performance and she seemed to be on the verge of a smile. One could even say that some of her *mudras* were aimed at the man. Was the crowd aware of this by-play?

There sat the King. He was smiling benignly at the crowd. No doubt his mind was more on the nubile young dancers scattered around than on the performance. Rama Raya had his eyes closed. It was the music for that one. He was writing a treatise, it was rumoured. Bhima shook his head in bewilderment—a scholar and an ambitious and ruthless statesman! How did such opposing streams run through his blood? There was a new Brahmin in the crowd not of these parts, he was sure.

Watching Achale, Bhima marveled how easily she could shift the energies or *rasas* from anger—*raudra rasa:* eyes spewing flames; to *bhayanaka*—fear the dying of Kama; to *shringara*—love and *karuna*—compassion, for Rati, Kama's wife's lament. Her coral tipped fingers, rivaling the dawn, flitted like bees, spread like bird's wings and unfurled like petals to evoke the moods, while her large and lustrous eyes, flashed, shimmered and glowed softly, drawing one's soul into her hands. The courtier Vajrabahu was looking bemused. The lady had surpassed herself.

As she danced, Achale wondered, for whom am I so adorned? She tried to summon the usual warmth of devotion to the Lord, but it did not come. Instead, some mischievous canker in her mind summoned up the image of the potter she had seen in the marketplace. She banished the thought as soon as it arose. Bhima, watching her, was wondering the same thing. Achale had long said that she was the Lord's handmaiden. But Ningi was giving out that she had evinced interest in the potter and sculptor, the descendant of Kai Dala.

Achale ended her dance with Shiva's creation of Kumara. While she danced, her eyes had scanned the crowd, expecting to see a new face and recognize through some intuitive magic, as yet undiscovered, the Unknown who had sent her the scintillating verses. She had seen no one new. Only Madhava, who had taken over the flute, had caught her eye and she had engaged in some silent banter with him which had added some sparkle to her dance.

A bevy of minor dancers immediately pranced in, their feet already moving to the quick rhythm of the movement that they were going to perform. Bhima checked to see if Ningi had gone off stage to assist his mistress, and then sat down to watch. There was a slight stir among the audience. A young boy seemed to have joined the dancers, which was not usually seen at such gatherings in the temple. Craning his head, he could see that the youth was Achale's brother. He seemed to be grinning at the flautist who was nonchalantly moving his head in time to the music. Bhima glanced at Achale's father. The man looked thunderstruck. At least he had remained seated. This augured well for the boy though his father could hardly do more as the King was still seated and seemed to be enjoying the boy's routine.

Bhima looked around for Achale and became aware that another drama was playing out behind the stage. The newly arrived Sangama courtier, Vajrabahu, was chatting up Achale, who seemed to be enjoying his attentions. As Bhima took his place at a little distance, ready to be of assistance if need be but not so close as to intrude, Achale smilingly turned to go and collided with a Brahmin. As she quickly stepped back in confusion and folded her hands in apology, the Brahmin turned revealing himself to be Bhadrinatha, the Brahmin collector from Alur who was always harassing Achale to pay the prostitutes' tax that *Ajji* had warned her about.

"Ah, Achale, no need to apologize. What does a beauty such as you have to hide," this with a suggestive leer at her breasts, clearly visible through the thin material of her bustier.

Achale was incensed, especially as Vajrabahu had not stirred from his place, obviously enjoying this quarrel. She hurled a *vachana* from *Akka* at Bhadrinatha:

"Why do you feel desire for this carapace, this shell filled with the anger and avarice, of *kama*? Know this and free yourself to experience God, in this, His Temple!"

They were creating quite a commotion, unheard of in the King's presence and during the festivities. Besides the King, a minion stood close by with a silken cushion bearing a silver plate on which rested a necklace studded with gems and a bag of coins. However, Bhima saw that rescue was close at hand. The new flautist was bearing down on them, the Brahmin whom he had noticed earlier, close by his side.

"Achalabbegaru," Madhava Shastry said, bowing low, "Well met! Truly spoke the poet who likened the sunstone afire in the sun to the effect of an insult offered to an honourable woman."

Bhadri was beginning to look ill at ease. Madhava introduced the other man as Venugopalachari. Achale, in spite of herself, was interested. She had not noticed the newcomer while dancing, which put her in mind of a more pressing query,

"*Acharare*, did I not notice you playing the flute? What happened to my regular man, what did you do with him? And how could you induce Kesava to dance at the assembly and the priest, how did he permit...?"

"*Devi*, we may be of different faiths but we all worship at one altar. It was only a matter of ascertaining the price of your regular man."

"Seriously, did you see my father in the audience? I was too anxious to take a good look at his face. Suppose he were to stop the dance? What a humiliation for the temple! Especially now that we have yielded our place as the heart of Vijayanagara to Tirupati. Even our King had his coronation at Tirupati."

"He also had a crowning ceremony at the Shiva temple at Kalahasti. He is a king. All his subjects had to be kept happy."

"At least your deity has not been forced to flee the *sanniddhi*." This from Venugopalachari.

"Sir?" Bhadri had joined the conversation. Madhava introduced Bhadri and Venugopalachari ceremonially.

"And what great good fortune permits Hampi to be graced by your presence, good sir?" Bhadrinatha was becoming embarrassingly courtly.

"My mission is no secret, sir." Venugopalachari revealed that the ceremonial idol of Vishnu had to be removed from Chidambaram and reinstalled at Lower Tirupathi for safekeeping from threatened depredations by the Saivites at the time of Kulottunga Chola II. "My fellow Brahmins want the idol of Devadidevan to be installed in Chitrakutam with full ceremony."

"Ah!" Bhadri fell silent but one could almost see the thoughts chasing each other across his mind.

"There are different legends associated with the temple but only one which explains the unusual feature of one shrine for two deities. There was a dance competiton between Shiva and Kali, so the duo approached Vishnu as arbitrator. He is supposed to have directed them to Tillai. Shiva, at a covert gesture from Vishnu, is said to have lifted his left foot towards the sky in the Urdhuva Tandava posture, a definite male gesture, which Kali, governed by the rules concerning female modesty, could not duplicate. Shiva thereby emerged victorious. Kali was appeased with the status of primary deity in another temple in the outskirts of Chidambaram. Shiva agreed to remain at Chidambaram, next to Vishnu's shrine" replied Bhadri.

"Ah, thus making this a Vaishnavite triumph," was Achale's derisive retort.

"The lady must admit that the legend seems appropriate to the situation," said Venugopalachari.

"But not on this day, the day that the *linga* first manifested itself, when the earth gets ready to throw off the shackles of winter and embrace the soft glow of the spring dawn, when life begins to break into bud and the earth uncoils even as a young woman, asleep in her lover's embrace, wakes up to greet the invigorating dawn with her arms outstretched, her limbs elongated, engulfed in the rosy blush." Not for nothing was Achale known for her insight and scholarship.

"You are talking about Brahma and Vishnu, setting off to find the source of the *linga* and Brahma's secret compact with the *ketaki* flower to defraud Vishnu and Shiva, by lying that he had met the flower falling off Shiva's head. We will never agree about the Trinity, which makes it easier for others to denounce our faith!"

Turning to Achale, Madhava then said, "That was good poetry that you danced to. It was good of you to introduce an unknown poet to the public on such an important day. "

"The verses were so good, I could not resist. There is no special merit in acknowledging that something worthwhile is so. "

The talk soon veered to the 4000 *Divyaprabhandams*, the songs of the Vaishnavite saints, the Alwars that Madhava was translating into Telugu. Scholarship held no interest for Bhadri. He bowed and withdrew.

"*Acharare*, what of your ambition to enter court circles?" Achale wanted to know.

"Oh, one thinks it is harder than Sanskrit, one calls it Telugu. They have no ears who cannot hear their language in my poetry."

"Oh, let it go, sir! The rasping caws of crows will silence the goose. But the crow is a crow and the cuckoo a cuckoo when spring comes."

They broke into laughter at the same time recognizing that Achale had capped Madhava's verse with the next few lines from the same piece he had quoted, Kavisarvabhauma Srinatha's introduction to *Bhima Kandamu*.

Achale also clasped her hands and turned to go with a mocking glance over her shoulder. However, the King was preparing to leave and the minion standing near Achale unceremoniously thrust the reward into Bhima's hands before running off to his Majesty's side. As the king placed his foot into the stirrup, and prepared to be lifted on to the horse, someone darted from the crowd and held the horse's reins before the guard could react.

"Manju!" The groan broke from Madhava. The King was impatient to be off, his brows were drawn together, his eyes flashed; the thunder was soon to follow.

"Sire," shouted the boy, "My mother's spirit has no peace. Her ashes flow in the river but her spirit is still unquiet." Madhava hurried forward. He now approached the King's steward of the horse, who listened to his murmurs. Achale could make out the words, chastise... punishment... *Shivrathri*. The steward gently disengaged the boy's hands from the reigns as Madhava held him close in an embrace. "Oh, well done, *acharare*!" murmured Bhima, from his place close to his lady, "To pass it off as a prank for Mahashivarathri, the usual child asking for punishment to evoke Brahma's punishment for lying." As the King's horse moved off in a cloud of dust, boy and man moved off, arms around each other. The poet now engulfed a weeping child.

"*Amma*, I don't understand—what chastisement?" asked Ningi. Bhima explained the legend of Brahma and Vishnu and the source of the Shiva *linga*. "To evoke that tale, children are allowed to play pranks and then confess, asking forgiveness on Shivarathri."

"So her son was allowed by the Brahmins to perform the last rites." Ningi voiced the thought in Achale's mind.

"They could hardly do otherwise, having accepted him as a miraculous being. In short, he is now acepted as twice-born," Bhima answered.

"In death she triumphed," murmured Achale. "I suppose he will now live with his mother's relative, Madhava." And so it transpired, as they heard later. But at that moment, Achale could only lament that the unknown poet had broken his promise to meet her after the dance.

Chenna came to on the back of a horse, only he was not sitting on it, he was slung across the saddle, tied to it. The pain was excruciating. His ankles were burning, so were his wrists, the effort to stay on the saddle was hurting his stomach, back and groin and his shoulders and arms were being pummeled by the horse's motion. The rope was cutting into his middle and he could hardly breathe. They seemed to be going on a journey to Hell itself, so long did it seem. He was careful not to make a sound. Let his captors think he was still unconscious!

At last, the horse stood still. He opened his eyes a fraction, for a quick look. However, he dare not raise his head. That would alert his kidnappers. All he could see was the ground and a portion of a building. It looked massive, more like a fortress. He closed his eyes again. He was hauled off the horse and carried on the back of one of the men, like a sack of coal. He hoped he was very heavy and had the satisfaction of hearing grunts of pain when the man had to climb what seemed to be stairs. He heard a door being unlocked and he was thrown onto the rough stone floor. His bones groaned at the impact. The door was pulled shut and then there was quiet. He could not understand what had happened and why one moment he was on his elephant watching the procession and the the next, here he was cooped up in the dark.

From where he had been left to lie, he could see a patch of sky. It was bright with sunlight, signifying that it was still probably mid afternoon. Suddenly, he jerked—a brainwave had made him tingle. He was an acrobat, a gymnast, flexible of body and mind. How could a few pieces of string present any problems? He began the series of contortions which would set him free—this trick had never been his but he had seen it done a hundred times in practice sessions and in the shows. After some time, he felt the bonds yield a bit and then give way. Slowly, he wriggled out of them. He propped himself against the brick wall and waited for the night.

The guards, meanwhile, sitting outside, were enjoying a break. They had decided to go down to the yard to stretch their legs after the grueling ride. Their voices floated up to Chenna:

"Why are we holding this fellow? He seems too puny to matter. What is he suspected of?"

"You know the Great Lord. He suspects everyone and everything! You know they say: what is likely to happen if they give a scorpion power? So he has always to be wary."

"And our Lord always follows his brother's lead."

"The great Rama Rayagaru! What else can his brother Venkatadhri do?"

"But what is suspected of this weakling?"

"Oho, so you have to ask? Really, you do not see beyond your nose! Did you not see this one seated on the elephant's trunk, half-hidden, watching? Maybe he is the King's spy. Maybe they suspect."

"He is a Dombra. Do you think they can spy?"

"They go everywhere."

"So, will the plot work? The young one, Sadashiva is just a boy."

"All the better for our Lord's plans. Did it not almost succeed last time?"

"With our Lord Kondoja helping, it might. He is lucky! A barber to rise up to overlord status!"

"Hmmm..."

There was silence for some time, while the guards sat down and settled themselves to roll and chew betel.

"Did you hear about the young saint?"

"What saint?"

"That one who was initiated by God Vittala himself. Over at Alur."

"Oh! I remember, I remember."

"Strange that *that* woman should have had such a virtuous son."

"Why do you say that? Do you know her?"

"You forget I come from Alur. Who has not heard of Thulasi, the beautiful young widow who had a son well after her husband was dust? She always insisted that he was Lord Madhava's son! Imagine! Now she herself is fodder for the Fire God. It is all the work of Narayanacharlu, her husband Srinivasa's heir. Was he not waiting to grab her husband's lands for himself when she was excommunicated? He did not care that she was left the income for life. Now he is after her *stridhana*, I'm sure. A fat parcel just outside the village which Boriah was cultivating for her. Easy enough for him to lay claim to it along with guardianship of the boy."

"Is not Bhadrinatha, lord of Alur, interested in the boy? I heard that he was telling anybody who would listen that the boy was a saint. Good for the Vaishnavites to fob him off and good for the temple at Alur, which he heads as trustee."

"Ummm...You are right. The *bapanoollu* always have some devilry up their sleeve. They do it to fatten their purses but pass it off as God's will. Did you hear of what Tenali Rama, the old King's jester did? He heard that the Brahmins insisted on fees of a solid gold cat to perform the obsequies of the King's mother, a cat-lover. He waited until his mother's death day came round. He insisted on giving each Brahmin a smack with a stick, in remembrance of *his* mother!

"Ha, ha, ha! I wish I had been there! "

"Anyway, it is up to Betappa the *taliyar* of Jogahalli to find the murderer or die trying."

"I don't envy him his task. Narayanacharlu is powerful." His voice dropped.

Suddenly, Chenna heard a commotion which seemed to be from the back of the palace, at quite a distance from where they were. He heard loud exclamations from the guards and the sound of running feet. A voice could be heard singing.

O Lord of Vaikuntha, come running, my heart yearns to see you..."

The song seemed to come from close by and then seemed to come from farther away, as if the singer was moving away and indeed it grew fainter by the minute. It was replaced by a tremendous crashing and cacophony as if huge stones were being hurled at the walls. Chenna was too shocked to worry about himself, stuck away somewhere within, when a battle seemed to be raging outside. He hoped that Bhima had somehow realized he was missing or maybe some of the young men from his troop, Basava or Venkatu had seen him being abducted and had come to spirit him away. Even as the thought took shape, he dismissed it as unlikely. No one was brave enough to encounter these paid villains for his sake.

He heard the guards leave their post and run. He reached up and caught hold of the window, tried to hook a leg on to the window ledge, succeeded and jumped onto the sill outside. He was just gearing himself to jump, when he saw a mendicant staring at him, with his fingers on his lips. He jumped and the mendicant moved forward, catching him, to break his fall. From the corner of his eye, he spied the guards, wrestling with a white dog that seemed to be pulling their spears so they were forced to turn away and aim kicks at it.

Still silent, the mendicant and Chenna moved quietly round the other side of the building and hid behind some bushes. The coast seemed to be clear so after a while, they moved slowly until they were far enough away to break into a run. When they were some distance away, the mendicant gestured to a tree and asked Chenna to climb it. He followed suit, and in a short while, the soldiers thundered by below.

When they judged it to be safe, Chenna and the mendicant climbed down and began their long walk to the town, going in the opposite direction to the guards.

They were joined by the white dog and the mendicant immediately began to sing Purandhara *dasa's* song,

O Chieftain of the crooked tail ,

Idle wanderer,

What did you thieve or forage to eat today?

Chenna was glad to be on the move again. He wondered about the mendicant and hesitantly, because after all what business had a Dombra with a sage, asked, "Honoured sir, what good fortune brought your reverence to this place to free this accursed Dombra?"

The mendicant smiled and began another song:

Tandanana, ahe, Tandanana...
The soul and the Divine are one....
All creatures are of the same caste under the sky
and everyone has Sri Hari as the inner soul.....
The king and the slave
Sleep the same sleep
The Brahmin and the Untouchable
Pace the same land...

Even children knew this song, composed by the great Annamaya, so Chenna found this easy to follow. Slowly it dawned on him that it was an answer of sorts to his question, though he would have to piece it out after considerable thought. He shrugged philosophically; this world was full of strangeness, if it had helped him for once, it was good. For now he was content to just walk the road to the city and pray the soldiers would not come back.

CHAPTER XII

MARCH 1996

Maya had been looking forward all week for the first class on Wednesday. So here she was, sitting on the chair outside the studio waiting for class to begin. The aunty-type had joined her; she looked so much like a familiar stereotypical housewife that she caught herself looking for the net shopping bag and then scolded herself for being a bitch. Her name was Uma. She had put on weight after her second child but, had always liked dancing. She didn't much like dancing with a partner but generally enjoyed the classes and hoped her husband would never get to see what they were up to when they did the salsa. Maya wanted to know more, but all she got was a smile.

They were joined by Maya's first partner, Sunny, the accountant, who seemed pleased he had caught up with her and they chatted, desultorily. Idly, Maya asked about the show, and if they were going to join up. "Who told you? For a newcomer, you know a lot," said Sunny, with a teasing smile.

"Oh, Thomas told me," Maya answered. The next minute, she could have bitten her tongue, as there was a distinct frost in the air, mainly coming off Sunny in chilly little drifts.

"You seem to be very friendly with Thomas. He told you all about the show, did he? So you are going the way of Tulsi!"

"Tulsi?"

"The girl who jumped. Paru told me you knew her."

Maya remembered that she had mentioned that Tulsi had told her about the class while they were all going down in the lift, after class, on the day she had first met Thomas. But the question still caught her off guard.

"Yes I did know her. Did you know her and what do you mean, 'her way'?"

"She used to go off with Thomas after class. Look where she ended up." So Sunny was jealous? Had he fancied Tulsi? This was getting more tangled than Maya liked.

"She used to 'go off' with Harsha also. I've seen them, in his car, once or twice. Whoever she was meeting, Thomas or Harsha used to wait at the lift for her to get changed." Uma broke in.

"That can't be Thomas. He usually waits for everyone to go and locks up," said Sunny.

"I've seen him waiting for Tulsi at the lift," insisted Uma. "In fact, on the day she died, I saw Thomas, waiting near the lift. He was still there, when I went down. I remember holding the doors for him but he motioned me to go ahead."

Maya sat up. Hadn't Thomas said he had gone in to lock up? What was he doing near the lift? "What about Harsha? Didn't he take class that day? Was he also waiting?" she asked.

"Yes he did take class but I didn't see him around after that. I thought he'd left. Did you notice?"

"No, I left early, had to be back in the office, I took the stairs." They were directly opposite the studio, while the lift was round the corner.

Maya needed time to digest all this, so she was glad when the class was called. With a little thrill, she saw that Thomas was the instructor. He got the class to sit down while he explained the concept of the show. He explained that Creation itself was a product of desire, for companionship. So the first dance was the Creation myth from the Brhadaranyaka Upanishad contrasted with that from the Bible.

The stage was split into two halves and the action was simultaneous—Pati and Patni and Adam and Eve. Eve would tempt Adam with the apple while Patni realized she was born from Pati and therefore, coupling was wrong. She hid from him in different ways, changing into various animals but he always found her, assumed the male form of that animal and mated, thus creating more animals.

He played them the music which he had composed by re-mixing short instrumental pieces. She thought she recognized some Carnatic bits like the *ragas bhoopalam* and *kalyani*. There were other bits which sounded like western classical pieces but what did she know? She was less than a beginner when it came to music. The applause which greeted the finish was genuinely enthusiastic and she could see Thomas relax.

"Now for the dance," he said, and began to call out the names of students. Since they were all beginners, they were assigned roles of props and group dancers. Maya found herself with Sunny in the Vedic group while Uma and Paru were in the Biblical group. The class progressed, positions were given and each group sat out while the other learnt the dance. In Maya's group, they were to mirror the actions of the principals which Thomas and Surilee danced for the session. By the time the hour was up, the enthusiasm was catching, even for Maya.

The day was not over, however. Maya had a date with Toni for dinner and a late night movie, which would keep her going till the next class and (who knew?) maybe a date with Thomas. With a little pang, Maya remembered Tulsi. She had been laughing with Tulsi's best friend Toni and had had coffee with Thomas who might have been Tulsi's lover, while poor Tulsi had died mysteriously. With a wry grimace, she remembered Tulsi quoting from the Tamil classic, *Tirumular's Tirumantiram:*

They called the whole village,
Keened loudly;
They removed its name;
Called it a corpse;
They took it to the burning ghat;
Burnt it;
Plunged into water;
It passed out of memory.

You wait, Tulsi, she promised, silently. I'll find your killer.

Toni was waiting for her, at the entrance downstairs, looking dazzling and exotic wearing a flowing fuchsia kurta, with a tight churidhar in orange teamed with huge gold hoops in her ears. She could see some of the other students from her class and even the other visitors to the building stop and stare at the vision, shaking their heads, bemused.

"So where shall we go?" Maya asked, as she navigated the traffic, waiting to slip into the smooth stream moving down the main road.

"We can go anywhere but let's go somewhere where we can eat something quickly; I'm famished and we haven't much time if we have to buy the tickets for the movie," said Toni.

"Which movie are we talking about? I thought we hadn't decided even this morning." Maya innocently widened her eyes.

"Maya, stop being so infuriating. We are going to see *Vijeta*."

"Oh, some nobody star kid showing off!" Maya groaned loudly. They had reached the turn off where they would either have to continue or turn left.

"Will it be 'Woodlands' or 'Cakes and Bakes'? Decide quickly, the lights may change."

"Ok. I guess *dosai* sounds good. Cheaper for you."

"Oh, so it's my treat?"

"I thought you knew. You mean it's not? I didn't bring any cash. I thought you know, leading lawyer, stinking rich, she can stand a stony dancer a meal and cinema tickets."

Maya grinned but kept her eyes on the road as she navigated the turn. They were soon parking in the huge lot. They decided to eat in the self-service area to make it quicker.

Soon, they were seated in the no-nonsense dining area, tucking into huge, crisp, golden brown dosas folded into neat triangles and stuffed with potatoes and onions. Small cups of sambar and coconut chutney were eagerly dipped into—the equivalent of Madrasi gastronomic heaven. They were not going to stop there and had decided on almond halwa and ice-cream for dessert. It was so cheap, it would be a crime to pass up such superlative food and neither thought of diets.

Maya filled Toni in about the new show the class would be doing. "Sounds interesting. What's the central theme?"

"He didn't say, exactly, but it seems to be about desire."

"He could follow it up with desire for liberation, *moksha*, you know and union with God—the theme occurs even in Christianity."

"Brilliant! Oh, Thomas invited me to coffee and told me that Tulsi was helping him with it late into the night at his house."

"See, I told you her social life had hotted up. So you're going out to coffee with the owner are you?" Toni gave her a knowing smile.

Maya went on, quickly, "Oh and listen, he said that he always stayed behind to lock up and did so even on the day Tulsi…jumped. But later I heard from Sunny and Uma—two people in class—that he used to wait for Tulsi near the lift and was seen near the lift, which by the way, is round the corner from the class, even on that day. And get this! Tulsi was seeing two of them at the same time—Thomas and Harsha. So I can't see Thomas after this. He's definitely a suspect."

"Makes him more interesting doesn't it? Oh come on Maya. Who's making the rules here? You're not even doing this officially. Take it as part of the investigation, getting close to the suspect; lulling him into a false sense of security, whatever," she shrugged.

"Hmmm… I'll have to think about this. Anyway, you're not surprised about Tulsi's high jinks. So you knew? You could have told me."

"Oh so I am a suspect now? Maya, I didn't know for sure. Tulsi was cagey the last few months. But she looked… elated. I knew there was a man in there for sure. She never looked like that before. I didn't know she had two strings to her bow! Enterprising as ever, Tulsi!"

"That's exactly it; Thomas implied she killed herself as her husband was bound to find out. How did he feel? And did Thomas know about the other guy? Did she tell you anything about her research?"

"No. It's like too much was happening in her life and she just wanted to enjoy it all by herself. And I let her be. I didn't want to be a busybody. She'd had enough grief in her marriage."

"How was her marriage, do you know?"

"He was not an abuser. Just a cold fish and severe, everything had to happen at a set time—a real anal personality. He didn't appreciate his wife's creative temperament or her joy in living. He wanted her to be this domestic goddess and wasn't really interested in the bedroom side of things either. So she'd lost out in many ways. Never could understand why she chose him. He was a good dad for Shibani and earned well but was by nature a saving type which Tulsi was not! I can tell you that."

"Oh?"

"Yes, we'd had words before on her spending of the office funds. Months before her death or I would be feeling really guilty! She had promised to reform and was getting better at keeping tabs on expenses and sticking to the budget." She signed to the waiter, and as they waited for the check, she continued, "Tulsi was a strange girl—bubbly and very creative one minute, but moody the next. She was given to long periods when she went all broody, usually when she was thinking up some dance. She was different this time and I was surprised. All revved up and excited, like there was something happening. She used to be 'strange' in another way too, you know. She used to have dreams. They used to be like premonitions-precognitive, I think they're called. She could see the future."

Maya was taken aback with this information. "Did she see her own death, I wonder?"

"I don't think so. If she did, she never said anything."

"I forgot to ask you. I came across the name Alamelu Maami scribbled in the file, but I don't know anyone of that name. Do you?" Maya ingeniously avoided mentioning the diary again

"Sounds like that astrologer Tulsi used to go on about. I'll hunt out her address for you if you want to interview her. How could she help you, though?"

Maya was caught. What could she answer without mentioning the diary? Luckily, it was rhetorical.

"Thomas mentioned that he thought she had jumped because the husband might trouble her about Shibani. He didn't file anything in the case. Do you think he was bothering her?"

"She never said a word about anything like that. My God, Anees and I went round and round with the question of why she died for days. I'm just completely baffled, Maya. Please let's forget it for now. Oh, look at the time! It's getting late. Let's go. I don't want to miss the first scene, I heard it's quite thrilling and I think the heroine is ravishing."

"Actually, I don't mind the star kid. The only thing is, they're getting younger and younger every year. Who'll we have to lust after at this rate? We're too young for cradle snatching. I'll have to concentrate on Denzel Washington and Harrison Ford," laughed Maya.

"Oho! So the craggy, male animal type is yours. I have to check out this Thomas to see if he'll measure up."

Maya laughed. "What's your type?"

"Anees!" She said with a tantalising smile.

Maya couldn't stop the involuntary "Oh! Did Tulsi know?"

"Of course. We've been together since we were students."

They kept up their chat into the theatre and then settled down for some serious escapism.

The court was stifling with its single fan and warm press of bodies. Her case was called and the junior, Kala, indicated to the judge that they were ready. Maya was representing a woman whose husband alleged mental cruelty and wanted to divorce her. He had been carrying on an affair with his secretary who was pregnant and wanted marriage. Maya's client had staunchly refused to tolerate a 'second wife', so here they were, all conciliation attempts having failed.

She thought back to Tulsi's case which had not yet come to trial and would now be infructuous. Now she found that Tulsi had been seeing someone else. Had the husband known? It had certainly started after she had joined the dance class, but after she had filed for divorce. Now she would never know what answer the husband would have given to the allegations in the divorce petition. Would he have revealed that he knew about it or was he in the dark?

From Tulsi, her thoughts naturally flew to Achale's Thulasi. What had such a playful, passionate woman made of her marriage to a strict husband? For that matter, how had Puttalakshmi survived her marriage to Achale's father? Such a capable healer, forced to practice on the sly, always watchful, apologetic, wanting to please him and anxious that she couldn't. Was that love? No wonder Achale wanted anything other than marriage.

She sighed as the case was called and prepared to stun the husband with her cross-examination.

Maya stopped to buy peanuts from the woman vendor outside the courts. Usually the woman would be half-asleep at this time, even though business was fairly good, if not brisk. Today, she looked very alert, but there was no smile on her face. She looked distracted and rather disturbed. Maya wondered what the matter was. The woman's smile was like a constant in her week.

"What's up, *ma*? Why no smile today?" Maya asked her.

The woman sighed loudly. "Oh, this government! They promise you things when they want votes, but after elections where are they? You tell me that!" She shook her head.

"You are a regular in these courts. Don't you know what to do when you have a problem with the government?"

"Madam, don't you think I would have done that? First they said: file a case in the High Court against the government. We'll ask them to take over the temple land on which we live. It seems there is a Government Office. So we filed the case. Before we finished the case, the temple had filed a case before the rent court to throw us out. Our case before the High Court was done for. We fought that case. Went on appeal, even. No use. When the other side has money, who can win against them? For thirty years I have lived there. Where will I go? Or my children? I paid the *Padriar* so much to get him to take my son in the English school. All a waste! This is all too much for simple woman like me!" While she was talking, her deft fingers were measuring the peanuts and shaping cones out of newspaper squares.

Maya felt very bad. There was little she could do, however, as all legal avenues had already been explored.

"Ponmudi Lakshmi, I was called. What will my name be now when I lose my birthplace?"

Maya smiled sympathetically as she collected her peanuts. She patted the woman on the back and went her way.

Maya had fixed a meeting with Alamelu Maami. But first, she had to write to Dr. Gopalakrishnan for an appointment. He was easy to find in the telephone directory, as he taught in a celebrated college and was the Head of Department. Would he tell her anything if he knew it was a murder and that she was a lawyer? She doubted it. People generally wanted to avoid any hint of the court or the police station. She decided to pose as Mridula, a housewife, interested in an old book.

Dear Dr. Gopalakrishnan,

I request you to advise me with regard to the provenance of a delightful old book I happened to come across in a second hand bookshop. Please forgive my presumption in writing to you, but you are an authority on the subject of Vijayanagara a history and I hope to interest you in my little problem.

I have completed my masters in Medieval History from Madras University, but my household responsibilities prevent me from pursuing my studies or my passion for historical research.

The book seems to be a cheap paperback, ill-preserved and yellow with age. It appears to be a Tamil translation of a medieval Telugu work, written by one Achaledasa. It has been printed by 'Anjali Printing Works,' though the date has been obscured by silver-fish holes: it is probably printed sometime in the 1930's.The cover gives the title 'Middle Time'. It seems to be about a dancer named Achalabbe, mentions one Manjunatha who performed a miracle at the Madhavaperumal temple at Alur, near Anegundi.

I appreciate that your time is valuable and if you would rather not answer, I will understand. However, a line in reply will be gratefully received.

She signed herself Mridula after the closing phrase and gave her office phone number and the house address. The Professor must be a dried old stick. She hoped she had been respectful, yet dangled some interesting information to tempt a reply. She left it for Kamala to post and went off for her appointment with Alamelu Maami.

The day had wound itself to a weary close and as she drove in the evening to her appointment with the seer, Maya was glad of the sea breeze. The hoary Parthasarathi koil, one of the 108 important shrines of the sect to which Achale's bête noire, Bhadrinatha Shastry belonged, jostled the shops with Muslim names and the palace of the Nawab of Arcot. Maya had gone to the Parthasarathy temple on December 31st with her mother and passed through the 'gateway to heaven.' The idol inside the temple was Krishna as the divine charioteer of Arjuna, the Pandava prince of the *Mahabharata*. Krishna had taken Arjuna easily through the battle lines, counseling him with the divine wisdom of the Bhagwad Gita but His face showed the battle scars.

Outside the temple, pedestrians darted through the gaps between the bumpers, cyclists inched their precarious way through the openings, not to mention auto-drivers who seemed hell-bent on a suicide mission on the narrow Triplicane road. Inside the temple, the priests chanted 1000 names of Vishnu in Sanskrit, but outside resounded other names for in the pure, undiluted language of the streets. That battle-scarred prankster Krishna might even have been amused.

She parked the car and got out. The house was one of the row houses common to this area. Great for maximizing space and gossip but minimizing privacy. Devotional music was playing inside. She removed her footwear outside, in the verandah, pressed the bell and waited for the door to be opened. The main door elaborately carved in heavy teak was open, but a lighter one made of hardwood with a simple grill insert, was shut and bolted from inside. The smell of good filter coffee, ubiquitous in such surroundings, was tickling her taste buds. Maybe, with any luck, the coffee was for visitors like herself! She smiled pleasantly at the girl in a half-sari who came up to the door—all the better to wangle a cup! The girl ushered her into a small room, furnished with a silky reed mat and some cushions and bolsters. She was asked to wait as Maami was at her puja and oh joy, coffee came in a steel tumbler with its accompanying small bowl. Smacking her lips as she savoured the coffee, she waited.

Maami came in, bringing the smell of camphor, holy ash, hair oil and sandalwood, a likable amalgam. She was pleasantly plump and dressed in a traditional nine-yard sari wrapped around her legs. She was smiling, but her eyes nevertheless raked Maya appraisingly.

"What is it, *ma*? Want to know when you will get married or if you will go abroad?"

"I... I came to ask you about my client, Tulsi...I don't want to know the future. I just want to ask what she had told you. You see, she's dead."

"One question—Rs. 500." The smile was in place, but had become implacable.

"Uh...OK." Maya hoped she had brought that amount with her.

Maami took Maya's left hand and pored over it. Maya tried to take it back, but Maami was made of stern stuff. She became immersed in calculations, after getting her birth time and date. Finally, from a small copper pot placed near her, she poured water into a steel tumbler, lifted it and poured it into her mouth. Maya watched in fascination as the liquid slipped down in a single stream until the tumbler was empty. Perhaps this feat was part of the five hundred rupees' performance. "What do you want to ask?"

"Uh... I came because my client Tulsi, who died mysteriously gave me a book—a story about a murder which happened in the past. The woman who was murdered has the same name as my client."

When she stopped for breath, Maami asked, "Tulsiaa...? Some time back a woman called Tulsi came here. She said she was having dreams after reading a book. The story she told me was the same as your story. So she died.... I saw death in her hand but I did not want to frighten her. I did not warn her. But you are different, child. You can conquer fear."

"Did Tulsi say why she felt the book was important? Apart from the dreams?"

"She said that she felt the dream was asking her to help the characters. Also that the problem continued in the present. That's what she said."

"The problem continued? What did she mean?"

"She did not explain further and I began to tell her about the future of her daughter. Route *maripochu*—shifted."

Maya got up. Maami held her hand and began to speak hurriedly, "Wait, wait. You are working; your career is going well. You are like a man. You make quick decisions, have a sharp clear mind and are not afraid of danger or a fight. There is something threatening you... the time is very near, be careful. Five hundred. Forgot, eh?"

"OK, OK!" Maya opened her purse. After much shuffling through pockets, her purse yielded the required amount. Maami gave her a book of Vishnu's 1000 names as a goodbye present. Maya was sure she had got it free from someone.

She blinked as she came out into the evening light. Tulsi was having strange dreams! The more she struggled the tighter she became enmeshed in the coils of this bizarre situation. What was she, logical Maya, doing in this twilight world?

Chapter XIII

Spring, March-April 1536

Bangaru's tail swished from side to side in rhythm with the swing which was carrying Achale almost to the top of the mango tree from which it hung. Each time the arc was complete, the scent of the mango leaves, sharp and tart, carried a delicious hint of the pickles to come from the tree. A warm golden glow bathed cat, mistress and garden. The yellow of the acacia, highlighted by the lime green of the *manoranjitham* below, echoed in the yellow heart of white flowers of the oleander plant beneath.

How peaceful not to be rushing to her duties for once! After the exertions of the recent few weeks, Achale had been given time off, so that the priest could train the lesser *devadasis* in their duties. From the swing she could see far into the horizon. The world was lush with a colourful palette. The green fields were striped with the rich brown of the earth. The sand-coloured tracks and the red, gray and coppery brown of the boulders were punctuated by bright flashes of the green bee-eater, the black of the double-tailed drongo, and the white from the paddy-bird.

Achale had no warning when her mother walked up and took over the swinging from the maid. Her mother looked preoccupied and was uncharacteristically silent. Achale allowed the quiet to stretch. Her mother would open up in good time.

After a while, Achale, unable to bear the silence, asked, "Did you come alone, Ma?"

"No, I came with Indra and Manju." Hastily, before Achale could ask, "Kesava has gone out to hunt birds with a boy from the village."

"And the children are with *Ajji*? I know she must be feeding them *ellunde, chinipalunde* and *karachikai*. If we knew they were coming we would even have made *holige*."

Her mother laughed, "Anyone would think we starved them at home. They went straight to the kitchen. They didn't even wait for *Ajji,* but started pestering your maids."

"Ma, if they hadn't you would have been worried."

"Ah, *that* is true!"

"Ma, let's go in and see what they are up to. How is it Indra is with you? Why is he not at school?"

"Ah, the guru's wife had a mind to come to the city for the celebrations. She brought him with her. They will go back tomorrow. Manju came over with Ranganatha and I brought him here. He is good company for Indra."

They went inside the house. *Ajji* and the boys were in the courtyard outside the kitchen. Achale hugged Indra, who had rushed to touch her feet. She watched in amusement as the little saint stuffed his mouth with sweet puffs, while her mother murmured, "Slowly, slowly, you will choke!"

Achale now thought to ask, "Where is *Appaji, amma*?" Puttalakshmi signed with her eyes while she told the boys to go out and play where some monkeys had gathered. A monkey stared unblinkingly at Manju, to see if he had any eatables in his hands. Disappointed, she began to comb her baby's fur, eating the fleas as she caught them. The boys ran past them, shouting, wiping their grubby hands on the stone walls, accompanied by soft remonstrance from Puttalakshmi, "*Putta,* wash your hands, see, the ladle is just there, in the water pot…don't touch your hair, ants will get in and it will itch...Indra, Manju…" Only after they had gone out, unheeding as usual, did she speak.

"He's locked himself up in his dispensary. I heard him shouting orders at poor Kenchappa. He takes on all the anger your father feels against any of us."

"*Appaji* pays him well for the trouble."

"Did he scold Kesava?" inserted *Ajji*.

"He spent nearly an hour with Kesava. I did not see him all evening and he did not come home for food. He must have eaten in the village. And today he went hunting early. Just drank some gruel with a black face."

Ajji spat the wad of betel she was chewing into the pot meant for that purpose. "Hmmm… all of us have to live with the decisions of our children, whether we like it or not."

Achale rolled her eyes, knowing she meant it for her and not Puttalakshmi.

"He'll come around. Times are changing. There is a great demand for dance masters. He can dance with Achale."

"Oh, and I must pretend my baby brother is my lover. I wonder what the old one will suggest next," muttered Achale, loud enough for *Ajji* to hear while her mother made hushing motions with her hand on Achale's arm.

"What's that? Lost the power to emote, have you my girl? As if the dancer represents the truth! You are His instrument to join Him in creating *maya,* illusion, with your actions. What does it matter who your partner in this exercise is? It is all illusion. That is all it is! You'd do better to apply your mind to the philosophy your gurus spent years teaching you than to pull it down to base desires."

"Ho, she talks, who would have me minister to the desires of very earthly suitors," muttered Achale.

"Practicing your *dharma,* whatever it may be, is better than ministering to your base desires."

"*Amma,* the desire to serve a husband is a woman's *karma*. What is so base about it?"

"And would you have her jump up every time the man comes in, who may be less talented, even stupid in the face of her learning and nod her head like a cow and spread her thighs for his inept fumbling?"

"*Amma,* that is what you decided was best for your daughter wasn't it?" There—it was out, no subterfuge.

"My daughter was an innocent; well read, soft spoken and tender-hearted. Better that she be in the keeping of a besotted husband than tie on the responsibilities of a *devadasi*'s life along with her anklets. I did not know then that his mild manner would change to stern gravity in a few years. I saw only harmony and security for my daughter."

"Such security that to meet my mother, I have to slip out on one pretext or another and I have to hide my lineage from the world." The dam had burst.

Ajji put her arm around Puttakshmi while Achale watched, flabbergasted. Somehow, seeing her mother cry twisted something deep within her.

Before the debate could get more heated however, Ningi created a diversion by appearing and announcing, "Acharyulu, the singing sage and *Ajji* Jakkini have arrived. I have asked them in but they insist on sitting at the banyan tree and having their meal there. Shall I send someone out there to serve them?"

"Achale, you go out and bring them in here. We are blessed indeed. *Ajji* Jakkini is a learned Jain nun, a *pravarthini* from the Tapogaccha University who is renowned for her mastery of logic and the *Jinagamas*. She moves around from monastery to seminary teaching and holding assemblies. It is good for you to serve them."

"Of course, *Ajji*." Achale went out into the garden.

They had esconced themselves quite comfortably. The bricks for their fires were in place and Ningi had already given them their rations of rice and vegetables. They were cutting them up, chatting companiably. The nun was in her usual unbleached handwoven coarse garments, her shaven head covered.

The nun was holding forth, Acharyulu merely smiling at appropriate intervals or shaking his head from side to side in agreement. Achale joined them silently and squatted on the stone seat, under the tree, listening to their talk. *Ajji* Jakkini was speaking of the last session she had attended. Acharyulu merely smiled as he listened but the expressions on his face, ever-changing, formed responses if one were willing to see them.

Finally, after her narration she turned to Achale. "I heard something…a new saint and a death. Is it true? I believe your neighbour, Bhadrinatha has a hand in the sainthood."

Here, Acharyulu felt impelled to say something so he sang Annamacharya's *Ekulajudemi*:

How does his caste matter,
If he knows the Lord?

"Are you referring to Bhadri or the saint, *dasare*?" Achale wanted to know.

"Oho, so you have suddenly become an admirer of Bhadri—even his wife, had he one, would not claim selflessness as his virtue. The boy is of course, too young. His innocence must be his recommendation," said *Ajji* Jakkini.

"He is a good boy, gentle and well mannered. He does not forget his mother." Achale replied.

Just then, Indra and Manju ran up. They sat down by Achale and Indra leaned on her, playing with her hair. Manju appeared absorbed in watching the rice grains bobbing up and down in the boiling water of Acharyulu's pot. He hummed under his breath in time with the bobbing grains.

"So you like to sing, Manju?" Achale asked. The boy bowed his head and hunched his shoulders, trying to hide his bashful head like a camel. "Did your mother like singing?"

"She used to sing me to sleep."

Here Acharyulu began to hum a well known lullaby *"Jo jo achyutananda..."*

"Yes, yes that one!" the boy cried. Achale took up the song and hesitantly, the boy joined in. *Ajji* Jakkini beat time with the pestle she was using to pound her roots into flour.

The music soon drew Achale's mother, grandmother, Bhima and Ningi. Even the cat Bangaru came to sit erect, his golden tail twitching in time to the music. Acharyulu's dog, who was never far from his master, lifted up his head as if to howl, but thought better of it under the scornful gaze of Bangaru and settled down again, his head on his front paws.

After the song, there was a pleasant lull in the conversation. The two young boys ran off. Achale broke the silence by saying, "*Dasare*, I heard something very strange the other day. The daytime players were performing at the Mahashivarathri festival and they said, that babies could be bought and bundles of cloth could become babies. Whom could they be referring to?"

Achale's *Ajji* spoke. "I heard tell that Queen Amalotpava Devi is pregnant, at last. Poor woman, she has waited long for this event to come about."

Achale said, "But Madhava Shastry mentioned that she had come to him for a love poem only last week."

"Oh, so he is selling his wares?" began *Ajji* Roopavathi and then she remembered the boy and fell silent.

The talk moved on to other things, mainly what *Ajji* Jakkini had seen and heard on her way, "There seems to be some activity near Kondoja's stronghold. A number of horsemen and clouds of dust." She had pounded her flour and now she was making some into dough, preparatory to rolling it and flattening it with her hands.

Acharyulu smiled and began to hum *Oh Chieftain of the crooked tail*...again. Bhima, who had seen Chenna before he had moved away with his troupe now joined in and recounted the acrobat's capture and escape, while Acharyulu smiled and nodded.

Ajji Roopavathi said, "*That* dog's tail will never be straightened. Always ambitious, he's now joined the Raya. Will this King ever sleep?"

Ajji Jakkini shook her head sadly.

"Chenna told me that the rogues guarding him were saying that one Narayana, who got Srinivasa Shastry's property seemed to be eyeing her property outside the village and was making noises of applying for the boy's guardianship to the King," said Bhima.

"In that he won't succeed. The poet Madhava seems determined to have the boy for Thulasi's sake. Seems he was her cousin." Achale put in.

"Another strange thing," Bhima said, "I saw Bhadri with that new Achare, Venugopalachari from Chidambaram."

"Yes, he was saying that his mission was to re-install the idol of Vishnu in the temple, which is now only dedicated to Nataraja," broke in Achale. "I saw him with Madhava at the Shivrathri dance."

"So, Bhadri must be trying to get the commission to re-install the idol. More money into his pocket if the grant is routed through him!' *Ajji* Roopavathi chipped in. "Manju will be very useful to him."

"Hmmm...Bhadri must be drunk with success. Everything seems to be going his way."

Achale was about to say something else, when Bhima broke in, "Strange, he looked unlike his normally dapper self. His sacred thread was broken and tied up."

Ajji Jakkini looked grave, "Achale, you must be careful. It was your maid who found the body. There are many political undercurrents around the murder. And there is a smell of money—someone felt she was a threat, Undoubtedly, there is money involved. I don't think it was passion which killed her, if it was murder."

"Why do you say that *Ajji*?"

"Passion is swift and sure, it leads to strangulation, stabbing, acts of violence. The killer does not seek to conceal, he wants to make his mark. Concealment and stealth only mean that the killer has something to gain by his secrecy. In whose way did she stand? The person who took such pains to make a murder look like suicide will not thank you to interfere."

"She was Bhadri's mistress, so they say..." Ningi's voice trailed off. The nun always made her feel a little uncouth, there was such an air of serene wisdom about her.

"All the more reason for Achale to take care. Bhadri is an enemy to be feared."

Ajji Roopavathi broke in, "Well said, *akka*, well said! I have been warning Achale that she should take a powerful lover. Vajrabahu, the Samgama is more than willing. Or else, she may end up disgraced —or worse."

Achale got up. She bowed to Achayulu and *Ajji* Jakkini and took her leave, saying she would leave them to have their meal in peace and she needed to practice some steps for the morrow. Ningi followed, glad to escape. The rest watched as Bangaru swished his tail and swatted the white dog. The dog yelped and scampered, tail between his legs to Acharyulu, who patted his head. Tail twitching, Banguru executed a flawless about turn and stalked after his mistress, jumping over the bushes which would flower into begonia, rhododendrons, musk rose and lily in late summer.

Ningi and Achale were sitting in the small balcony which overhung the backyard, just out of Achale's room. Achale's chest and back were bare, covered only with a thin cloth. Ningi was rubbing her back with medicated oil smelling of camphor, turmeric, and pepper—Puttalakshmi's special concoction. Achale had been complaining of a slight heaviness in her head and Ningi wanted to make sure that no cold would mar Achale's voice when she had been invited to perform at a special function to mark the opening of the temple at Lepakshi. Bhima had communicated his own doubts about the provenance of the invitation—who else but the giant potter they had met at the bazaar outside the temple before the Mahashivarathri festival could have engineered the invitation? Ningi had retorted that her Achale did not need any one to push forward her name, it would have been considered anyway. But Bhima had laughed knowingly and infuriatingly.

Now she said, "This smell reminds me of the day I found the corpse." She continued rubbing the oil into Achale's back in broad strokes.

"Which smell?" Achale wanted to know, dreamily. The balcony looked out over the fields, green and glowing in the late afternoon sun. In the distance, a man slept under a tree. The cows tethered in the courtyard underneath could be heard lowing and harrumphing as they swished away the flies. The warmth and the hush had made them relaxed and sleepy.

Achale's mind was ranging over the day's events. She could never understand her mother's relationship with her father. To live in constant fear of displeasing someone, and yet continue her daily existence, outwardly calm and collected. Good thing she preserved some dignity by distributing her free medicines. And they had married for love. This was not the life for any woman. And yet, this was the lot of nearly every woman. It was even worse, sometimes, if the husband had concubines, or was an opium addict, or a drunkard, like several of the nobles.

Thulasi's life must have been like her mother's. From all accounts, Srinivasa character was like her father's. No wonder they were friends! Thulasi, according to her mother, had been brimming with life. Even adversity had not dimmed her ardour—from all accounts, she had taken up with Bhadri and so secured a liitle comfort for herself and her son. She had kept up the mystery of his birth till the end. What unquenchable spirit! Yet her life had been snuffed out like a lamp by the wind! It was too bad that her murder should go unavenged and that her little son should never know peace. Perhaps she could help the poet find her murderer as he seemed determined to do so. She suddenly realized that Ningi had spoken of Thulasi.

"What smell?" she asked again, more alert.

"Camphor. There was a strong smell near the body."

"Maybe she had rubbed the oil on herself."

"She rubbed the oil to ward off a cold and then drowned herself in water? Not likely."

"I wonder how she really died? We must ask Betappa."

"Still talking about that death? If you had followed my advice you would have been too busy to bother. Your feet would have been heavy and your belly full," Achale's mother came in. Ningi quickly gathered up her paraphernalia and made an exit. Puttalakshmi sat beside her daughter and stretched her legs.

"It's time for me to go home," she said. "*Ajji* is preparing some food for me to take home. So I don't have to cook today or tomorrow. You know your father. If the dinner's not on time…!"

"The Brahmin loves his food."

"Exactly! As they say, if a Brahmin gets angry, the roof is likely to catch fire."

"How do you stand it, Ma? Imagine a reasonable person wanting things to always go his way or else…"

"He is otherwise a good husband. Doesn't abuse me, takes care of my needs. Respects me despite his reservations about my background. I can deal with his small quirks. Don't you have to deal with Sundari or Bhadri?"

"Ummm…" Achale wasn't about to carry this farther. She could forget her problems as soon as she walked in to her home. She didn't have to deal with them all day.

There was a drumming of quick feet and the boys, Indra and Manju entered.

"*Ajji* asked us to find you. She has packed everything and the carter wants to set off as soon as we can, as it looks like it will rain." Puttalakshmi pulled Indra onto her lap. "We'll go. Putta, did you have a good time?" Indra lolled back, pulling at her upper garment, playing with it like a puppy. The cat Bangaru hoisted himself onto the balcony ledge. "Aii!" Indra was off after it.

Manju sat down shyly, a little distance from the women. "*Akka*," he said. "Did you use camphor? I can smell it. My mother loved that smell. She used it often. Whenever her limbs ached or she had a slight chill. I smelt it on that day..." his voice trailed off. Achale was silent. She did not know how to broach the subject. But the boy seemed impelled to continue and perhaps he took their silence for sympathy, or perhaps Puttalakshmi reminded him of his own mother.

"She went to the Madhavaswamy temple in the evening. She said she had to meet someone. I waited. I thought she had gone to get some rice or something. She often went like this and came back with rice or ghee or whatever we needed. But when she came back, she was ill and could not talk properly. She began to vomit late at night and kept shouting that she was burning. I went out to call Rangi *akka*. Her house was not very near, and it took some time to wake her. She asked me to give her water and she would come in the morning. When I came back my mother was not there. Many times in the night when she went out, she used to tell me not to ask questions or tell anyone. So I didn't."

"You did not tell Betappa this?" asked Achale. Manju looked down and shook his head. Achale thought that it was not likely that Betappa, of a lower caste, would have questioned the Brahmin boy.

Later, as she watched the lanterns on her mother's bullock cart blink at her through the dusk, Achale cuddled Bangaru and stroked his fur. It was a strange world. Women of ability could not pursue their dreams or even recognize them. Perhaps, this was the lesson the Divine wanted them to learn—the pursuit of dreams was possible if one was prepared to pay a cost, if one was a woman. Why was it not so for a man? *Ajji* Jakkini said that following the right path would free one of all constraints but that involved cultivating detachment. Could one be detached and follow one's dream? Shankara wanted one to focus on purifying the self- did that mean one could follow one's dream but strive for perfection? It was all very puzzling. What did one really want? What was *her* dream?

Maya put down the book with a sigh. It ended there. From here on, she was on her own. Time enough to think about it, tomorrow. She settled down in bed, but sleep eluded her. The window was open. It was a full moon night and it hung in the dark blue sky, yellow and radiant. The tree outside cast dancing shadows of its foliage on the wardrobe beside her bed. The leafy clumps bobbed up and down and Maya tried to hypnotize herself to sleep by watching them. There was one particularly rounded clump which remained still. Dreamily she thought that it looked like a head. She cast a lazy glance at the window, and sat up suddenly. There was a beautiful half-grown kitten on her window sill. She got up to shut the window, but before she could react, it shot through.

When she turned around, the cat was sitting on her sofa, cleaning itself. It looked at Maya through half-closed lids and resumed grooming. Maya was astonished. She knew it was an honour to be a cat's pet. But what was this cat doing here? Did it belong to someone else? She resolutely deposited it outside and made to shut the door. The kitten put a paw in the doorway and widening the gap, walked in. It wound itself around her legs. It couldn't have made itself clearer, if it had spoken—it wanted to stay with her. She shook her head and went off to locate a basket and some old clothes for the cat's nest, but found it at her feet, in her bed, a few minutes later. Resignedly, she warmed her toes on its back and went to sleep.

Maya opened one eye and blinked. Something was kneading her chest, miaowing with its pink mouth wide open. Her mind was still shrouded in sleep and she wondered lazily how Bangaru had jumped out of the book. In her half-awake state anything seemed possible. The cat nipped the tip of her nose and she was suddenly wide awake. A voice in her head seemed to mock: read about a cat, woke up the next morning and found one on your bed? And you still want to pretend everything's normal? Shut up, she told the voice. Go on like this and I'll be so scared, I'll be looking over my shoulder every minute! She couldn't repress a little frisson, however. The phrase *ghost walking over my grave* came unbidden to her mind. Oh my God, she thought. This cute, cuddly thing was definitely of this world and if it was a coincidence, it made for a nice, warm one. Anyway, better not to let Pat and Meena know about this latest development. Or Mridula.

CHAPTER XIV

APRIL 1996

Maya was ready in plenty of time for the next class and was almost the first one in the door. She had found herself practicing the steps in her head and humming the tune the whole day. She was back to partnering with Sunny. Harsha, coming in a little later, called Uma, and assigned her to Sunny, while he took Maya's hand, giving it a squeeze as he did so.

"You smell good. What is it?" He leaned a little into her.

"Something my brother got me from one of his trips."

"Ah, your brother! So...no boyfriend?"

Maya didn't answer. His behavior was too familiar and she did not know if she wanted to encourage him. He gave her a little shake and tried to look into her eyes. "Hey! What's up? Okay, don't answer. I take it that there is some hope for me." Then they had to do a line dance. He held her hands on his shoulders, instead of putting his own on the shoulders of the person in front

I haven't seen you around for some time." She hoped the change of subject would work.

"Yeah, I've been busy. I had to go to Singapore."

"Wow! Business or pleasure?"

"A bit of both, actually."

Finally, it was time for the rehearsal and Harsha held her hand throughout the instructions. Thomas made them do the steps they had learnt in the previous class. As he checked on Maya's steps, Thomas gave her a smile and mouthed "Stay after class." Maya felt a giggle rising and had to work hard to suppress it. All this male attention was definitely a pleasant change from the usual! The surprise package however, was Surilee; nothing Maya did was right. In the end, Maya got her to a corner of the class and asked bluntly, "What's wrong?"

"You!" Surilee exploded. "Stay away from Thomas. Just when I thought he was mine, you had to join and he's off after you. Don't you know he likes the thrill of the chase? That's all. Don't get your hopes up. You have nothing I don't, and everything I have is much better than you!"

Maya had to acknowledge that she had got it right. Surilee was much the curvier and prettier. But Thomas wants you, not her, she told herself. As for his dropping her, that could happen, anyway.

She found Thomas patiently waiting for her, sitting on the window ledge. She stood outside and watched as he locked up, noting that he was meticulous about opening doors like the props closet, before locking up. Would such a meticulous man have missed an intruder on the night of the murder? Maybe he hadn't even started when he had seen the body, so all the intruder had to do was wait until he rushed down, to slip out and down the stairs, unseen. Yes, she was sure that was what must have happened.

This time, instead of the coffee shop opposite, Thomas took her to the beach. They went to a café which, mercifully, was close to her flat, so going home would be easy. They settled down and ordered coffee. Maya began the conversation with, "Is this about Tulsi?"

"Tulsi! Where does she come in?"

Maya decided she had better come clean before it was too late. "Tulsi was my client. It was she who told me about the class. I was handling her divorce. Now she's dead and I don't know why."

There was a moment of surprised silence before Thomas spoke. "I see. Why didn't you tell me this before? You don't think she jumped, do you? Am I a suspect? Does your telling me now mean I'm somehow cleared?" His narrowed eyes now glittered and Maya realized that black depths could ice over.

"Look at it from my point of view. I didn't know anything about you. How could I trust you? I have to cover my back too, you know. I could be next."

"So, now you trust me. What, you think the husband conveniently bumped her off? But I was there that day and I can swear the husband never turned up." He looked curiously at her.

"So who else was there that day?"

"Let me think. The instructor that day was Harsha. The usual crowd of students: Sunny, Paru, Uma and all. No one else."

"There was a gap between the students streaming out and your going in, wasn't there? You said Tulsi was already dead, wasn't she, when you got in to lock up?"

"Yes. I usually check their accounts as they go past. That takes time. But on the other hand, no one can leave without my seeing them. I sit where you usually see me, at the front desk. Everyone has to go through the front door. Why would anyone want to kill Tulsi? She was such fun and so helpful." He shook his head. "It doesn't make sense."

"You really miss her don't you?"

Thomas was beginning to look confused. "Hey, what is this? Are you asking if there was something between me and Tulsi? Please, I like a quiet life. I didn't want the complication of dealing with a woman who was not yet out of her first marriage." He grimaced, "Too much baggage!"

He patted her lightly on her shoulder. "Forget, it. I don't want to keep thinking about it. So what do you think of the dance for the show? Did you like it?"

"Oh, the idea is great!" Maya beamed.

Thomas said, "Do you know love is something almost all cultures agree on? But most cultures classify two types—erotic love and unselfish, pure love. Like the Greeks spoke of "pure love", agape and eros, sexual passion. But for Hindus it is *kama, karuna, prema, bhakti*—devotion, leading to *moksha*, salvation."

"So the language of love differs but the words mean the same. Strange, no?"

Maya was almost afraid to exhale. Was this leading up to something? But she was to be disappointed and they parted at the restaurant gate. Maya was secretly glad—she would like all the stories to be cleared up—Thomas with Tulsi, Thomas with Surilee—before it morphed into Thomas with Maya.

Srinivasa Shastry was standing in the court for the formal hearing which would lead to the petition for divorce being dismissed as abated, since Tulsi was dead. The man looked as he usually did—collected to the point of appearing remote. But some men were like that, absolutely frightened of showing any emotion. He stood perfectly still while Maya told the judge that Tulsi was dead. He produced the death certificate. His lawyer was not with him, probably deeming that he could handle the formal hearing on his own, which was a blessing as Maya could speak to him alone.

As they filed out of the nearly empty courtroom, Maya turned to him and asked him to have coffee with her. The India Coffee House was not far so they walked there. Maya cudgeled her brain for small talk, but could come up with nothing. Finally she asked about Shibani's whereabouts and was told that she was in school. Maya asked how she was. Srinivasa said that she seemed to be alright but had become very quiet. They had reached the coffee shop and Maya went to buy tokens for their coffees—it was mid morning but suggesting a snack somehow, considering the topic of discussion, seemed tactless.

Maya debated how to begin but Shastry saved her the anxiety by starting. "Tulsi's mother told me that you are not happy with the verdict of suicide. Have you found anything to show it was an accident, then?"

"It doesn't seem likely to be an accident unless she had a death-wish and climbed to sit on a window ledge three storeys high." She regretted the callous tone as soon as it left her tongue, but the words could not be taken back.

Shastry made a production of stirring his coffee. Maybe he wanted to control his outrage, and Maya could have hit herself. Rubbing the witness the wrong way was not the way to conduct the best cross-examination.

Finally he said, "I know, but I did not want to acknowledge, even to myself that it could be murder. Someone must have forced her to climb up on to the ledge. What threat could have driven her there? It must have taken enormous strength to hoist her on to the ledge. Tulsi was not a light weight. She was strong from her dancing and as tall as you. She did not have that kind of enemy."

"So she had some enemies?"

"None that I knew of unless you called me her enemy, but it was she who wanted the divorce, not I."

"Did she tell you about her dance class? Not Ghungroo but Footloose?"

"No, Shibani used to chatter about it, but by the time she joined the class, she was living by herself and I was shut out of her life." He didn't sound angry, just full of regret. Maya shrugged; she did not want to get sidetracked. "Did she mention any of her classmates to Shibani?"

"No, Shibani only told me of a dance they were planning as a show, something about a lotus."

"Oh, that was for Ghungroo. When did you hear of her death? I never knew till the court clerk told me. I hadn't heard from her in a while, so I assumed no news was good news. Shibani was with you that night wasn't she?"

"Yes. The police phoned me the night of the murder. After that they questioned her neighbours and the dance class people and went to Ghungroo. Shibani had phoned the flat the previous night, before we knew about Tulsi but couldn't get through. We assumed that she had gone out with Toni, especially as Toni could not be contacted either. I told Shibani not to worry."

Maya checked her watch. She had a hearing in fifteen minutes and needed to get the papers and get to the court hall. "I'm sorry, I'll have to go to another case now, but you'll let me know if you hear anything, won't you?" Shastry promised he would.

Somehow, he had conveyed an impression of despair, tightly leashed. Poor guy. Perhaps he wasn't such a cold fish after all. He did not act as if he knew about Thomas or Harsha and Tulsi. What would it do to him to find out so late? She hoped he would not be devastated. Yet how could she just let it all go? Didn't the truth count for something in itself? Was he capable of murder?

The evening held a surprise for Maya. A letter from Dr. Gopalakrishnan was lying on her desk.

Dear Madam,

Unfortunately, I will be out of town for some days as I have been invited to conduct a series of lectures at Oxford. Your mention of the book has interested me, however. I remember having seen it, a long while back, though I cannot recall where. I also cannot recall off hand, a poet called Achaledasa but I promise to look him up for you on my return.

However, I can add this to your pool of information—Achale was a devadasi *at the court of Achyuta Deva Raya [1529-42]. She is mentioned in the inscriptions at the Virupaksheshwara Temple, as being the recipient of a grant of land for her upkeep from this King. She is also mentioned as having constructed a well for travelers on the road to Hampi. She was reputed to be very learned. Her father was the court physician.*

I will get in touch on my return.

Maya was disappointed. She already knew this. Tulsi had discovered that Manju was a real historical character. Maya couldn't begin to even duplicate the hours of research Tulsi must have put into it, not to mention that she couldn't read Telugu or even ancient Tamil. Searching for news of the murder would be like sifting through a haystack and Tulsi had not been able to come up with any historical data on it. In fact, Thulasi was not even mentioned, it seemed. The Chola rulers, Vikrama and Kulottunga II, were worshippers of Nataraja, who was their family deity. The

Vaishnavites seriously feared danger to the ceremonial deity, which was taken to Lower Tirupati for safe keeping. It was reconsecrated in the first half of the sixteenth century. But in the book, she had just read that a man called Venugopalachari had visited Hampi, trying to get a royal grant for the return of the Govindarajaperumal deity to Chidambaram. Had she found anything on that? Maya searched in vain for references to the murder, but found nothing

CHAPTER XV

APRIL 1996

Back in her office the next day, Maya called Kamala. "Could you get me a copy of the toxicology book? I'd like to look up poisons."

Maya spent the next hour going through the gruesome pages of the Medical Toxicology book and searching through the internet. Ningi had noticed a smell of vomit on finding Thulasi's body. The boy Manju had mentioned in the book that Thulasi had been complaining of a burning sensation. Then she had wandered out to the bathing *ghat*. Maybe she had wanted to cool her body. She must have been in considerable discomfort from the burning and might even have been dehydrated from the vomiting. She could have been disoriented with all those severe symptoms. She couldn't avoid going through all the pages of stomach turning detail, but found many interesting. There was a section on poisons and their use in the old days when forensic science was just developing in British India.

She found a whole chapter on poisons and went through all of them. When she came to cerebral poisons, *datura fastuosa* (dhatura) she found that it came in two varieties which grew commonly on waste ground. The seeds were poisonous. She read with growing excitement—here were the symptoms the boy Manju had mentioned!

The symptoms usually appeared within half an hour after swallowing the poison. Vomiting often occurred immediately after ingesting the seeds, especially when they were crushed, as they produced gastric irritation. Dryness of the mouth and throat, a burning pain in the stomach, followed by giddiness, dry, hot skin and drowsiness were the other symptoms.

So Thulasi had been poisoned! There could be no doubt about it. Who could have the motive or the opportunity? This was a real puzzle as there simply was not enough information to hand. Even Achale knew nothing and as of now, did not care too much about it. She had more interesting concerns.

What about Tulsi, her own client? She had better look up shock on the internet. She keyed in 'fall from height' on the search engine and within a short time she had a medical article on shock causing death in such cases, most of which were related to the construction of buildings. Deaths from shock were usually due to hemorrhage from vascular rupture, a tension pneumothorax or a spinal cord injury with loss of sympathetic vascular tone. These terms were new. From what she had read in the post-mortem, there was no mention of a spinal chord injury. She decided to check the definition of vascular rupture. This time the search results were disappointing. There were articles on muscle rupture or vascular surgery, but as she clicked on a few, she realized that the term simply meant that blood vessels had burst. She had better luck with 'tension pneumothorax'. Air got trapped in the lungs, pushing the other organs in the chest against the other lung, affecting the flow of blood to the heart. The result—low blood pressure, shock, and death.

The post-mortem on Tulsi was silent on the condition of the lungs or on internal bleeding from any rupture. The mechanics of death seemed unclear but there was no doubt it was caused by shock. Having decided that death was due to shock and not from any injury, the forensic doctor had handed it over to the police to decide whether it was suicide or murder. Seeing that the husband had no complaint of dowry harassment against him and that she was going through a divorce initiated by her, they had closed it as a suicide, as there was no shadow of a motive against him.

With a sigh, Maya put away the book and went back to her legal briefs. At least these had straightforward answers which required no sleight of hand.

Maya had set up a blackboard on an easel to scribble notes on any tough case so she could see the bigger picture. Various notices and greeting cards were pinned up all round. On this board, she wrote the heading MURDER and underlined it for good measure. Then she drew two columns and headed one Thulasi and another Tulsi. In the first column, she wrote Shibani and Manju in the next—both children were keen to find their mother's murderers. Next had to be 'dance' for both. Then she hit the full-stop. Perhaps she should write Srinivasa Shastri/Shastry in both—the coincidences were getting a little unnerving. However, if it could provide a key to Tulsi's death, so much the better.

Next came the manner of death, so drowning went down in one and fall from a height in the other. Another pause while she debated what came next and as the chalk hovered over the board, she knew; so, 'suspects' went down. She added Bhadri, Rama Raya, Amalotpava Devi and Narayana for good measure, though she knew nothing about them. They had been mentioned so far, so they might have a bearing on the murder. In the next column, which was much easier came Thomas, Harsha, Surilee, Srinivasa Shastry and she was forced to add: Toni(?). The last row dealt with clues—the smell of vomit, body burning, absence at night, unable to talk, rambling, camphor, pregnancy, riots; open studio were her jottings. She stepped back and looked through them. They were interesting and she hoped, comprehensive.

Pregnancy and vomiting generally went together. But it was not Thulasi's pregnancy—it was Queen Amalotpava Devi's. So then perhaps it was some poison; with symptoms like vomiting and burning body, it sounded like she had been poisoned.

In Tulsi's case, the husband and Toni were not there in the class. However, they may have paid someone to do it. It was a very long shot.

Maya laid down the chalk with a sigh. She had not considered the argument for Tulsi's death being a suicide. I'd better do some research on the internet, she thought.

Suicide, she read, on the webpage, was neither an illness nor a condition, but a range of behaviour including ideas and actions. She scrolled down until a series of causes and typical behaviour was listed: mood swings, withdrawal, preoccupation with death, settling affairs, etc. Tulsi had exhibited none of these- She was having two affairs with personable young men, cared for her daughter, had set in motion proceedings to rid herself of a relationship gone bad, was choreographing (and enjoying) two dances, and learning new skills—all evidence of a happy life, the opposite of suicidal behaviour.

Scrolling further down, she read some protective factors, chief of which were family support and cultural beliefs against suicide. This she did not know for sure. Tulsi had been much like Maya; religion did not play a big part in their lives, except as a way of enjoying a family get-together on festival days. She knew that Tulsi had celebrated all the major festivals—Tamil New Year, Diwali with a feast and fireworks display, Dussehra with a small doll's exhibit, and Pongal, the harvest festival. This was so she could pass on some family traditions and culture to her daughter. What had Shibani said? She remembered the small, piping voice, drenched with sorrow, saying Tulsi had kept out the ingredients for a cake she had promised to bake for her, Shibani. Loving her daughter so much, would she have promised something she knew she wouldn't be able to do? That was not like the Tulsi she had known. It seemed quite clear that it could not be suicide.

Tulsi had been having strange dreams. Toni and Alamelu Maami had both confirmed this. She had read somewhere that déjà vu was what the experience was called. She got herself a book from the library as Kamala was nowhere around. Déjà vu, she read, was the experience of encountering a feeling of familiarity when dealing with new situations. It usually was accompanied by a feeling of eeriness. Dreams were usually associated with the state.

That Saturday, Maya updated Pat and Meena on her latest findings. "Look, I asked Pandian to get the board in here. I need your help."

She turned the board, with its matrix of the two murders, towards them and asked them to take a good look. Did they have any ideas?

They both squinted at the board for some time.

Then Pat said, "The question we have to ask is why—motive and opportunity," she said, in the best detective tradition. "Let us examine motive in Tulsi's case: Thomas. Does he have a motive? What do we know about him? He was using Tulsi's knowledge of classical dance to choreograph his show. He and Tulsi were having an affair."

"He says he wasn't. Too messy was his reason," Maya put in. She continued, from where Pat had left off. "Did Tulsi find out something about his past? He is just running a studio which is not very well known. He is not a celebrity. What could she have discovered? Next—opportunity. He was there in the studio, though people say he was near the lift. He says he was locking up when he looked down and saw her body. So, the murderer must have been around, as there was no time for people downstairs to ask around and find out who had died and the police had not yet come on the scene. He left it open and went."

"So the murderer must have come out from the hiding place and run out," finished Meena, triumphantly.

Maya smiled in appreciation and went on, "Or, Thomas did it and is lying. The husband or Surilee, both of whom had reason to be jealous, could have been lying in wait. But Thomas says no one could have gone in without passing him and only the students were there with him and Harsha. He did not mention Surilee, but we can't cross her off. Two people saw Thomas near the lift on that day waiting for Tulsi. The motive may have been jealousy, as Tulsi was seeing Harsha also, if we think Thomas was lying about the affair. Next, we have Harsha. He was having fun with Tulsi. Why would he want to kill her? Toni and the husband had no opportunity unless they got it done by Thomas or Harsha. I can't imagine Toni's motive. She seems sad enough over Tulsi's death.

OK let's do the other one. I've already brought you up to speed on this, haven't I? Bhadhrinatha was Thulasi's protector—Achale's father warns her obliquely be careful of him and Ningi mentions that it was well known that she was his mistress. He is ambitious, pushing Manju as a saint so his temple will gain fame. Probably he is in charge of the temple lands and revenues as commander of the surrounding country," Maya summarized for them.

"Maya," Meena interrupted, puzzled, "He was a Brahmin—did they do such jobs in those days?"

"It was not like Vedic times with each caste having set jobs. It was more like now, with different castes doing various things. Anyone could be an administrator or serve in the army, only money and sagacity mattered. Why, Kondoja, a barber was Rama Raya's minion and became powerful under him," said Maya. "I bought some history books and have been reading them," she explained when her partners looked surprised.

"So back to the Badhri motive—no idea. Opportunity—we don't really know. Wait, there is another suspect—Narayanachar, the reversioner who gets the property and wants guardianship of the boy to get his hands on the *stridhana*. I'll have to check the law on this. Though opportunity again, we have to find out. As for Amalotpava Devi and Rama Raya, I can't imagine either the motive or opportunity. We'll have to see."

Pat clapped. "Maya, this is just like being in a movie!"

The tribute to Tulsi finally came around. Toni, as promised, had remembered to reserve two tickets for Maya, who was looking forward to the dance. When the morning dawned, drenched with rain, she could not suppress a pang, like a disappointed child.

She switched on the radio and was flooded with music: a song composed by A.R. Rahman, from the film *Bombay*. She hummed along, uplifted by the swingy rhythm. It was not so bad after all, even if it rained, she would be snug inside the theatre or the court and the ride back would take care of itself.

Maya decided to ask Thomas to go with her. Now that she and he had come clean about their relationship with Tulsi, she could ask him with impunity. Maya slipped into the round, graceful space of the Museum Theatre at Egmore, savouring the warm embrace of an old friend. Maya looked at the audience. As was usual at such performances, there were plenty of foreigners and youngsters. She glanced at Thomas. Like her, he was fascinated by the architecture and was smiling to himself. Encountering his glance, she smiled at him and he squeezed her hand in reply. Embarassed, Maya withdrew it.

Maya had been waiting for this dance. She did not know why, but she couldn't shake off the feeling that it would tell her something, point her in the right direction. This was a piece of Tulsi she had left behind for posterity. The weird and wonderful excitement, which was making her heart pound and her breath come in short gasps, was becoming unbearable.

The curtain lifted and her heart leapt up into her throat, choking her. It was Hampi and that was Achale, standing before the Virupaksheshwara Temple. The figure moved and Thomas's leaned across and whispered, "That's Toni, isn't it?" As she nodded, her heart began to slow its thudding and she was able to take a long, calming breath. Get a grip, girl, that's only Toni, she told herself.

Toni as the *devadasi* finished her dance and stole out to meet a bearded, well-muscled lithe young man. Was that the potter? The potter it proved to be. Their duet was supposed to be stylized love-making and the chemistry sizzled. Next, came a courtyard scene—Achale must have gone home. A supple Brahmin youth, teased and flirted with her, presumably Madhava. They argued. Toni's expressions, her quick footwork were superlative and she got a loud ovation at the end of a long series of steps. The young man dancing as Madhava then held the floor with deft footwork and sparkling gestures. The background score picked up and the singer launched into Annamaya's song on offering camphor to the Goddess. The male dancer's arms encircled her. With a brief struggle, Achale surrendered and they danced, arms entwined, offstage.

Maya felt herself let go as Achale drew her down, down into Hampi, with a flick of her eyelash and a snap of her fingers. The smell of jasmine and camphor tickled her nostrils. She was floating on a river of memory, her scalp prickling, her senses disoriented.

The programme wound its way to a close. It took some time for Maya to realize that it had ended. Not until Thomas flicked her cheek and made big eyes at her, did Maya come back to herself. "Come, the theatre's almost empty," Thomas tugged at her arm and Maya sighed, almost put out at having to come back to earth. "Let's go backstage and congratulate Toni. You haven't met her. You'll like her."

It had been really eye-opening, especially as Toni had managed to introduce the lotus dance in the story. A singer in saffron, who was probably meant to be the Acharyulu of the book, announced each stage of the story with the appropriate song. She rose to go backstage to meet Toni.

"Toni, I'm speechless! It was brilliant, beyond brilliant.... Tulsi would have been so proud."

"Except she would have been Achale. You really liked it?"

A tall woman, dressed in jeans and a t-shirt, her long hair loose and liberally threaded with silver, smiled and interjected from a chair at the back of the room. Maya had somehow missed her when she entered, perhaps because all her attention had been on Toni. Toni had that effect on people. Even Thomas looked dazzled.

"Maya, this is Anees," said Toni and Maya introduced Thomas to both.

"Oh we loved it. Didn't we, Thomas?"

"Woman as Goddess. Quite different from our dance of woman as mate," said Thomas.

"Toni, I wanted to ask you—you had a verse about doing your duty which is like the lotus leaf; pristine, I think the commentary said. What made you think of Parasurama there? I always thought that story so gory and so heartless. His father wanted him to cut off her head because she looked at another man. He did, but asked for her life back and she got a mare's head! Must doing your duty mean your heart plays no part? What about mercy?" asked Maya.

"I have always thought that an extreme example. But Tulsi insisted that it was like pure logic and the heart played no part in—Doing your Duty—in capitals, you know. She said my mind was stuck in the twentieth century so I couldn't understand that concept. I don't think she approved of it, mind. She thought all that unnecessarily cruel. But she perhaps thought that it played a big part in the psyche of the ancients."

Thomas chipped in with a doubt of his own and the conversation turned technical until they said their goodbyes and turned to go. Maya had a very important question but did not want to ask Toni in front of Thomas. She waited until Thomas had left, then doubled back again, from the car park, hoping Toni had not left. She had not.

"Toni," Maya said breathlessly, "Did Tulsi script the dance with choreographic movements written in or was that you? Could I have a look at the script?"

Toni hesitated. Clearly, she didn't want it out of her sight. Quite apart from its being Tulsi's legacy to the school, it was school property.

"Please?" Maya pleaded. "It's important to the investigation."

"Toni, I think Tulsi would have wanted Maya to see it," Anees said, gently.

"OK. Sorry, Maya, but I'm really possessive about school stuff. Here it is. Don't bother returning it; it's just a photocopy." Right up to the last minute, Toni's hand hung on to the script, until Maya had to pull it away from her and Toni laughed, to show she had been joking.

They all turned to leave the dark theatre. Maya quickly said, "It's late. I've got a packed day tomorrow," and scampered for the car. She couldn't wait to read the script.

She was disappointed. The script contained only annotations of dance movements and brief references to the storyline.

But her disappointment was short-lived. The morning's post brought her a thick envelope with a hurried scrawl from Dr. Gopalakrishnan.

I found these among my papers while I was clearing my desk. I do not recall the source, but it seems to be about Achale. I am sending you a copy in case you are interested.

Maya took the papers he had sent home with her. Later, as she prepared to read them in bed, she saw that it seemed to be a typed copy of a bit of the paperback, but translated into English. As her toes curled around Bangaru's warm fur, she thought dreamily that it was as if Tulsi had meant her to read the papers.

CHAPTER XVI

MARCH 1536 (UGADI)

A lone cuckoo was calling in the rose garden, hidden among the acacia and fig trees which grew along the far corners, like a wall against prying eyes. The rose and jasmine bushes, stood like fat, untidy stragglers at the end of an army of plants, with bricks edged, in between.

Ningi, taking a short breather, checked whether they had been watered. It was not yet hot, but the rains had not set in. Bangaru joined her, gracefully sliding into his usual pose, sphinxlike, but with front paws tucked in, eyes half-closed. The twilight made his fur appear dark brown with tawny highlights and his resemblance to a tiger was intensified.

Poor Achale, she was still closeted with the musicians, fully dressed, unable to enjoy the last of the daylight. Ningi got up. She had to see that the lamps were lit in the inner courtyard; the young girl in charge of the lamps was flighty and inclined to be too interested in watching the men. They would already be assembled on the cushions and mats, according to taste—Brahmin scholars, mingling with merchants and nobles, Moorish, Arabic and Persian traders and soldiers, all waiting to experience Achale's art and be transported for a brief while, to a world of love and longing, wit and philosophy, far removed from their everyday cares.

Ningi glanced around, making sure the guests were being served by the attendants—*panaka* made of pomegranate and sweetened with jaggery was being served in copper tumblers with *sikarane*, fruit salad; copper plates spread with plantain leaves had sweet meats such as *karachikai* and *sakkare burude*. Gusts of sweet smoke from silver incense burners perfumed the air. Blazing copper lamps placed at intervals in wall niches threw interesting shadows and picked up the glittering eyes of one whom Ningi recognized as the potter from the bazaar and surely, the Brahmin with the silken shawl and gold *kulayee* on his head was the poet of the bathing pool! Two of Achale's admirers in the same place! There were going to be fireworks! Better to warn Bhima. Ningi hurried away.

Achale was going to shock them with a male dancer, her brother, Kesava and then confront them with the work of an unknown poet to gauge the reaction of the audience, before she tried it out elsewhere. Ningi wondered if the day's takings would be profitable after all. It was a good thing there were two people who professed to be her admirers. She might need them after this performance after all!

She went out to the second courtyard where Bhima usually would be found at this time of the day, having a hookah with Balla, the cowman. She hoped he would be sober enough to listen. But Bhima was not with Balla, who was snoring near his cow. Betappa and Bhima were hunched together, next to the elephant stable, talking earnestly. As Ningi came into view, Bhima called to her and made place for her, next to himself. For once, Betappa did not look at her. Otherwise he would be leering at her breasts. He was instead sitting with his head in his hands, so Ningi knew that it was serious indeed.

"Betappa has received the king's summons. He has to find the murderer within two months and report his progress within a week to Bhadri's chief watchman, the *taliyar*. You know what could happen if he has no progress to report."

"He will lose his land."

"Ningi, Betappa says something else. Very worrying. It seems the summons was delivered by Rama Raya's man. His horse trappings had the symbol of the Aliya's house. Betappa feels that the Aliya is interested in the murder. "

"I heard talk in the market place. That Janamma who sells fish said that the Aliya hates all *devadasis*. Maybe someone was not true to him at some time, no one knows why. She said that, he especially hates our Achale as she is so rich and accomplished. She sells fish to everyone, doesn't she? She must have heard it from his household. I wanted to tell you but the preparation for this evening drove it out of my head. *Ajji* is right. Achale needs a protector. What can she do—one woman against his might?"

Betappa spoke. "The situation between the king and himself is not so good, you know. That one roams around like an uncaged tiger and see his supporters—the *nayaks* of Adoni, Kurnool, Awuku and Nandyala! The king has the Salkarajus, it is true, but he must always sleep lightly. Just as the donkey knows not the fragrance of camphor, so also, the Aliya does not realize the purity of your mistress. He must equate them to prostitutes! But how did he light on Achlabbegaru, you tell me that?"

"They will say it is because Ningi discovered the body that suspicion attached to Achale. The old one warned of this. She said Bhadri would make trouble for Achale."

"Ah, say that! The patient wanted rice with milk and the doctor prescribed it. Then we must watch out."

Ningi couldn't keep silent any longer. "If the dog barks, will the heavens hear it? Why should we care about the idle rumours spread by wicked people?"

"This is no longer rumour, Betappa has been asked to act! if he does not, then Bhadri as *karyakarta* to the king, can simply act on suspicion and imprison Achale," Bhima looked very grave. "We must warn Achale. She has to be careful."

"*Anna,* why don't we help Betappa? I go everywhere with Achale, we can speak to people that he cannot question, like Manju. We can find out the truth in two weeks not two months." Bhima looked thoughtful at this suggestion.

Betappa said, "There is talk of an astrologer in Anegundi. They say he knows how to read faces and carries with him palm-leaf horoscopes of all in Vijaynagara. He can tell past births and predict the future based on that. He also throws shells and reads faces. Let us go, *anna*." Bhima nodded because Ningi was motioning him to come with her. He excused himself and followed her, the midges from the beasts were stinging sharply and they had all scratched hard as they talked. It was time to move indoors so Betappa must be induced to leave. "The potter is here. So is the Brahmin poet," Ningi whispered worriedly. Bhima understood. He whispered back that he would be there as soon as Betappa left, after a meal. It would be prudent to be extra gracious to Betappa at this time.

Kesava was watching Achale's dress. They were going over the programme. He was already dressed. Taller than Achale, he would make a striking foil. Even he could see that though she was dressed simpler than usual, she looked exceptional.

Achale was speaking. "My guru used to say that each *raga* possesses a particular mood or flavour and the duty of the dancer, singer and musician is to find it and release it. You must take the audience with you towards God, by releasing the devotion, within them, through your dance. Then you will gain salvation in both this life and the next."

"Tell that to my father. If you listened to him, I am more likely to attain hell here on earth."

"Patience, my lad. We are on the first step now and soon we will reach the summit. It will be you then, saying this to your pupil. But you must work hard—no more prancing off to the fields. You will have to live with me, if *Ajji* permits, and I must find a dance-master who is willing for you to apprentice with to him." Kesava bowed his head. The thought of at last breaking free of his father's oppressive control was too much for him.

Bhima could have told the poet that he had no chance as soon as the potter entered Achale's field of vision. Her eyes had closed momentarily and he had seen her chest rise and fall quickly. He had followed her glance towards the source of her disquiet. *Ajji*'s eyes had glittered ominously as she sat behind the curtained embrasure. She had picked up the signals, he knew, as had Ningi from her alertly angled head, as she too watched, at *Ajji*'s feet. Just a glance and peace had fled the house!

Virabhadra was sitting at ease. He was dressed like a commoner, wearing only a thin shawl over a loincloth, the usual foot-long head dress and the *linga* in a pouch round his neck. He sits like a prince, sculptor though he may be. Whence this strength, this majesty? Bhima mused. He cleared his throat, preparatory to keeping his guest occupied till Achale refreshed herself and joined them.

"Achalabbe Devi has gone to change. Will your honour like some refreshment? The hour is advanced and this house would be honoured by your partaking of a poor meal." Bhima bowed politely. The potter had been lost in his thoughts, but now he sat up straighter, and leaning sideways towards Bhima, spoke.

"Such an establishment must cost a lot to keep up, eh? If she does not have a patron, she must be hard pressed to maintain this lifestyle. Of course, people pay for the privilege of watching her dance..." he mused to himself. Bhima did not know whether to be affronted or to answer seriously and then decided that the courteous course would be to take the question at its face value. "Yes, the household is expensive to maintain—we have animals as well as servants, but we manage. The King has been generous with land, which we rent out and she has many engagements. *Ajji* Roopavathi lives with her and adds her considerable income, to ours. We do very well."

"I heard talk that there is some trouble with Rama Raya. There is a rumour that he has turned against your mistress and wants to get her in trouble as the murderess of that Brahmin lady who died, that new saint-child's mother."

"Where did you hear this, sir?" asked Bhima, eager to verify Ningi's story.

But the potter dismissed it with a wave of his hand, "It is common knowledge in the bazaar." Bhima knew that Ningi's fisherwoman would have spread the story. That did not make it untrue, however.

"Tell me, would the lady sit for me? I need to know. I have to finish a sculpture for the Lepakshi temple being built by Virapanayya, Nayaka of Penukonda and his brother Veeranayya." Bhima looked alert. These were known supporters of the Aliya. So, the potter had not come out with the truth. He must have heard talk even at Lepakshi or from someone in the know.

"Tell me, will she agree? It will take only a few hours, but I must sketch her before I work on the sculpture."

"She will be down soon and we can ask her," Bhima was non-commital. Achale might be flattered. She was changing before their eyes, better not to make any decisions for her.

Ningi came first and directed the placement of the seat and the attendants with fans. Then Achale entered. She had changed her garments for those of plain silk cloth. A faint fragrance of roses and sandalwood wafted in with her.

All Achale's sophistication had deserted her and she was as tongue tied as any girl. The classes in deportment had never failed her till then. When she had seated herself, the potter spoke.

"I have rarely seen such a talented performance. The room was bright with lamps, but the stage glowed even brighter, with the brilliance of lightning and we were deafened by the thunder of your art."

Achale had got her breath back and with it her wit. "You mould your words as you do your pots." Her eyelids fluttered coylty and she darted glances from beneath them even as birds do their tongues when they sing. "Our house is honoured by your visit."

"Lady, please forgive the rudeness of this humble potter and let us begin again. I am Virabhadra, the sculptor."

He held up his hands, those strong, long-fingered hands with square fingertips and smooth knuckles.

"I can use these hands, rather than a maul or chisel. But sculpting is the way I hope to make my name. I have been commissioned to sculpt some pillars and figures at Lepakshi temple. Naturally I agreed, being named after the deity and hailing from near Anantapura."

His gleaming smile flashed, his eyes like pinpoints of light in the night sky. "I would like to sculpt the perfect woman, a Padmini *jati stri*. The waist should be small, perfect and the navel placed at the apex of a perfect triangle from the waist. The breasts should rise as Harsha said, compact and high, proud to be held close to her heart. A Padmini *jati stri* is slim where she should be, heavy where she would give the most pleasure and full of lip, promising the nectar within."

"You seem to be well-versed in the masters. A poet and a sculptor-potter—there are no end to your skills, it seems."

"One cannot sculpt without some knowledge Devi; would you deny me *jnana*, when you have it?"

"What we have right now, to satisfy your hunger, is food. Please honour my humble table and grant me the grace of feeding a guest tonight."

Achale watched as Ningi directed a table to be brought and green banana leaves placed on a silver platter. She was relieved to see that two kinds of pickle, tender mango and radish, a side-dish of fresh yellow pumpkin, *katogare* or lentil soup, neem flowers, chicken and partridge with fragrant boiled rice, *chitranna* (lemon-flavoured rice) and *mosaru butti* (curd rice balls) were served. A meal which would not have shamed a queen! She had worried that they would have nothing much to offer an unexpected guest, but *Ajji* must have cooked for Kesava.

When the meal ended, she motioned him to sit on a swing suspended from brass chains with her. As she took out betel leaves, and areca nut shavings from a chased silver box to roll a *tamboolam* for him, she said, "They say the temple is very beautiful."

"Yes, it will surpass all others in beauty."

"Viranna sent a messenger, asking me to dance there, when the renovation is complete."

"That is still in the future, though we are working hard to complete the *mandapa*."

"There is talk that the Aliya's men are brewing trouble in Gooty for the King."

"As long as the two factions are at loggerheads, this will go on. Will the peace he made at Raichur, hold? Will the Adil Shah or the Qutb Shahs never strike? Who can guarantee these things? If one is King, one must expect war."

"Sir, you did not answer my question earlier: whence your love of poetry?"

"My parents scorned the *gurukula*. They were Virasaivas and took Basava's *vachanas* about some Gods being worse than dogs to heart. They sent me to the village school, but my friend the priest's son took pity on me and taught me Sanskrit and Telugu. *Devi*, I came here to ask you to sit for me. Future generations would be lost, if they never were to see such beauty."

"And what of your wife? Is she learned? Does she fit the idea of a Padmini?"

He smiled to himself, which Achale saw and immediately felt foolish. She had betrayed herself. The answer, when it came was gentle. "I have no wife." He moved a little, so they were sitting close, his arm rested on the cushions along the back of the swing, his foot grazing her thigh. Achale half-turned to him, one leg tucked up, her hand extended now, with the betel leaf-roll. He took it, one hand cupped round hers, the other accepting the betel leaf. Her hand trembled briefly and he felt warmth shoot up his arm, catching even him, who was used to beauty, by surprise. This was a woman worth winning.

"Where will the sittings take place?"

"With your permission, here. I will make some sketches and a clay figure and take it with me to Lepakshi."

He began to play with a lock of her hair, unpinning the knot, so it fell in profusion down her back, rivaling the night, soft, cloudy, smelling of incense and her own musk. Achale stirred, but could not get up, her legs were unwilling to follow her commands. She followed Virabhadra's strong fingers as they gently stroked her bare arm and went to her shoulder. His lips followed, leaving a trail of fire. She moved and shivered.

"I am afire…each glance… every touch.." he murmured. It was if he knew that she needed the goad of words. His mouth now found hers, but withdrew almost immediately. Like a moth to the flame, she turned and with a small moan, fastened her lips on his. He gently traced her nipple through her bodice. Her mouth opened in a groan and his tongue found the nectar within. The fan clattering from the attendant's hand, while she sagged in sleep, roused Achale. She broke off and stood up. She put out her hand and he took hold. Hand-in-hand they climbed to her room, while Bhima watched, his heart in his stomach and his soul taking flight in despair. Ningi looked up from her position on the floor, half-asleep and caught the look. She glanced quickly at Achale, but Achale was oblivious. Already, they had stopped their progress to embrace, before continuing. She settled down for the night. *Ajji* would have a lot to say. Meanwhile she could at least get some sleep.

As soon as they entered the room, Virabhadra pulled Achale to himself and pressed his lips on hers, hard. When they broke apart, she said, "Gently, my lord potter, this body has not felt a man's hand before." His eyes glittered in the flickering light of the lamps, as he muttered hoarsely, "Lady, the time for gentleness is long past. This is not Virabhadra but Gajendra before you, now." His hands unknotted her garments with practiced ease. She had never been naked before a man and her sophistication had dropped away with the garments, so she clung, limp as a plantain stalk. He grasped her waist and swung her on to the bed. "Peerless one, we will go slowly, though all my instincts cry out for the swift conclusion of this wonderful game." He rubbed his hands over her body, kneading it slowly like he would clay for his pots, while he bent and delicately sipped the nectar from her navel. She moved and murmured his name, hands clutching blindly at his shoulders. Her earrings gleamed in the lamplight, while they slipped about and swung drunkenly as she moved her head from side to side.

"What, are you a tailor?" Achale murmured as Virabhadra covered her nipple with his thumb tip, all the while cupping it with his open hand, as if he was measuring it, while his long little finger caressed the tender spot where her armpit merged with the top of her breast. For answer, he took her nipple in his mouth, while his hands performed the rite of squeezing her pyramid of pleasure. With his chest he rubbed the down which pointed arrowlike to the pinnacle of desire, while his legs pressed hers apart. As she moaned, his mouth covered hers while his tongue explored the sweetness thus within his reach. His hand now moved to untie the final knot of her girdle. Virabhadra took in his breath sharply. Even for one as experienced as he, this was a new departure in the match of love and he showed his appreciation by anointing her with his tongue, so when at last, he spread her thighs and raised her hips, for the final move, she was more than ready, she wished for the conclusion as surely as he.

The cuckoo had begun its usual work of calling to its mate. Not to be outdone, the crows cawed loudly, as the pale light of a new day was seeping through the dark stain of night. The moon, which had lain all night, wrapped in the dark embrace of the night, now stirred and gently disengaged, drew up the pearly veil of light and prepared to flee before the bright rays of the sun. Achale, threw out an arm from under the soft silk blanket, and sighed, still deep in sleep. The soft skin of her inner arm, rosy with sleep, still bore marks of the potter's head. Her hair, tinged gold by the rays streaming in through the window, lay spread in abandon on the pillow, but a few tendrils snaked on to her breast unwilling to be separated from the tender curve of her neck.

Ningi stole in. Virabhadra had left in the early hours of the morning, waking up Bhima to light his way. Now it was time for Achale to wake up. Achale was on leave from her duties at the temple. She could tease Achale best by her silence. She could not, however, resist humming Annamayya, the poet of Tirumala's immortal words:

Paluku tenela talli…

O mother, sleeping from her exertions with the Lord…

Ningi kept to her resolve until Achale came out of the bathroom. Then she began humming another of Annamayya's songs,

Her breasts bear the nail-marks of the Lord, shining like half-moons….

"Aren't you ashamed girl, singing about Goddess Lakshmi to describe wordly matters? This is why they say, it is better not to educate the lowly too much," Achale was scathing to cover her embarrassment.

"*Chikkamma*, what do I know of love poems or love-play? All I know is what is sung on the street. And what you dance."

"Talking to you is like talking to a monkey!"

She had found a crescent mark marring the smooth cream of Achale's thigh, her lips swollen and red and a dull red bruise on her breast. Oh she would have her work cut out, masking all this from *Ajji*'s sharp eyes. How many love bites would she not have seen as Simhapuri Roopavathi? They dressed, Ningi taking care to cover the potter's depredations.

Achale was nervous. *Ajji* was waiting to serve her breakfast as usual, the attendant had said. There was no Kesava to distract her and make her discreet. Ningi and Bhima she did not consider. All was lost. They went down to the courtyard by the kitchen. *Ajji* had placed herself on her usual seat and was fanning herself. Achale, touched her feet, after praying at their household shrine, and went to sit at the seat which had been placed for her. There was a porridge of rice and lentils with ghee. Achale pecked at the food, stealing looks at *Ajji*. There was an ominous silence there. While Achale was drying her hands on a towel, the storm broke.

"Did I lavish attention, spare no expense on tutors, write away my fortune and manage your affairs only to be thrown aside like an unwanted shoe, girl? If you do not want me, you have only to tell me. Not take your pleasure where you will and expect me to become a madam to a common harlot. Have we come to this?"

"*Ajji*," Achale, threw up her hands and covered her ears. "Please, not a common harlot. I have no wish to sell my wares. I simply..."

"Oho, your mouth you turned aside, you shut your ears to his persuasions but he undid your dress and your bodice split on its own, is it not?"

"You injure me in that you take me for a fool. Love stole on me. You were young once, did you never feel, *Ajji*?"

"Hai! Listen! She felt love. And are you a common slave girl, to yield to love's importunities? You are Achalabbe, granddaughter of Simhapuri Roopavathi, fit to consort with kings as Chinnamadevi has shown *devadasis* to be. And you yield to a lowly potter like a fool. It will be all over the market place in a week. And you not only fed him, you did not get anything in return. I would have found you a patron worthy of you. Now, we must settle for something less. Maybe a landowner or a commander if we are lucky. What is the use of a stove burning after the food is eaten?"

"So it is true! You *had* lined up that courtier Vajrabahu for me! Next, you will have me pay Bhadri's prostitute tax. Do you remember what Vita, a character from *Mrichchakatika* says, *Ajji*? 'A courtesan is like a creeper growing by the wayside, a well from which all passersby drink.' Would you have me be like that, loving one, serving another and dancing before a third master?"

Achale did not wait to hear her grandmother's response. She hastily, touched *Ajji*'s feet, motioned to Ningi and they climbed into the cart and were off over the fields.

CHAPTER XVII

APRIL, 1536 (HOLI)

The rolling coracle stopped at the landing ghat of the bazaar and Achale, Bhima and Ningi got out seeing Kesava, Indra and Puttalakshmi waiting eagerly for them. Kesava had been dispatched earlier to Nagalapur to bring his mother to Hampi. They had decided that they would go the big bazaar street outside the Hazara Ramachandra Temple from Virupakshapura through the western gate, the wares were always the best there and the festivities, the magicians, the acrobats, snake charmers who would have gathered there would be the best in the city. They could browse through precious stones, knick-knacks and the finest cloth. They set off in a carriage that Bhima had arranged earlier.

As they were passing the Malyanta hill, by the bridge over the Turuttu channel, Ningi said, "Bhimanna, you were going to the astrologer with Betappa, what did he say?"

"Like all astrologers, this one too proved very wily. He insisted that there were signs that a big change was coming in all our lives."

"Did he say anything about Achale's marriage?" asked Puttalakshmi.

"I told him to see but he insisted that a change was coming and would not say more."

"Maybe he is losing his powers" put in Ningi. Bhima shrugged. The astrologer had been anxious to see them leave after he had told them that a change was coming.

As they neared the market street, they could see clouds of saffron rising in the air as people sprayed colour from spray guns. Everywhere, there were men and women with clinging wet garments and beautiful garlands of sweet smelling flowers. Indra and Kesava were eager to start and leaped down from the carriage even before it came to a stop. Bhima suspected that Kesava's eagerness came more from a wish to see exposed female shapes close-up than to play. They had brought spray-guns with them which they filled up from the huge pots which were placed at the wayside, and were soon lost in the crowd. Puttalakshmi was not worried. Kesava would keep an eye on Indra. The women desultorily aimed a few sprays at each other for form's sake and eagerly approached the ornament stalls for the real business of the day. Later, they would buy some snacks and sweetmeats from a vendor to keep them going till they could enjoy a picnic meal with the food Ningi had brought from home.

Bhima wandered into the crowd. Achale would be occupied for some time and would not need him. A familiar figure inched its way through the crowd. He stopped here and there as if to get its bearings and then continued. Bhima recognized him, even though he was dressed like Bhima himself. It was Vajrabahu. He had a shawl covering his upper body and an ordinary *kulayee* on his head. Bhima followed him through the crowd; Vajrabahu seemed to be looking for someone or something. Finally, near a crowd watching a *fakir* playing a pipe and making a rope rise straight up, Vajrabahu stopped. The rope stood firm like an iron rod, even when the *fakir* tried to bend it. A small boy who had been in charge of the basket put down the lid and began to climb it, one hand over the other. The crowd went mad and coins began to rain down on the cloth spread on the ground. Bhima was watching Vajrabahu, who had stopped and appeared to be searching for something.

In the middle of the crowd were some Kalabhras and Kalamukhas, distinguishable from their macabre ornaments of bones and skulls and ashes smeared on their bodies. They approached Vajrabahu. Taking advantage of the general commotion, the group disappeared behind some conveniently placed carts. Bhima could not get nearer without attracting attention, so he had to remain content with watching until the group broke up.

On the way back, they heard singing: "*Show me the path to Vaikuntha!*" and they knew Acharyulu was somewhere nearby. Soon he came into view. They would have given him a lift in the cart but he declined and kept pace with them, easily.

The passengers who wanted to be dropped at the first city gate were sitting in the front of the cart, so the space at the back was free for Achale, Ningi and Bhima.

Bhima said, "I saw a strange thing today,"

"Oh, *anna,* was it the snake charmer? Everyone was talking about his rope trick!" Ningi broke in.

"No woman, stop your chatter and listen. This is important. I saw Vajrabahu wearing ordinary clothes, as if he wanted to blend in with the crowd. He was talking to Kalabhras and Kalamukhas and they went behind some carts as if they did not want to be overheard."

"The courtier and these strange death-eaters! I wonder... what a strange assortment! What could they have in common?" Achale wondered.

As they were discussing the incident, Acharyulu continued to sing. Suddenly, Achale's ears alerted her brain. Was there a pattern in the choice of songs?

"*Why does a commoner want to be King?*" Acharyulu finished the song. He broke into another song, this time in Telugu by that '*Sankirtanaacharya*' Annamayya.

"*Chikkamma,* I think the *dasa* is trying to tell us something. See how he is singing different songs. *Ajji* Jakkini said he wandered around as a spy. Maybe he has seen something. Maybe he saw you, *anna*."

"Why should an ordinary man want to rule? Something to do with kingship. He followed it up with taking shelter in Achyuta of Venkatadhri; Annamayya's song. So is he saying the King is false?"

"*Chikkamma,* but he said take refuge in Achyuta so someone else is being false."

"He is continuing, with another song by the dasa Purandara ... *Yellaru maadavathu*."

"Ruling to fill the belly. He must have seen Vajra and the Kalabhras. Vajra must be trying to depose the king. He has two powerful foes, then: the Tirumalas and Rama Raya. Who is he, of what family that he is trying for kingship?'

"Yes, it seems to add up to Vajra. He is of the Sangama clan; they, that ruled Vijayanagara once, before the Saluvas and Tuluvas seized control. They say he can trace his line back to Sri Pratapa Devarayudu," said Bhima.

"This is the best time to try to wrest the crown with conditions so unsettled. And the Kalamukha *mathas* feel slighted at the importance given by Sri Pratapa Krishnarayudu to Tatachari of Tirupati, the Sri Vaishnava and Vyasatirthagaru, the Madhva *dasa*. The Sangamas worshipped Shiva as Virupaksha as their family deity, which these Tuluvas have changed. But this is the first time since Sri Krishnarayudu died that conditions have been so settled and we have been able to conduct so many festivals in peace. Must he be King? Can he not serve the King?"

"In these troubled times, when one does not know what the morrow will bring, the desire for advancement is very urgent," sighed Bhima.

Acharyulu was singing, a song of Kanakadasa's, this time. It was wonderful, the way he could string songs like a garland of flowers to make his meaning clear to any dolt, thought Ningi. Aloud, she said, "What are the words… I did not catch them."

"A beggar mistook an elephant for the King and garlanded him. He is now singing Purandara *dasa's* song, '*Who helps anyone?*' He ran to a tree to shelter from hot winds only to have it fall on him, he is saying."

He is warning us that Vajra is proceeding to his destruction. The foes ranged against him are too strong, thought Achale.

"Vajra may be asking for trouble. I will ask Chenna to keep an eye out. There is a fair at Jogahalli. Chenna's troupe will be there. The next meeting may be at the fair." Bhima reassured her, as if he had read her mind.

Achale was in a reckless mood that night. There were very few visitors. It was as if someone had warned them off. She could very well guess who it could have been. Bhadri must have done his job well, implied among her regulars, the traders and jewelers that she had fallen in disfavour with Rama Raya. It mattered not that she still had the King's favour. Only this morning, he had come to the temple, informally, with a small retinue and gifted her shawl as a special mark of favour. Some rumour must have come to his ears and as usual, the competition between Rama Raya and himself must have prompted him to grant her this indulgence. She shrugged off the sight of just two of her admirers, one an old poet, whom no one had any use for anymore and who had stopped composing his doggerel long since; the other was Madhava Shastry, her admirer of the pool side. She made her obeisance and sat down.

No matter; the small audience gave her license to simply sing instead of dance. She played the single stringed instrument with a bow made of goat string and bamboo. Indicating the song to her small band and with a slight, challenging smile at Madhava, the Vaishnavite, she began to sing a song composed by the shepherd from Kaginale, Kanakadasuru, '*Dasanaagabeku, Sadashivana, You have to be the servant of Sadashiva*'.

She follwed it with one even more provocative by the same *dasa*,

'*Ellaru maduvadu, Everyone works to satisfy the stomach*!'

And when she came to the part, which described a *devadasi* with accompanists dancing to satisfy her belly and for a piece of cloth to cover her shame, she got up and mimed the words, ending with a laugh.

As she ended it, Madhava broke into, '*Kshirabdi kanyakaku*' by Annamayya, describing the offering of camphor to the Goddess at Tirupati in appreciative detail.

From the admiration emanating from him in waves so hot, they burnt as white as the camphor he sang of, there could be no doubt that he meant it for her. He had effectively capped her taunt of singing to Sadashiva. Achale smiled in embarrassment, as she bowed her head and clasped her hands in acknowledgement and launched into the *mangala* song, which closed the concert.

When she was eating her meal, Ningi informed her that the poet wanted a word with her. Achale was tired out with worry about her next course of action and what the ominous lack of visitors meant to her own safety. She was in the mood to refuse, when she remembered that she had to give a discourse at Alur to a group of Sri Vaishnava women and she would like to discuss the content with him. Also, here was a golden opportunity to discuss the murder and hear what he had to say. As Ningi had said, her only hope now lay in trying to solve it. However, her brain was not so numbed by tension that she could not feel apprehension at the implication of the poet's action in staying back. He may have heard of her tryst with Virabhadra. Such news could not be suppressed and the bazaar was probably ringing with it.

So it was with a slightly strained smile, that she went in to Madhava and supervised his meal. She made sure this time that the betel leaf was served by a maid, while she sat a little farther away from him, on a seat. No dangerous swinging this time!

"Your man told me you are going to Alur to deliver a discourse on the occasion of Sri Rama Navami, Devi." Madhava himself gave her the opening.

"I would like your help, Acharare. Andal, in her *Nachiar Thirumozhi*, in the second set of stanzas, calls Sri Ranganatha 'man who is called as Narayana'. Is Andal playing on Nara (man) and Narayana (abode of man) contained in the sacred chant, *Om namo narayan*?"

"Yes. Andal is also saying that that Nara the disciple can reach the abode of man through the *acharya*, Narayana. In the Vaishnava tradition, the *acharya* who performs the initiation is everything, for he takes our sins. In the Sri Vaishnava tradition, women are allowed to speak the sacred chant, *Om Namo Narayana*. The *acharyas* initiate both men and women and people from all castes. That is why our Ramanujachariar, on being initiated, went to the top of the *dhwajastambha,* the sacred pole of the temple, and shouted out the *mantra,* so it became available to all. Our saints, the *alwars* have sprung from all walks of life. Andal's *acharya* is Vishnucitta, her father Perialvar. She also is telling us that she is pierced by longing for union with the Lord. The *acharya* implanted the sacred chant in her, through her right ear, and it entered her soul."

"So that is the meaning of what she says in the fifth decade that he entered her and 'sowed' her ruin."

"In the third chapter of the Gita, Krishna likens lust obscuring the mind and senses, to fire covered by smoke or a mirror covered by dust. Krishna then goes on to say how by taming them and concentrating on spiritual intelligence, one conquers lust, the enemy of self realization."

"So Andal, a young girl, just blossoming into womanhood strings together sensual verses, while bringing out the sexual longing and anger to be merged into her consciousness so she may attain self-realization and her soul, oneness with Krishna. This is shown as sexual union. Since God is male, the devotee is always female. Ah, this is an excellent interpretation."

Achale got up and bending touched his feet. His teaching had really opened her eyes. When she sat down again, she asked: "How goes your work? And is there any progress in uncovering your sister's murderer?"

"The work goes on a little slowly. Meanwhile, I am still in search of a patron to admit me in the King's court." He smiled at her.

"Don't you know, achare, this *devadasi* is fast becoming an outcast, a fugitive. Rama Raya's men are lying in wait for me. Did you not see the empty room this night? I have to help Betappa solve the murder or Bhadri, who is of course behind all this, will see that I disappear. You will not benefit from being seen as my protégé. Today is Holi but you find me here, instead of in town, enjoying the celebrations. Bhima refused to let me out of his sight."

He looked concerned. "Devi, I will help in any way I can. That Narayana is trying to take the boy from me. The boy likes me and by staying with him, I gain a place to live. I think we should investigate his movements. Then there is Bhadri, but he had every reason to want her alive. She was his woman."

Achale debated whether she should tell him about the new piece of news they had just discovered. There was no harm in it. "We also saw Vajrabahu, the Sangama talking to Kalabhras and Kalamukhas. There might be something in that connected to Thulasi's death."

"I don't think Vajrabahu knew Thulasi. What reason could he have for her murder? There is much to ponder."

"When I am in Alur, I could talk to the women and learn something. I think I will send a message to Vajrabahu to meet me there after the discourse. He seemed to admire me though he has not visited this house."

There was a caterwauling from the rose garden. The door to this garden had been shut and the cat, Bangaru wanted to come in. Achale pushed open the door. The cat incalculably went silent and sat hunched outside, refusing to come in. Achale went out. There was no moon outside and it was a dark night, but the torches illuminated the garden. The heat had released the smell of the roses and mingled with the jasmine, their scent intoxicating.

Achale felt a warmth behind her and realized that Madhava had come outside. Softly, he said,

"Is that a waterfall of jet silvered by the night,
Or are those my lady's tresses,
Released from their braid
To flaunt wantonly through the night,
Enticing my poor senses
With their scent
And the promise of pleasure?"

The moment she heard the verses, Achale knew that he had won. This was the Unknown Poet who had set her imagination thrumming with his verses at the Mahashivarathri celebrations.

Achale moved a little, but he followed, not touching her, but letting his breath scented with betel and spices caress her. He must be doing more than selling love poems in the Soolai bazaar, thought Achale.

"Limbs turned liquid gold with sandal,
Oh Saree, why are you so cruel,
Hiding the pots brimming with nectar below.
Blow wind and let the sharagu fly!
Oh Waist, if you are an altar to my lady's beauty,
Let me worship you
So I may enter the gate way to heaven."

His fingers hovered over her shoulder but did not touch her. Achale could feel the heat emanating from them. He let his finger tip set the tassels, which tied her bodice at the back, swinging. Achale's bodice felt constricted as if her breasts had suddenly become heavier. They longed for that fingertip. Stop it! she admonished herself. Your body wants release, a voice whispered through her mind. Your soul is your own. You are the hand maiden of God. Such union is permitted to you, as your bridegroom can never enjoy your body, only your soul.

"So what if the lips like tender leaves,
Breasts like mounds of sweetmeats
Topped by a single rose,
Thighs like the pillows of the love-god
Neck like a swan,
curved and enticing,
Are turned away?
Can I not slake my eyes
On the feast before my eyes
And imagine the rest?"

His thumb had now taken to gently rubbing the nape of her neck, visible where the hair was parted to fall in front. He let his other hand wander over her back, leaving a trail of fire at each touch of the finger tip.

"My *gurudakshina, devi,*" whispered Madhava, demanding payment. He picked up Achale, suddenly grown weak and unable to walk, and carried her up the stairs effortlessly. This poet has surprising sides to him, thought Achale with the part of her brain which could still function.

By the time they had reached the chamber and shut the door, both of their garments littered the stairs. Madhava put her down against the wall near the door and sank down on his knees with a look of awe. He bent his head and began to kiss her feet. Achale swayed from the heat of his lips, so he gently tugged at her arm and lowered her to the floor. Fleetingly, she thought, if *Ajji* could only see me now, taking my pleasure on the floor like a slave girl, before giving herself up to the exquisite sensations his lips and hands were causing. The poet, true to his calling, worships at my altar, she thought. No kneading or pummeling; only fluttering kisses until my senses are so inflamed that I am ready for him, nay eager, for consummation. She writhed under his practiced hands, offering up her breasts. When she opened her mouth in a sigh of pleasure, he immediately covered it with his own and turned her over, supporting her hips while he pierced her with his embrace. I thought we had covered the four positions, the potter and I, but the poet has taught me a fifth, she sighed to herself.

After a brief nap, she found herself astride him, her dangling gold earings grazing her cheeks with her rhythmic swinging, while he encouraged her by cupping her breast with one hand and steadying her waist with the other. She wondered, before she slid into ecstacy, is this Achale, the virgin bride of the Lord?

Much later, before her eyes closed in sleep, she thought to herself, he has spent his time in the Soolai Bazaar very profitably. All the pictures in the Hampi palace to educate young girls about the pleasures of the bed did not cover even one of the caresses that Madhava had displayed that night. Nor the strength of a man who seemed indefatigable or what such attentions could do to a girl's ego, not to mention her heart.

Achale was expecting much more from *Ajji* so the ominous silence was hard to interpret. With timid glances at her grandmother who was bent on only showing her profile—the haughtiest part of her—Achale could only bolt her *ragi* balls and milk. Even Ningi had no repartee. *Ajji* had finally succeded in shutting up even that irreverent damsel. Ningi entered to say that the cart was waiting.

Ajji finally spoke: "Ningi, you may tell your mistress that I am remaining here only to serve my grandson. This house has now turned into a bawdy tavern with the only difference that no money changes hands and your mistress is giving away her youth and beauty free. That I had to live to see this! Worse than a common harlot! Now that Bhadri will have a free hand. Mark my words, he will ask for her favours and now that he is allying with Rama Raya, saying no is not going to be easy. How will I face her father? He will lay everything at my door! Poor Lakshmi! How is she going to face his wrath? Tell her to pray hard that he hasn't heard. Though it must be all over the bazaar now. Not one but two! Can we trust them to keep their mouths shut about such a prize?" She shook her head in disgust but could not prevent a tear from straying down her cheek.

Achale was touched. How the old one must be worrying! She bent down and touched *Ajji*'s feet before she could withdraw them, then hugged her. "*Ajji*, it will all come right. Don't worry. I'll play them both against each other until they ask me to marry them. Then I'll decide what to do. All is not lost."

As they hurried down the street leading to the temple Achale once again cannoned into Virabhadra and this time, his arms clasped her for a second to his breast before he steadied her and let her go. Even in that brief meeting, her treacherous heart had stopped and was now drumming fit to burst out of her bodice, while her skin was singing. While his hands had been gentle, his eyes raked her form and finding the love-bite on her shoulder, stopped and narrowed. "*Devi*, well met! But perhaps, you are disconcerted rather than overjoyed?"

"Disconcerted?" Achale was playing for time, which she did not have much of, as the morning hymn had started. "Let me go forward. I am late. Please meet me at the back gate in an hour. We can talk then, undisturbed." Pushing him gently, she hurried on.

It cannot be said that her mind was on God as she went through the motions of the dance and the ritual sweeping of the sanctum. If the priest noticed, he said nothing. It would not do for him to say anything against one who had the King's favour after all. Impatiently she waited for the daily puja to wind down and taking her share of the *prasada*, she almost ran to the back gate. She need not have worried. Virabhadra was there, looking like a thunder cloud, arms crossed, eyes half closed and mouth in a straight line.

When he saw that the street was deserted except for them, he pulled her roughly down beside him on the stone seat and pushing her upper garment aside, showed her bruised skin. "What is this? I thought you did not take lovers. Did Kama come down then to spend the night? Or perhaps it was that reprobate, Indra. If he could seduce Ahalya, and let his wife Ṣachi be importuned by an usurper, he would not have been able to resist you." Achale was touched. Even in his anger, he did not want to believe the worst of her. "I could not refuse. It was *gurudakshina*."

"So it *was* the poet!" he burst out. "*Devi*, I have no weapons against such a consummate flirt. He is welcome to you." He brought his raised palms in a salute and left, his strides becoming longer and longer as his anger carried him away from her. Achale was left desolate.

The cart was swaying from side to side, winding its jerky way along the rutted cart track. Talking was difficult, for which Achale was glad. She couldn't have taken Ningi's chatter just then. It was nearly a week since the altercation with Virabhadra and he hadn't come by, not even to fix a date for the sittings. Only pride prevented her from sending Ningi to him, to find out what was up. Pride, which acted against Ningi's finding out about the quarrel and from seeking out Virabhadra herself. Though her nights had been spent very pleasantly with Madhava, some part of her being ached for Virabhadra's understanding.

The problem of course was that she did not understand her own actions herself. Despite her aching heart, despite her despair at Virabhadra's anger, she continued in her dalliance with Madhava. Was it that she needed Madhava and merely felt sorry for hurting Virabhadra? No, it was more than that. Her body longed for their union of that night to be repeated. She was happy if he was happy. She felt safe in his arms. There was something about him which inspired trust. What then of Madhava? Did she perhaps take pity on him, away from home, friendless, a poet languishing without a patron? All that, but more importantly, he fulfilled a need for beauty within her, with his poetry. His appreciation of her form and his importunate wooing struck some chord within her. She needed both. The only problem was that each demanded fidelity. That was, as things stood now, difficult for her to promise. She was a *devadasi*, her only *dharma* to serve God. Chastity in the sense of fidelity was not expected of her. That was her mother's chief concern, but she need not make it hers. *Ajji*'s was a more thought provoking suggestion as it was more immediate. Rama Raya was certainly an opponent to take note of. A protector would come in useful. But at the end of the day, resource was a better friend. After all, who would be the best protector? She would have to look to Salakaraju Thirumala. And even he had not been able to help Achyuta Raya, when he had been imprisoned last year.

The cart ground to a halt. They had reached Alur. A group of women had been waiting, and as they got down, they came forward with the plate of coloured water and the lamp to welcome them. The formalities over, they were escorted inside. The bossy looking, plump matron who had wielded the *arthi* now hurried to take charge of the introductions. She was Rangi, the chief priest's wife. Then the attenuated woman with the absently sweet smile was Lalitha, the *vaidyar*'s wife. The rest were wives and daughters of minor officials. Bhadri did not have a wife, so Rangi was chief in consequence here. They went into the main hall of the temple to pay their respects to the deity, who was decked out in sandalwood and from there they commenced to the hall where the discourse was to take place.

The discourse was over and after a good festive meal, where lemonade and lentil salad were some of the main items, they sat down to gossip over the *tamboolam*. Achale had been looking forward to this as a means of information about Thulasi and was racking her her brains for an opening.

"*Akka*, your discourse was brilliant," a young bride opened the proceedings. Rangi now spoke, "We had never heard Andal's first stanza of the *Thirumozhi* interpreted in such a way before, Andal is actually giving women a way to achieve salvation."

The woman called Lalitha chipped in. "And the steps, *akka*! You have simplified things for us: one, get an *acharya*, two, surrender to both the Supreme Mother and Father."

The bride spoke again, "Henceforth, I will always try to say *Jayamalakashmi* while I work."

"You should always say, *Namo Narayana* instead," Rangi admonished righteously.

"*Akka*, the Mother will open the heavenly portals much faster," the bride protested.

"Humph... Thulasi was used to surrender..." an old woman who was pounding the areca nut in a brass mortar said, "First to her husband, and then to Bhadrinatha... what did it fetch her?"

"Grace, *akka*," Lalitha rushed into speech, but the old woman was continuing as if no interruption had occurred and Achale was praying hard that she would be allowed by all these well-meaning but ill-advised women to finish what she had started.

"Little enough all the men in her life cared about her, except the little boy and what can one so small do against his own cousin, Narayana, who rushed to usurp all her husband's lands? Overnight, his wife went from eating gruel to serving rice pudding on a silver plate. Thulasi had wanted to fight, but Bhadri advised her against it. Who would listen to an outcaste? Then she surrendered to Bhadri's desire to turn Manju into a saint. Like any mother, she wanted a normal childhood for the boy. Who listened to her?" slow and bitter tears were scouring her withered cheeks and she paused to wipe them, which gave the women time to hustle her off and cover up the moment by offering around the betel plate.

"That little Manju is such an unassuming little boy. Saint he may be, but the pranks he gets up to! He tied the tails of Jegga's two cows; took the flowers off little Rakki's plait and garlanded the cows and then got them to face opposite directions. He gave them each a prod and fell down laughing when they tried to run off, pulling at each other, with surprised expressions on their poor dumb faces. And the questions he asks! Another Nachiketa, says my husband!" The young bride's face was alight.

"Just as Krishna, the little prankster grew up to teach Arjuna the eternal truths in the Gitopdesa, so also will Manju lead us in the future" prophesied Rangi, somewhat pompously as was her wont.

"Ah, take some sugar, *akka*. If Bhadrianna had been here, he would have given you a gold chain," slyly interjected one of the women.

"What you say is true. And if he gets the grant to the Chidambaram temple, he may even afford to give away ten."

Ningi was standing outside the *mantapa*. It was time to take leave, and Achale did so. "*Chikkamma*," said Ningi, as they walked out of the temple. "You had asked Vajrabahu to meet you. He is here." Achale hurried to meet the courtier. She met Bhima instead. Madhava was with him. "Devi, quick, we must leave on foot. The achare will show us the way. Rama Raya's men are lying in wait. Acharyulu heard of it and told Chenna, who has brought me the news. They mean to waylay us and take you prisoner. It is God's blessing that the dombra understood Acharyulu's songs correctly."

"Devi, this way, but first, remove your clothes. I have brought you some coarse clothes. Give me your jewels. I will keep them safe. I will wait for you outside."

The next half an hour was tense. Hugging the Brahmins' Quarter where the soldiers dare not penetrate, they made their way over the fields, towards Anegundi, led by Madhava. Chenna had told Bhima about a fair that was happening at Jogahalli at some distance from Achale's house, where his troupe was performing. It would be easy to lose themselves at the fair and thence gain their cart which would be waiting on the Nagalapur road. Even so, Achale was not relishing the prospect of staying with her mother, within her father's sights, but it could not be helped. Rama Raya dare not approach her there, so she was safe. Vajrabahu was waiting for them with his carriage and after introducing Madhava, they parted.

The fair was very crowded. Villagers for miles around had turned up to watch the various amusements in their finery. There were the ubiquitous buttermilk vendors and vendors of puffed gram, roasted peanuts and freshly cut mangoes. It was festive and despite the tension of their flight, Achale, Ningi and Bhima could not help but be beguiled by the holiday atmosphere. Vajrabahu looked relaxed, untouched by their apprehension. He stopped the cart at the entrance and they got down, joining a group standing around a ram-fight. The foreheads of the rams were shining with the lime juice and other concoctions smeared on them.

"Come and see, ram fight, *tagarina mota*!" the beater shouted, while a drummer standing near the rope strung between two poles, shouted, "watch the elephant climb and dance!" Chenna was there, smiling and as he caught Bhima's eye, he nodded to indicate that he would follow Vajra, if necessary.

They stopped to watch and marvel as Bhima the elephant climbed a pillar thirty feet high, beating time to the drums and cymbals all the while. It was some time before Ningi noticed that Vajrabahu was missing. She darted to the front of crowd and was relieved to see that the dombra had also disappeared. Bhima was standing a little at a distance, keeping watch for Rama Raya's men So far, they had evaded them.

A slight commotion at a puppetry booth a little farther away caught the attention of both Bhima and Ningi at the same time. A horseman had alighted and seemed to be searching. Moving back into the crowd, Ningi went up to Achale and murmured, "*Chikkamma*, don't look back. Just move slowly, as if you are looking for some other thing to watch. Rama Raya's man is searching the crowds." Achale moved unhurriedly as Ningi advised, to the edge of the crowd. Joining a group which seemed bent on enjoying themselves, they hid in the middle, with Bhima keeping watch. The crowd made its way from stall to stall. The horseman was back on his horse, and was scanning the crowd. Ningi dare not look up. Achale with her plain clothes may not be recognized. The horse's hooves moved nearer. Ningi forced herself to act normally. Their group was now standing before a vendor of snacks. Ningi engaged in bargaining with the woman. The hooves clattered away. Slowly, they moved with the group, until they could see the exit. Bhima had slipped into the fair crowd, dogging the horseman's footsteps and he came back to report that the horseman had slipped out of the fair. They had to wait. The horse man could be lying in wait. An hour went by before Bhima reported that the horseman had got back onto the road, to Hampi. They slipped out of the exit and gained their cart which was waiting patiently outside the fair. The cartman turned the ox's head towards Nagalapur and they were on their way but not before Ningi had decked the cart and the ox with flowers, while pulling off all costly ornaments which would give them away.

They had gone some way, encountering not a soul except innocent wayfarers bound homewards like them, when Ningi felt it was safe to talk. "I was sitting with the village women, *akka,* while you gave your discourse."

"You would have done better listening to the discourse."

"*Ayyo!* What has this dunce to do with discourses? I'd rather serve you well. I wanted to see if the village women knew anything about the dead woman. They had no complaints. She was industrious and worked her lands well. She paid them good wages and filled their bellies. They could only work there since Bhadri allowed it and influenced the panchayat to do likewise. You can imagine, *Chikkamma*, what they made of this strange attitude of the overlord. No one was in doubt of *that* relationship. But what even they could not explain is the extraordinary behaviour of Boriah, that goat herd. It seems that boy Manju, really is a saint. He seems to have bewitched Boriah, who used to bring him lambs, strange plants growing in the forest, small birds. Boriah would leave these once a week on their verandah and would hide behind a tree to see how Manju received his gift. Manju loves animals so these gifts always pleased him and Boriah would go away smiling while Thulasi watched from the doorway, saying nothing. It is really very peculiar but then, odd things keep happening to that boy. Yet he is so normal, playing pranks and games with other children."

"I don't know what to make of that boy!" Achale marveled.

"Saints have odd ways. It is not for us ordinary folk to decipher their behaviour. Look at Acharyulu! Can anyone do anything other than marvel at his astonishing variety of conversation?" This was Bhima's contribution.

The servant must have run inside as soon as the cart had appeared in the distance because Puttalakshmi had come running out.

"Achale, *putta*, is anything wrong? I heard some talk in the market and I was so worried...!"

"Amma, we'll go in and I'll tell you everything," said Achale soothingly. She put her arm around her mother and they went in.

Chapter XVIII

April 1996

When Maya returned to her chamber from the court, the clerk told her that Thomas had called. Maya didn't use the pager, though it was the most popular electronic device to hit the market,since cell phones were unreliable and unwieldy newbies. She could collect messages when she reached the office after all. Thomas returned the call in half an hour and soon, Maya was heading out of the office for an evening out with Thomas. She tried but failed to kid herself that this was mere investigation. This was pleasure, pure and simple.

Thomas was standing under the Triumph of Labour statue on the beach, looking pleased with the world in general and smiling at a child who was running on the grass. He waved as Maya found a space to park and came down the steps to her. Maya did not like wetting her feet and getting sand all over herself, so she sat and watched as Thomas surged into wave after wave. Suddenly, she was also running, forgetting wetness, sand, everything but the exhiliration of clinging to Thomas while the water crashed around them. Thoroughly wet, they sat on the sand to dry off. It was April, the weather was getting quite warm so drying off would be quick. A small boy was selling boiled and seasoned chickpeas and fried rice flour twists, which Thomas bought along with tea from another vendor who had a steel can with a spigot perched on his cycle.

"So, you said you wanted to discuss something. Is it about the dance?"

"Must there always be a reason for us to meet? How old are you Maya? Haven't you ever been on a date before? Or are you a stay at home type? "

"Hardly. I did my postgraduation in Social Science from JNU at Delhi, before I settled down to law. I'm turning thirty this year. And you?"

"I'm twenty-seven. And you didn't answer my question."

"I've had my share of casual relationships but never anything serious. Never met anyone, I guess." Well, it was not exactly cradle-snatching, so no one could accuse her of that!

Then she remembered the TV show she had seen. It seemed such a long time ago. "I don't see that actor in the classes," she commented casually.

"You think Raghu has time for us now?" Thomas sounded bitter.

"What was that about a show Surilee mentioned and Harsha doing a solo?"

"God, that was embarrassing! I had arranged a private show of dancers from my troupe for a dance director who was looking for some dancers. On the day of the show, we waited forever for Raghu, the actor, who was just a nobody then, to show. When the director came, Harsha did the solo which Raghu was supposed to have done. We later heard that someone had locked Raghu in the control room on top. Raghu claims he never saw who it was. He just received a message from a guy who looked like a mechanic to go up to the control room on the terrace as someone wanted to meet him there. He was locked in and no one heard him banging until the next morning. The dance director didn't choose any of our guys, but Raghu was seen later at a college function and became a star. Surilee was in a strange mood the night of the interview. I was actually terrified that she would reveal all this on TV! "

So that's all it was and here she was imagining some great secret crime. However, if there was someone going around locking up people... could it have been Harsha, to get the solo and impress the dance director? If so, the actor had had the last laugh. Still, if it had been Harsha, it showed that he could be quite ruthless.

There was a small silence while each thought their thoughts and then Maya came up with, "You know, I wanted to ask you—did you used to wait for Tulsi after class?"

Thomas let out a whooshing sound and took her firmly by the shoulders. "What can I say to convince you that Tulsi and I talked about the show, but that's it? We were both passionate about dance."

She looked down, a little shy, and muttered, "The students all say you were close."

"We discussed the dance, Maya. Besides, I don't think she was fully over her husband, yet."

"But they say that you were waiting for her near the lift on the day she..."

"Was I? Maybe I was. I remember I had missed her coming out. I thought she had left the class. I wondered if I could catch her at the lift. I wanted her to hear the music we had mixed."

Maya slumped a bit, in relief. The explanation had been so simple. No wonder he had forgotten.

His arm stayed around her shoulders as he said, "Forget it." He gave her a little shake.

"I've been reading Nammalwar, in translation. Have you read him?"

"No. A bit of Andal's stuff is about it."

"There is this verse from *Tiruvasiriam* where he says, 'he grabbed me, my body trembled, love pierced me.' Get the imagery?"

"Amazing isn't it?"

"What makes them come up with such images you know, after all the different words for love and everything?"

"I think a devotee imagines he or she is a bride because the union of the soul with the Lord is like marriage. It's a metaphor, meant to make the image real to devotees. It is not meant to be erotic."

"Ah. Strange how these different schools—Virashaiva, Advaita, Dwaita and Vishishtaadvaita—unite when it comes to expressing devotion and salvation. Merging, union, two halves becoming whole—same imagery, different God, different paths."

"You seem pretty well informed about all this stuff."

He replied with a shrug, "I did Political Science, Philosophy and Social Science in my degree course and my thesis now is on secular poetry and dance."

Maya was impressed. This was a thinking person and sexy too—intriguing!

"So how about if we have Nammalwar after *pati* and *patni* in the dance? We underline this by explaining the marriage hymn: be my partner in life and rituals, etc. Don't you think we should stop there?"

"Sounds good," agreed Maya.

"So, what say we go to my pad and we have a pizza after all this brilliant work?"

"I'd say you have yourself a deal."

As it happened, they ended up sharing more than a pizza.

The next day, when she walked into the Saturday meeting a little late, she thought she saw her partners hiding smiles. As soon as the clerks and others were packed off, her partners pounced on her. "Maya," began Patricia, "nice night?"

"What? It was OK."

"How does she do it?" asked Meenakshi.

"Do what?" This was from a suspicious Maya.

"Oh, I've almost forgotten. The kids insist on sleeping with us, so it's just grabbing a minute or two, in the bathroom or in the afternoons on Saturdays," Pat offered.

"I meant look so fresh after a sleepless night and a hurried bath in the morning after a quick getaway." Meenakshi made her eyes big and innocent and Patricia giggled, "Just my own problem surfacing from my consciousness, I think."

"But in this case quite apt. How do you do it?" Meenakshi wanted to know, again.

"Will you two stop? I'll come clean. I know it must be some strange telepathy or maybe you two have taken to snooping on me in your dreams. That's voyeurism and prurient!" Maya snapped.

"Dirty mind yourself. Here we are saying you're looking good. Very toothsome," Meenakshi leered.

"Alright. I spent the night with Thomas."

"Where's my hundred?" Patricia opened her palm and Meenakshi coughed up.

"You horrible lot!" Maya shook her head.

"Was it good?" asked Patricia.

"You mind your own business."

Meenakshi sighed. "Poor girl. She'll learn. If it's like this now, how will it be later on? Maybe she'll get lucky and just be able to chalk this up to experience."

"Shut up!" Maya picked up the heavy glass paper weight and tried to chuck it at Meenakshi but Patricia held her hand, though she was giggling so much, it was difficult for her to maintain her grip.

"So how did it happen?"

"Nothing, we went to the beach, to just discuss the dance script, and then we a pizza and then..." her voice trailed off.

"Hear that Pat, one thing led to another. Oh Maya, you'll just kill us. You are such a kid. Just listen to you, so dewy-eyed, defensive. Just tell us to go to hell."

"Go to hell."

They finally settled down to the meeting, but no one could talk about work and there wasn't that much to discuss, since there was barely a month for the vacation. They settled that they would be going to Wynaad in Kerala for their usual girls' only trip. Pat could get away only for a week but Meena and Maya wanted to stay longer, so they rang up their travel agent and fixed it up.

Afterwards, Meena asked, "Maya! You never said a thing about Tulsi's memorial dance. What was it about?" Maya told them.

"Toni gave me the script. Tulsi's written annotations about choreography with the story in the margins. But Dr. Goplakrishnan, the history professor I had written to earlier, sent me some pages. It's her writing. She had met him, it's in her diary, but he doesn't seem to remember where he got them from. It's like a story. She's actually gone a little further. It's like she was there. So vivid. I wonder... Toni told me once she used to dream about the future. I think I already told you that Alamelu Maami said Tulsi had dreams after reading the book. Maybe she dreamt this, even."

"So what's happening now? You told us Achale had talked to Manju and found out about Thulasi's last moments," Pat put in.

"Yes and its getting more interesting. Achale's fallen in love and slept with her lover, a potter."

"Wow! Like dream, like reality, eh? OK, OK, I won't go there," Pat laughed as Maya gave her a withering look.

"Her Granny got upset because a virgin had a higher chance of getting an aristocrat—even marrying one. They went off to celebrate Holi. Then she got seduced by the poet. She's deciding between the two now. There's a plot on. Vajrabahu, the courtier her grandmother wants her to marry, wants to stage a coup," Maya summed up the last few chapters she had read.

She remembered something she had been meaning to discuss with them. "That potter of Achale's, he spoke of possible war between his district and the King—faction fights, they aligned with Rama Raya's faction, maybe. Krishnadeva was fighting all the time. If not with the Bahminis, it was with break-away dissidents. So was Achyuta'. It seems so strange during these settled times."

"Maya, what settled times? Look at Kashmir; have we ever had peace there? Assam's problems could not be solved for years. The North East is always a problem. Then there's Tibet and that border. We have had ongoing self determination struggles in Uttarkhand and Jharkand. It goes with the territory." Pat was dismissive.

"And now of course, there is no concept of justice and everything is a question of how to play it for the media and electoral gain." Meena sounded disgusted.

There was a short silence. Then Meena, looking a little downcast, said, "I didn't want to speak of it earlier, because it would spoil all the fun but..." she hesitated, then started again, "I'm sorry but access puts Thomas in the loop and if Tulsi didn't tell him about Harsha and her affair, and he had found out or even if she had told him and he was jealous, then he has motive as well." She looked really troubled.

"Maybe you could cool it for a while with Thomas," Pat suggested, gently patting Maya on the shoulder.

Maya shook off Pat's hand. She had convinced herself to trust Thomas. It was terrible of Meena to make her doubt him now, just as she was starting to like him more and more.

Later, as she lay in bed, Maya thought back on Tulsi's script. Achale's life was getting more complicated all the time. She had fallen in love twice. She had to appease one of them and decide what to do: continue with two strings or detach one; if so, which? What persecution! Poor Achale! And where could an innocent woman go, then? Come to that, could a woman trust the police even now? Things hadn't changed all that much really, for women—not in India, anyway. In any case, Achale's love life was better than Maya's. She could not contact Thomas until the murder mystery was solved, which it looked nowhere near. But why, oh why, had Meena now put this embargo on Thomas? He seemed so intellectual and sensitive. He and Maya were a good fit! She had allowed all her instincts to take over and had stilled all her earlier doubts. All her doubts had come crowding back. Couldn't Meena have let it be? Her love life was secure wasn't it? Why did she have to mess Maya's up? This was much worse than the mystery, thought Maya bitterly.

How would she find out what happened next? Tulsi's case had reached a stalemate. What could she do? She sighed and turned over, closing her eyes.

Chapter XIX

May 1996

Maya was on the phone with Mridula. She needed to get more information on Achale and Manju. Tulsi's steps needed to be retraced so she could see what Tulsi had seen, if anything. She needed to find out where she got the book from. Who better to comb the archives than an M.A. student who could pretend to do research? She could surely wangle a letter from some professor. She would tell Mridula that she wanted to solve the murder of Manju's mother.

Mridula sounded eager. "Maya, this is a godsend. I am so tired of this domestic routine and the kids and Shreyas are getting on my nerves. Shreyas with his constant clock-watching, like I have to punch in my hours and the kids with their picky eating and gourmet demands. I need a holiday!"

"OK just go on holiday to the archives and I'll come on Sunday and give them all a piece of my mind and tell them you are the best cook ever, or better still, I'll treat them to my cooking, after which they'll value yours as they ought to."

Mridula laughed and rang off, promising to Xerox or copy out all relevant documents, whatever was possible. She could easily manage the letter as it happened that one of her old classmates actually worked at the archives. It was all shaping up very nicely.

Maya had a surprise call that night. Anees rang to tell her that she had located some photographs Tulsi had given her. Tulsi had been hoping that Anees, who was in charge of costumes, could copy the costumes for the lotus dance. They were temple sculptures and Tulsi had actually found time on the weekends when she was free, to visit Hampi and Lepakshi. Anees had shoved the pictures in a desk drawer and forgotten about them. She had been rummaging there for something else, just a little earlier, when she had come across the photos. She promised to post them the very next day. Maya couldn't help feeling a thrill. Somehow, the finding of the pictures seemed significant.

Maya's mother was a lecturer in a city college. She was also an expert cook. Maya watched as she made *dosas*. She did not have just *dosas* and *idlis* up her quick fix sleeve. She could rustle up, with no apparent effort, quick snacks which even her junk food-crazy and ad-zapped grandkids would eat with joy.

"Soon, we'll be unable to go anywhere. I don't know how you'll manage. Its time for elections and they'll be blocking roads with their meetings, extorting money and we'll have to pay both sides while hoping someone new and uncorrupt would dare to stand," her mother said.

"They are saying some superstar is going to announce his support for the opposition—that's the latest rumour," Maya added her bit.

"Oh, but let's talk of something else, politics is always a fruitless discussion." Her mother abandoned the topic for another,"So you are going dancing, now?"

"Yes Ma, and if I meet someone, you'll be the first to know. Mridula has been busy, I can see."

"Maya, *kanna*, you know Seethamaami next door? Their priest, the *jeeyar*, wants to see you. He has some problem. I told her you would help." Maya made a face. This was unusual. Usually they went to the more orthodox lawyers.

The noise at the club was deafening. Barely were they in the door when Toni whirled onto the floor with a man in skin-tight jeans and a fitting white kurta. Was that an earring gleaming on his eyebrow? Maya caught herself; she sounded like her mother! But the truth was, she was conventional underneath.

Maya looked around. She knew no one and Toni was busy dancing. The air was heavy with smoke as well, never a good thing with her and it smelt like it wasn't just tobacco. She squinted and made her way towards a table where there seemed to be drinks. Dutch courage wouldn't go amiss. She was halfway there, squeezing past gyrating bodies, when she felt herself grabbed and a male voice shouted in her ear. "Maya! Who have you come with?" Squinting upwards, she realized it was Harsha from her dance class and felt immediate relief. Here was rescue—someone she knew who might even ask her to dance. "I came with Toni," she shouted back. Harsha held her arm and led her off to a little nook where the music wasn't as deafening.

"I haven't seen you in this crowd before."

"Toni insisted. Have you been coming here long?"

"These are the guys I hang out with. Tulsi used to come here sometimes. Thomas told me you were her lawyer."

"So you knew her well?"

"She was a looker and loved to dance. She really knew how to live. She was a riot. I miss her."

"Were you surprised by her suicide?"

"I wasn't expecting it. She was such a happy person."

"I can't believe it myself."

They were still talking rather loudly, but the conversation had taken a somber turn. They were quiet for a moment, and then Harsha steered her to the floor where he held her close, moving to to a fast number.

"I heard that you were seeing Tulsi," said Maya, leaning close to his ear.

"Tulsi told you?" His grip on her hand tightened. "I saw her home a few times, gave her a lift, you know. She was worried about the kid. What case were you filing for her?"

"Didn't you know? She was divorcing her husband."

"Yeah, yeah, she mentioned that he and she were separated. I didn't know it had gone so far." He seemed about to say something else but checked himself.

"So, does our dancing together mean we are an item?" Maya joked.

"I didn't think we were dancing." He wiggled his hips and did some salsa steps. "Does that make you feel better?"

Maya laughed, "I think we should have some drinks."

"I can get you more than that, if you want."

"Drinks will do just fine, thank you."

He looked down at her seriously, one hand on her arm. Then he smiled and looked as though he was going to blush.

"OK. Before I go, I want you to know that I really like you Maya. I could go for you in a big way. Don't say anything now. Just think about it."

Toni joined them with Anees. Harsha smiled, raising his drink, to both. "I would have come up earlier but you seemed preoccupied," said Toni, grinning. Maya rushed to speak, to stall more wisecracks from Toni. "What do you expect, when you rush off, abandoning me? This is Harsha from my dance class. He was also a friend of Tulsi's." Harsha smiled, but seemed distracted. He wandered off to get more drinks.

Anees led the way out to the porch. She sat on the parapet which circled it, while Toni grabbed a stool and Maya sat on a chair, resting her feet on the parapet.

"You look like a kid, not Tulsi's hotshot lawyer. Toni told me you're not convinced it was suicide. I can't imagine why anyone would want to murder her."

"It may be jealousy—Tulsi was having a scene with Thomas and Harsha."

"So that throws the field wide open, except that if she was murdered at the class, it could not be the husband. I've seen Harsha here with Tulsi before. They used to dance together, but there were no vibes there. He never held her like he was holding you."

This was a new one. "Did she tell you anything about her research?"

"Not a thing. Toni here knows more than I do."

"Who is this guy, Harsha? I wonder what he *really* does for a living. He may be an instructor at the school but he looks well-heeled. From what I've heard, he lives the high life—expensive clothes, travel, dope, parties, the works!"

"I wonder what else he does?" said Toni.

"Who knows? And if she did, Tulsi never said a thing to me," said Anees, shrugging.

What connection did this have with Tulsi? wondered Maya. Of course, he might have been better boyfriend material than poor Thomas. Did this make Thomas jealous? Had he been lying about him and Tulsi?

Toni suddenly got up and pulled Maya back inside. "Come on, let's dance! Show me what they teach you in that class!"

The phone was ringing as she let herself into her flat again. It was Srinivasa Shastry. He had a piece of information for her—Shibani had told him that Tulsi had been talking to someone on the phone and had mentioned Ponmudi. Maya picked up the cat, Bangaru and twirled around her living room. She was getting somewhere, but she still did not know why Ponmudi was important in the here and now and to whom?

CHAPTER XX

JUNE 1996

Maya was ready to call it a day, but met Kamala as she entered her chambers. She was told that she had to go in to the office as they had rung up with the news that an old priest wanted to see her and had been waiting since lunchtime. This one she had to meet.

She noticed him as soon as she entered the office and hurried in. She rang the bell and told the clerk to send him in. She knew that this was no ordinary priest, or *jeeyar*. He was the head of a Sri Vaishnava *math*. But what was more intriguing was that he had been a bench clerk with whom she had had many friendly run-ins as a rookie. Then he had been transferred and though she had seen him around the campus, they had exchanged no more than smiles. He had come in his usual uniform of saffron clothes, with a long staff and Maya could not suppress her embarrassment. He had come with some others, dressed in what she thought of as 'normal wear.'

Maya folded her hands in greeting and then settled him in a chair with a wooden seat to spare his sensibilities with regard to defilement. The *jeeyar* smiled in acknowledgement and immediately launched into his problem.

It seemed that the *matha* was under a trust but the funds were administered by the Hindu Religious and Charitable Endowments Board. In theory this should have worked perfectly—the government body to see that the administration was kept up without corruption by the trustees for the benefit of everyone, even the Scheduled Castes and the Trust and the *jeeyar* to take care of the religious duties and ceremonies. But as in all the systems in India, corruption saw the funds trickling away into the pockets of officials and the *jeeyar* was left high and dry, without funds to even cement the roof against leakages. Maya promised to go through the papers and see what she could do.

Before he left, she asked, "Swami, do you not find this strange, after being in the judicial service?"

"Child, I always knew that one day I might have to assume these duties. A *jeeyar* finishes his karma towards his family and then takes up the mantle of a *mathathipati*."

Maya had a brainwave. "Swami ," she blurted out, "I wonder if you know where the *matha* of another *jeeyar* is located. The first *matha* head was a widow's son who had his initiation by a miracle, after submersion in a temple tank at the Madhavaswamy temple at Alur in Karnataka."

"Everyone knows this. You are talking of the Ponmudi *matha*. A very old *matha*, established by the great Kandadhai Ramanuja Ayyangar of Tirupati, at Anegundi in Karnataka." It was as easy as that. There you go, Maya thought. The connection she had been looking for.

Maya had her second miracle that day, when Anees' photos arrived. She wanted to shout and share the photos with someone, so she sought out Pat and Meena, who saw the look on her face and freed themselves from what looked like grueling client interviews and followed her into the conference room. "Look! Achale!" she said and thrust the photos at them. The Padmini *jati stri* stood there, her face a perfect oval with its rounded chin, lotus shaped eyes, small sharp nose and tiny mouth, her waist as slender as a wrist, and over everyhting floated the massed clouds of her abundant hair.

Maya thought, Is she for real? I wish I could have spoken to her.

"So, do you think this is her?" Meena asked.

"Probably, though I'm sure she was much better in the flesh."

"Didn't you say she was deciding between two men? I'm surprised there were only two."

Just as Maya had got to the door to leave for her dance class, the phone rang, so she went back in to answer it. It was Mridula.

"I know you're leaving for your bumps and grinds with sexy men, much good though its doing, but you have to hear this. Manju's *matha* has a branch at.... Ponmudi." Maya chorused the name with her. "Hey, how do you know?" Maya told her about the *jeeyar's* visit.

"Oh, but listen, you won't believe this. I saw Achale's name mentioned." Mridula sounded excited.

"Did they say what happened to her? Rama Raya's men are after her. She is in hiding. Poor thing, she just wants to keep dancing and end up giving discourses."

"A career woman through and through!"

Maya laughed. Mridula continued, "Listen, I decided to try the Chidambaran temple inscriptions and found quite a lot of stuff, though I had to really read up secondary sources in the Connemara library reference room later. I went to the University library, even.

It took a lot of time, but I found it, a reference to Venugopalachari and Manjunatha."

"Great! Was he the grantee? Then Bhadri would have gotten rich!" Maya interrupted.

"Achyuta did give a grant in 1539," Mridula went on, "but Bhadri's name is not mentioned though Manju is mentioned. I found out that no one acted on the grant until after Hampi was razed in the battle of Talikota, when Krishnappa Nayak... wait..." she paused, presumably to check her notes, "in 1599, carried out renovations and the re-installation of the missing idol."

"So Bhadri might have swallowed the income from the grant!" Maya exclaimed.

"Well, like I said, he is not named. I looked up the gazetteer and found a reference to Manjunatha establishing a *matha* and giving a grant to Chidambaram. It went on and on about the incident in the temple tank and how he became famous, etc."

"I wondered what he turned out to be," mused Maya.

"He was apparently really good at his studies, and knew the answers to all kinds of tough questions people put to him," she concluded.

"You said you found a reference to Achale?"

"Yeah, you know my friend Sitalakshmi, who works at the archives? She told me to check up a private collection, donated to them. Some Telugu film actor, who collects old Telugu manuscripts. I can tell you, I was really happy I learned all the South Indian languages in case I had to do research. Of course, that was before I met Shreyas..." trailed off Mridula.

"Get to the point, I'm getting late!" Maya growled.

"I found an old book on temple dancers. It mentioned Achale in connection with the Padmini *jati stri* and said she was the model for this Lepakshi sculpture and that she had set some dances to poetry, new pieces, which are lost now, but were very wonderful. They mentioned that one Madhava Shastry had composed them and he later became a famous poet."

"Nothing about what happened to Achale?"

"No."

"Hmmm. How's Shreyas?" Maya could not resist asking, changing the topic, even though it was going to make her late.

Mridula giggled. "Oh, Shreyas is grumpy, but I just ignore him. Who has time with all the juggling? Hey, Sitalakshmi told me that this college had started part time M. Phil courses. I'm going to join up."

"Good for you!" So some good had come out of it all. "Thanks, Mridula." She put the phone down and headed out the door.

She wondered what Achale would do. Puttalakshmi's life was dead boring, so Achale's dream life was much better, but life with the potter would be exciting. She wished she could meet someone like him. He sounded exciting. Thomas sounded a little like him and his lifestyle was cool. She liked self-assured men. Then she grinned inwardly as she remembered that Shreyas had been self-assured, God-like, before marriage. Perhaps men and marriage were not suited!

When she reached the dance class, they were almost finished with the warm up and Surilee, who was the instructor, glared at her, while Thomas frowned from the back of the class. Head down, highly embarrassed, Maya slunk in.

They were going to start with the show practice and Maya was curious to see how Thomas had choreographed the dance.

They had finished the *pati* and *patni* creation myth, which actually came in the middle of the program. Thomas explained that they would now be interpreting Nammalwar's hymn about God filling him and taking him over.

Thomas had got a friend of Surilee's to set it to music and a band Thomas knew had performed the number.

The composer had set the lyrics to a kind of fusion of Carnatic instrumental set in a fast paced *raga*. The dancers wove in and out of turns and half-turns, finally moving as one. Maya watched Thomas dance with Surilee and marveled that she felt no pang.

The choreography was complicated and the non-professional dancers looked terrified as they took their places. Maya looked around for Sunny, but found he was already taken by Uma. She looked around for Harsha. Might as well have a familiar person to share the tough dance with, then she could forget about the partner and concentrate on the steps, she thought. But Paru beat her to it.To her surprise, Harsha turned Paru down, telling her to find someone else and took Maya's hand. Paru threw them angry glances but Maya was left wondering whether to be flattered or sorry. Was it her imagination or was Harsha getting extra physical? But as she danced, her mind kept slipping to Achale and she only half noticed when Harsha held her close enough to feel his chest, or pressed her hand while holding it. If he was getting some wrong signals, too bad.

Harsha was doing a good imitation of possessiveness, now that the dance required them to change partners for a few turns then swing back. He was glaring at poor Sunny, who obliviously grinned at her as they muffed a step and found their place again. When she went back, he held her even closer, making it difficult for her to move. She was glad when the dance finally ended.

As they disengaged, Harsha caught her arm. "Maya, have you thought about it?" Maya was caught off guard. What was he talking about? Harsha gave a gusty sigh. "OK. You don't have to say anything. I know when I am beaten." He walked off.

Thomas hurried up, as she was leaving. "Maya, I called a few times but.... didn't your office tell you? How are you?"

She forced herself to smile, feeling like a heel. "I'm OK but we've been very busy—a big new case, very hush-hush, so I've been working hard."

He shot her a look, "Hard work or is Harsha working on you?"

"Excuse me?" Maya was taken aback

"Had to ask.That was quite a tight grip he had on you." He gave her a long look.

"Didn't you see me wriggle?"

"So, are you free tonight?"

"No, I'm sorry, Thomas. I have to go to my mother's for dinner." She wished she was better at lying.

Perhaps he thought she was cooling off. He was stone-faced. "Fine. See you," he said curtly. He walked off and Maya followed, feeling awful.

Maya looked around, but Harsha had disappeared and she found she was glad. She needed to grill him about Tulsi, but she half-feared he would turn up and want to take her out and she would have to give some excuse.

Maya was waiting in court for her case to come up. Idly, she doodled on her pad and was unsurprised to find that she had written Ponmudi in Romanic script and had begun to decorate it with borders and curlicues. She was bored. She wished she had more time to give to the mystery but on second thought, time would not be a gift for what would she seek without a clue? However, the feeling that both mysteries were somehow connected was getting stronger.There was the strange repeated coincidence of the place Ponmudi in the past few days. And the existence of the *matha* somehow strengthened the connection. It was frustrating not to be able to find out more about Achale's story.

The lawyers were sitting around a table, right under the judge's nose, in various moods—forced repose, complete relaxation or controlled impatience. The lawyer next to Maya had been drumming his fingers on the table in a very irritating manner and she had been searching for a polite way to tell him to stop it, when he noticed her doodle and said, "Why Ponmudi? Are you thinking of buying land there? Most of the prime property is owned by a *matha*. Two large factories are coming up. The land values are already triple what they were a year ago. But no fear, the *matha* had leased out the land and is fighting cases to evict the tenants. I heard that one big chunk is now ready to be vacant and sold, which means the suit will be decreed soon and the tenant bought off. Some big real estate company is behind it, I'm sure. They are ready to lick the pot clean." Fighting to keep the excitement out of her voice at this jackpot of information, Maya just said, "Oh, is that so? There's no way can I afford land there."

After her case had been dealt with, Maya almost ran to the chamber. She called Kamala, the only person she could trust to do exactly as she said. "Kamala, you have to go to the Ponmudi sub-court and find out from the records section who the buyer is for the *matha*'s lands and what is the plaint in some of the suits. Get copies if you can. Do we know anyone in the section?"

"Yes madam, I know a clerk there. Patricia madam has many cases in Ponmudi. She was protesting against the slum eviction."

Thank God for Pat's contacts. "OK go then. I'll be waiting for you."

"Madam, I'll go straight home from there. It may be very late and there is a direct bus to my house. I'll see you in the morning." Maya sighed. So be it.

As Maya dipped her Irani biscuit in her masala chai, she ruminated on what she had found out till now. Tulsi had mentioned Ponmudi on the phone, just before her death. Thomas had locked up, but the motive was still unclear unless he was jealous of Tulsi and Harsha's closeness. Harsha had seemed to be on friendly terms with Tulsi but according to Toni he had not chased her the way he was chasing Maya. There seemed to be so many different angles and twists to this tale. She would have to make sense of them all, somehow.

There was no doubt that he could be ruthless to gain his own ends. Witness his role in Thomas's embarrassing incident, which had inadvertently been revealed in the TV interview! If Thomas had done an Othello, shouldn't he have been devastated? True, hardly had Tulsi's ashes cooled when he had started coming on to Maya but callousness may not amount to murderous intent. Anyway, he had said that Tulsi and he were not an item. As Kamala had suggested, the murderer could have slipped out while Thomas waited for Tulsi at the lift as was his wont.

So if one was looking for a strong motive, one would look at the money angle. But Tulsi did not have that kind of cash. She sighed. It all came down to the mysterious Ponmudi and she had to possess her soul in patience until Kamala came back with the information.

At lunch, Selvi came in with a message for Mridula. Dr. Gopalakrishnan had called. Could she see him that afternoon? Maya wondered what the old man had to tell her, but told Selvi to confirm the appointment for four o'clock.

The University had a huge campus of several acres set on the edge of a small wildlife park. Monkeys ran onto the road, screeching at cars. Deer lazily pawed at the grass. Maya smiled in delight.

It took her some time to find the History Department, which was tucked away at the back. Dr. Gopalakrishnan had requested a meeting in his office on the first floor of the Research Institute.

A young man was seated at a desk, dressed in a polo-necked T-shirt and jeans. Perhaps he was a doctoral research student. "I have an appointment with Dr. Gopalakrishnan," said Maya.

"Hello. I'm Dr. Gopalakrishnan. You're Mridula?"

Maya hesitated. She had to tell him the truth. There was no other way.

"Good afternoon. I'm Maya Vikraman. Mridula is my sister. I felt that you might not help me if you knew I was a lawyer. I am investigating the death of my client, Tulsi. She fell from an open window. Her family feel that foul play may be involved. I found this old book among her papers." She took it out and showed it to him. She had taken the precaution of going home for it. "It's incomplete. The last few pages are missing. I found your name among her papers as well. I would be very glad if you would help. Please forgive the deception." She waited with considerable trepidation for his response.

His eyes narrowed when she had mentioned murder. Now he studied her for a while, before saying, "I usually don't like it when

I'm not given an accurate picture of things. But I have to admit, I'm intrigued. You're forgiven." He smiled and said, "Let's have some coffee. Or would you prefer tea?"

"Coffee will be fine, thank you." Not everyone made tea like the Irani café.

While they were waiting for the coffee, he examined the book. He looked up. "I recollect now, someone came to see me. A woman. She said she was a dancer, doing research on *devadasis*. I showed her my private library.This book was one of them. I didn't recall its provenance when you wrote to me. Its been years since I took a look at it." He went over to the cupboard. Maya's heart was thumping hard. Would he be able to find the rest? He ran his hand down to about the third shelf, and then began searching through the titles. Halfway through his hand stopped and then came way with something.

"Ah, I thought so. Here's the rest." The sheaf of papers fitted in neatly. "Do you want to read it? I'll make a note." He did so. Perhaps he had decided, better safe than sorry. After all, Tulsi had taken it without his permission and he hadn't even known, till now!

"I have not found any more about Achale than the information I have already given you. I have been very busy since my return."

"Professor, there is just one small thing. Could you tell me if there was a plot to overthrow Achyuta by the Sangamas and one Vajrabahu? Another thing, did Achyuta have a son by his Queen Amalotpava Devi?"

"Amalotpava Devi was not a chief wife. She put out a story she was pregnant but it was discovered to be a false alarm. The Sangamas did not lead any coup of which I am aware."

"Professor, this Achalbedasa, could it be one Madhava Shastry who became a court poet?"

The Professor said he would look up the information for her. and they left it at that. She thanked him, promising to tell him more when she knew and drove back home.

It was late at night, when Maya settled down to read the next installment of Achale's tale.

CHAPTER XXI

JUNE-AUGUST, 1536
MONSOON

At her mother's house, Achale's days had slipped into a routine. Waking up at three in the morning with her mother, after a hasty flick of their teeth with a neem twig, they would trudge along with other women to the temple tank for a bath. This was the worst thing about this house—one had to urinate on the heap of ashes in the outer courtyard, or use the neighbouring common for more elaborate ablutions, hoping there was no one about. After all that came the business of cooking, while Ningi added to the household's help after all there were only two slaves, a male and female to manage the household.

Puttalakshmi was chief cook however, and now Achale sat in the kitchen with her mother, frying *dosas* on the griddle, while her mother stirred the lentil soup which accompanied it and the maid ground the coconut and green chilllies for the chutney which was to be served with both. The sun had risen and they both felt the urgency of the situation as Achale's father would be with them in a few minutes, his bath done, the morning *puja* and meditation finished with. Any minute, they would hear the bell which signaled that the camphor flame was lit and the *puja* was ended. She quickly checked whether there were at least five *dosas*, while her mother lifted the *idli* moulds from the copper steamer. "*Ayyo* Ranga, is the chutney done? I am putting the mustard for seasoning in the oil," Puttalakshmi shouted, as the bell began to sound and unusually, Achale's father called for his daughter. "Coming, *Appaji*," Achale hastily handed the ladle over to the maid and ran. It turned out that he wanted her to sing, so she did, choosing a fairly long song, so her mother would get some time to finish cooking breakfast.

Later, sitting on the swing after they had eaten and the morning's cooking was done, Achale reflected: suppose she was married to Madhava, she would live her life like her mother. The poet may well marry another, more powerful Brahmin girl and set her up as chief wife. Madhava, being a Brahmin, was supposed to practice restraint and might restrict himself to two wives, but for Achale even the thought of loss of precedence was galling. Probably in course of time, after her body had thickened in child birth, he would not even visit her bed and woe betide her if she had only daughters, he may even set her aside.

The potter was more likely to be faithful. He seemed steady and respect for her emanated from him, while the poet was cocky and claimed intellectual superiority. Life with the potter would not be boring. They would always be moving and they had an equal love of beauty. But she would have to give up the comforts she had become accustomed to; she did not know if she was adroit enough. She knew though, that she did not want to lead a life tied in matrimony. It was too limiting. She would prefer to keep her present status and move gracefully to that of wise woman giving discourses. Now Rama Raya had interfered with that plan. Maybe she could still win if they all bent their efforts to finding the murderer. Then *Ajji*'s dire predictions notwithstanding, she could continue with her present lifestyle, as long as she kept the favour of the King. Later she could always run a dance school with her brother and give discourses. One thing was certain: she had to somehow placate Virabhadra. Her nights, as long as she remained in her father's house were bound to be lonely, but she had to make provision for the future and Virabhadra had to be part of it. To give him up entirely would hurt too much.

Ningi had gone to the market to buy vegetables for Achale's mother. They were needed for the evening meal and Ningi had jumped in with an offer of help. Truth was, she could not bear the enforced vegetarianism of this household and had thought that while she was there, she would find a lady selling *ragi* balls with fish curry, or better still, a Turk may be selling those divine fried pastries filled with meat. Her mouth watered at the thought. Achale's father earned well, but it was still a strain to feed additional guests and there were three of them—Bhima, Achale and herself, come for an indefinite stay. If she was lucky, she might find a mess of greens on the wayside to bulk up the next morning meal. This was not Achale's household, running on two plump purses. It would not look right for Achale to offer to supplement the household funds, either. She thanked her good fortune that she was merely a slave, and need not have such worries.

She had reached the vegetable market and had a fine time bargaining with the vendors. She bought some plump brinjals. Achale's mother did them well, fried in oil with only some chilli powder. This was the rainly, *Mithuna* month, and the skies were swelling and rumbling. Achale's mother was careful not to use too many lentils or root vegetables or any heavy substances like coconut or milk. The food was pungent, astringent, and light.

The shopping done, Ningi was free to search out a vendor of snacks. By dint of some wandering, she found one, her pots lined up before her on their rings of twine. A few copper *arakasus* changed hands, while Ningi took her time choosing. Suddenly, she felt a hand on her shoulder. "Ningi! Fancy finding you here! Well met!" Oh, *Shaniswara*! Surely you must have worked overtime to hand me over to the biggest gossip in the kingdom, thought Ningi. Aloud, she said, "Malavva, well met! I was sent on an errand to her mother by my mistress. And you?"

"Oh, my head needs some clearing! I met that Bairava, that wastrel who leeches on unsuspecting village bumpkins who come to the city and strips them of all but their clothes and leaves them high and dry at the end of it. Might even strip them of that if it was worth his while! We got talking and the rascal convinced me to buy him some arrack. One thing led to another and the dawn found me in the fields, with a sore head and a sorer nether region, curses on him! Parted with more than I bargained for and got nothing in return."

"Sit down, *akka*. Let me buy you some hot bean stew and these mutton puffs."

"Mutton indeed! Cat meat, more likely!" Malavva muttered while the vendor gave her some dirty looks, but she sat down and they were soon munching and sipping away with gusto.

They moved a little further away from the vendor and had a good gossip. "What of you and the Virasaiva? Any joy?"

Ningi sighed, "Can a jackal do anything else but bay at the moon? He desires my mistress and I am as dust before her."

Malavva patted her hand, sympathetically. "Fortifying yourself against the cattle-feed tonight, are you?"

Ningi smiled sheepishly as she nodded, "So, we heard something about bundles turning into babies—it was a performance of daylight actors."

"Ah, those empty vessels will say anything to make the most noise. But do you know, that woman whose body you found, her relative, the one who got all her husband's lands, he visits Queen Amalotpava Devi frequently. I've seen him myself stealing away late at night from her private apartments, with a shawl over his head and no turban, as if he was a common labourer. But you must be the one to tell me, *kalli*! Your belly must be full of news, take care it doesn't burst like Ganesha's. It seems your mistress has broken her famous abstinence and is taking lover after lover! What happened? Has the treasury run dry? I thought she was spending too much, when washing all those costly hangings and saris— unheard of! And what jewels, to rival the sun and moon! But they say her star is falling and Rama Raya has his eye on her and you know he has no love for *devadasi*s, even though our King and his brother thought they were queens outside the palace."

Ningi cast about for a safe tidbit to give her. Malavva's eyes were gleaming like a crow's and her head was eagerly cocked to one side. In the end, she decided it would be safer to talk about Achale's romantic life rather than her political predicament. The second might lead to her discovery. Safer to throw the other tidbit to satisfy Malavva's slavering. "*Akka*, don't tell anyone this. I know my mistress's reputation is safe with you." Like all gossips, Malavva sincerely believed she was the soul of discretion.

"Tell, tell! Nothing will pass these lips, you know it."

"My mistress is in love with a penniless poet! Her *Ajji* is very angry but she can do nothing. The other is just rumour."

"A penniless poet when she could have the King! *Ayyo*! But such is the foolishness of women and the craftiness of men that they can steal your heart and more, giving nothing in return. Poor *Ajji*, what plans she must have had and now they're all just dreams! Just like Queen Amalotpava Devi! She dreams of a son who would be the King's heir. He has only one son, an infant, he needs more heirs. But so it always is with these great men! How they must envy the beggar on the road who can produce eleven sons by just looking at his wife! The King with 500 women has only a single heir! Maybe he is tired from all those battles! If he has an infant, then the Queen becomes Regent. They gave me ten *varahas* to put it about that she is pregnant. Who more likely than the washerwoman, washing the monthly soiled clothes, to attest to the truth of a pregnancy? I can smell burning sometimes, when I go to the inner chambers. Soiled clothes must not be seen for nine months! Ah, such is life. Queens may lie, but if a poor woman were to do it, then it is: impale her as an example! But sometimes, the string that ties the flowers can also reach heaven, so it is the humble washerwoman who is needed now." Ningi could hardly wait to tell Achale and Bhima. Hastily, she said something about having to go and escaped.

Achale was sitting on the swing in the inner courtyard and thinking of her house. By this time, the lamps would have been lit, whereas here, her mother and the slave were still trimming wicks and filling the lamps. By this time in her house, she would have been dressing, the evening's entertainment planned, as it was Wednesday. Yet here she was, in hiding, not able to hold her dances for fear of her father and of discovery. Of course, unable to tell the

Virupaksheshwara head priest the truth, she had claimed severe illness. The priest might have believed the tale, as he may have thought the illness was of the soul, having taken a lover after such a long period of service to God. Yet here she sat, robed in simple garments, just a string of flowers in her hair, minimal unguents and more important, nothing to do or look forward to. She could sing, however. On this thought, her eyes brightened. "Ningi!" She called for her *tanpura*. But the Ningi who came in had other things on her mind. "*Chikkamma,*" Ningi had just paused to wash her feet and deposit the bag of vegetables and provisions in the kitchen and had come straight in to her.

"*Chikkamma,* I met Malavva in the market," she began.

"And you told her I was here? Where have your wits gone, girl? In ten minutes, the whole world will know."

"*Chikkamma,* do you think me such a fool? I have better sense than that! Did you know that the widow Thulasi's relative, Narayanachar, who got the property, is the lover of Queen Amalotpava? They are lying that she is pregnant. We don't know why. We should find out."

"It seems we have heard nothing but plots, the past few days. First Rama Raya and Khondoja's plot against the king, then Vajrabahu's plot and now this!"

"*Devi,* why this talk of plots on this wonderful night when clouds like rutting elephants frisk meaningfully in the sky, buffeted by the playful wind? Ah, the scent of the earth rises sharply, mingling with the chaplets of *Malti* and *Kadamba* in your hair that tremble with each sentient breath you take. Would that I was a flower to nestle in your cascading tresses…" Madhava's voice had lowered to a murmur for her ears only as he came in and decorously seated himself at a safe distance, while Ningi took up the fan and fanned him. He had free run of the house, since his brother was serving under her father.

"Ningi, tell us what you mean. Let the *acharya* hear as well." So Ningi told what she had learned from Malavva. "Hmm... Bribing her to say the Queen is pregnant means there has to be a delivery soon. But how will they get a baby and from whom?"

"What does Narayana gain out of this? His star is rising. First, the widow's pregnancy, then the boy's sainthood and a bid for trusteeship of his lands, now a queen in his coils," said Madhava.

Achale was struck. "This has been very convenient for him. Was it because Thulasi somehow stood in his way that she was killed? Or worse, was he the father of Manju?"

"*Chikkamma*, what if she revealed that? How would it have damaged him? His boy is a saint and since he came out of the pond with the sacred thread, he must be the son of a *dvija*."

"Yes, it certainly seems as if a Brahmin was his father. People suspected Bhadri but were too scared to speak, but if Narayana had fathered a son by a widow and had gained her lands on her husband's death, would not the community rise against him on coming to know of it? Would they let him profit from his misdeed? The boy is innocent, but the father?"

"Bhadri, suspected to be the father, is just allowed to roam free!"

"It is the rare man who can tame an elephant. People just throw up their hands, but for the sake of peace, do nothing. Besides, won't Alur gain if the temple becomes important through his exertions? You heard how the women talked, Ningi."

"True, true."

Bhima came in then, and he also looked big with news. But he was not Ningi, so he spent some time observing the niceties, making polite enquiries after Madhava and talking about their escape. The entire incident had flown out of their minds with Ningi's news, so they now mulled over it, wondering what Chenna had learned. They soon knew, for Bhima had been busy and in his painstaking, methodical way he had followed up Vajrabahu's trail. Chenna had heard the Kalamukhas and Vajrabahu deciding on a meeting with their *mathadhipati* to discuss ways and means.

"The courtier has to be stopped. He is no match for the Aliya and will lose his head to no purpose. Better for him to retire as a courtier than to attempt this foolishness. Don't they say that it is better to say no in the beginning than face disgrace later?" Madhava sounded unusually vehement and Achale wondered if it reminded him of his own frustrated ambitions. Or was he thinking that furthering them could be accomplished by exposing Vajrabahu? That way was despicable, though many ambitious men had feathered their own nests in the same manner in the recent past. She must deflect him, but how?

She said, "The disease should be advertised, the family scandal suppressed. Why should we tattle about this? Let us tackle it at the root and pull it out."

"That's it!" said Bhima, approvingly. Madhava looked thoughtful, no doubt, wondering how to turn it to his advantage.

As if on cue, Puttalakshmi came in. She looked flustered as she announced that Vajrabahu wanted a word with Achale. Though her husband was a well-known *vaidya* and had many clients among the merchants and courtiers, he usually paid house calls, so their own house was not equipped for receiving such sophisticated guests. Achale, feeling sorry for all the trouble her presence was causing, tried to reassure her without making it too obvious to Madhava. "*Amma*, I'll see him here, Ningi will see to him." Puttalakshmi withdrew with a relieved look on her face.

Vajrabahu came in with a swagger which quickly changed to discomfiture when he realized the poet was also sitting there. "*Devi*," he proffered a wreath of tiny carnelian roses intertwined with thin gold chains, winking with diamonds like dew glittering in sunlight so the effect was of a garland of glowing roses. Achale wanted to laugh. What a contrast between the poet and the courtier! One used words for everything, as a profession, even to make love to a woman and the other was tongue-tied, even when he needed to speak! "Raya, welcome to my father's house. We left you rather abruptly the other day, but we were being chased by the Aliya's men and needed to escape."

"Escape! Why?"

Achale allowed Bhima to explain. The courtier looked preoccupied, which overlaid weightiness on his normally awkward manners. Through the narration, he sat, pulling at his moustache, until Achale wished she could put him out of his misery. How to broach the subject? Would he be driven to something rash, like letting out their whereabouts to the Aliya's hooligans or would he trust them? But wait, how had he known of her whereabouts? Surprisingly, he stooped and whispered something to Bhima, who stopped in the middle of a sentence, before he pulled himself together and nodded. He signaled to Ningi and they left the room. Achale then introduced Vajrabahu to Madhava and served them both the *panaka*, which Ningi had brought earlier, cool from the earthenware pot in which it had been made and scented with vetiver. Vajrabahu drank thirstily, as if to gain courage and Achale saw Madhava glance at him quizzically. Then Vajrabahu burst out, "Devi, how well do you know the Kalamukhas and Kalabhras? Are they to be trusted? You know several of the important courtiers. You cannot admire the Aliya and you know the present King hides behind the shield of the Salakarajus. You would surely support a more valiant monarch? Maybe one day, you may even be Queen, if you support the right person."

Valiant he may be on the battlefield, but diplomacy obviously made him nervous. Taking pity on him, Achale possessed herself of his hands. "Raya," she began gently, as if she was talking to Indra, "Vijayanagara surely needs a valiant King, but if a lion is caught between a crocodile and a snake, it would not be considered pusillanimous in him to retreat."

Madhava added his bit, "Raya, why seek enemies, if you have anger? With friends you need no medicine for danger. With kinsmen, why ask for fire to keep you warm? Go back to Kampili, but before you do, ask the king for a *nayakdom*. Then you can be secure in your own kingdom." He was thinking, two birds with a stone. Achale was looking too sympathetic. For days she had not mentioned the potter. Maybe his skill in love and song had driven the other away. With this suitor's departure, she would be his for the asking. My peerless girl, you would be heaven's blessing in my house, he thought.

Vajrabahu looked like Acharyulu's white dog when he was thinking, his brow furrowed and his eyes watchful. He had taken back his hand and was pulling at his moustache again. Achale, perhaps worried that his luxuriant moustache would soon be lying on her floor, patted his hand. "We'll find a way for you to save face." The eyes looked confused, then relieved, before the shutters fell. Madhava however, saw a gleam in Achale's eyes, before she lowered them. It did not need a genius to figure out that Virabhadra was the best person to meet the Kalamukhas and Kalabhras to disabuse them of the need for the plot. But for the *nayakdom*, some other way had to be found.

Vajrabahu spent a little more time with them before he left with the poet and from the way his hand sought the poet's shoulder it looked fairly certain that the two had become comrades. Achale was glad of this unlooked for result of Vajrabahu's plot as she was sure the poet was astute enough to use it to his advantage and gain entry to court circles. Vajrabahu had revealed that he had met her father at the court and got her whereabouts from him.

Her heart was singing as she called Ningi to her and asked her to give Virabhadra her earring as a token that they must meet on a matter of urgency. Ningi left on her errand but came back a bare half an hour later with the news that Virabhadra was waiting for Achale outside but she had hesitated, as he looked disturbed and unkempt; quite mad, actually. When the potter came in, Achale saw that this was quite true. He looked thinner, his stomach, normally well muscled looked shrunken as did his cheeks. There was thick stubble on his cheeks and his hair was matted. Thus far he had always dressed simply but had been well groomed.

"*Achare*, please come in and sit down. The girl will fetch you a drink immediately. Shall I arrange for a meal? You look troubled."

"I came to tell you that the sittings cannot be held for some time. The Nayaks of Gooty have rebelled. The King has gone to subdue them." A muscle twitched near his eye. His hand shook. From the strong smell of arrack that had accompanied him she guessed he had been on a drunken bout. Achale knew that what he needed now was comfort, but later, he would need distraction. She had to act soon. It was evening any minute now; her father would come in and she would be lost. She went out and sent her mother's slave to find Ningi and Bhima as quickly as if her life depended on it. Terrified out of her wits, the girl ran as if all the denizens of the underworld were after her. Ningi appeared right away, followed soon by Bhima, by which time, the potter had had a drink of lemonade. He was carefully maneuvered out into the garden, with the other two standing guard, as Achale held him to her breast and soothed him. After a while, he was smuggled up to Achale's chamber through the back door, bathed tenderly and fed by her. Much later, while he sat chewing the betel leaf, Achale broached what was on her mind:

"Vajrabahu, the Sangama courtier was plotting to seize the throne with some Kalabhras and Kalamukhas."

"Was plotting?"

"He has been advised that it would be better for him to go back to Kampili and seek a nayakdom instead."

"Your powers seem to be limitless. You can soothe a man, administer to his appetites, arrange his comforts and even direct his politics. I have made some sketches of you from memory, for the sculpture. Shall I show you?" He took out the cloth bag he had slung across his shoulders on coming in, which Bhima had carried upstairs. He was a skillful artist and had caught her playfulness and intelligence. The potter must indeed be besotted with her if he could draw so well from memory, thought Ningi, looking over her shoulder. A page showing her three quarter face, her eyebrow raised, her lips smiling playfully, fluttered to the ground. No one seemed to notice, so it disappeared into a fold of Bhima's *dhoti*.

Achale brought the topic back to the plot by saying, "We wondered if you could talk to the Kalabhras. Assure them that Vajrabahu would be the wrong choice and no match for the Salakarajus or the Aliya."

Virabhadra was stroking his beard, and came out with, "I think that can be done. After two meetings with him, they must have their own doubts."

"They may not take too kindly to your knowing the whole story, so you take care," said Achale.

Virabhadra grinned, "Devi, I will. As I said, you would make an ideal wife. You see, now my welfare is uppermost in your mind, even while you have skillfully overturned Vajrabahu's plot and arranged his life for him. My humble home will be honoured if you set your right foot in it and make it yours."

His grin had faded and he looked very serious and intense. "I have taken you by surprise; I can see the confusion in your eyes. I am not a poet. I cannot offer you a position in court. Yet my skills are not unrecognized and I can promise you a house quite as large as this, or if you prefer, I can live where you will, or in your house. Don't answer me now. When my mission is accomplished, I will meet you. Until then, let me have this night, so we each have something to remember."

As Achale's confusion deepened, Bhima and Ningi left the room, Ningi to sleep outside and Bhima to guard the corridor. For a brief moment Achale wondered what her mother would tell her father, then too many urgent sensations took over and deluged thought. Later, after Virabhadra had made his stealthy way home, she thought sleepily, whatever it was, it had kept her father downstairs.

It was the next evening. Achale was back on the swing. In a few minutes, her mother would join her. She was just giving the last instructions of the day to her slaves. They could now do what

Puttalakshmi liked best before going up to bed. Then they would wake up at the first *jama,* before dawn and the day would start again, just like the previous day.

Her mother joined her on the swing and they moved in harmony for sometime. "Achale, child, Ningi told me that the potter had made you an offer, what are you going to do? Madhava will also ask you I am sure. He is just waiting for an appointment in court and you have now arranged it haven't you, by putting him in touch with Vajrabahu."

Achale did not answer immediately. She wished she could just sing. But her mother could not be brushed off like that. "*Amma,*" she began slowly, "I love the potter. He is a good man, knows how to treat a woman and will listen to me. I will be free to pursue my desires and can have a dance school if I wish and give discourses. He will be gone most of the time, as his job requires him to stay near his sculptures. But I can't explain the yearning in my heart. I do not want to be bound to a man, even one as superior as this. I want only to call Virupaksha my lord. As for the poet…" she explained her reservations.

"Still singing the same song, Achale. Why is it not possible to serve two masters?"

"*Amma*, why should I serve two masters?"

"Achale, do you not want children?"

"Did *Ajji* not have you when she wanted? All in good time. You have taught me well."

Puttalakshmi sighed. With a grown up daughter, it sometimes better not to argue. Life would teach her, and she had to be patient until she learned.

She began to sing a Purandara *dasa* song she had heard Acharyulu sing:

I put my parrot in a gilded cage but it flew away....

Achale said, "*Amma*, listen to me; Amalotpava Devi is telling everyone she is pregnant when she is not. Ningi found out from the washerwoman. Narayanachar, the man who inherited Thulasi's acres has been seen visiting her in secret. Do you think *Ajji* can meet her and find out the truth? She knows her as she knows all important persons in this kingdom. Had she anything to do with Thulasi?"

"Achale, you forget. Your father is a *vaidya*. He often sends me with preparations he has made up. He has a new unguent which will preserve the skin from darkening in the sun's rays. Though this is the rainy season, at times the sun's rays beat down mercilessly. I will go and see her and pretend that the unguent is for her and find out the truth."

Achale reached out and gave her mother's hand a grateful squeeze. Regardless of everything else, she knew Puttalakshmi would help her till the end.

CHAPTER XXII

SEPTEMBER, 1536

"*Anna*!" as usual, Chenna rushed to speak as soon as he saw Bhima.

"Slowly, slowly, young one. If you rush through all things, life will lose a lot of fulfillment," Bhima said with a grin.

"Oh, *anna*, you are always teasing! Let me tell you, it's not only I who am fulfilled but all the lucky women who enjoy my custom. You can ask in the marketplace."

Bhima chuckled at the lad's indignation. "Eh, see him strut his way up to the tree-top, young cock! What you have done, even your Bhima has accomplished. Now tell me what you came to tell."

Chenna's eyes gleamed. "I was passing through Jogahalli with my troupe again. I just wanted to check on our lady's foes so I went past the temple fields. I saw them there. The man who followed us on the day we escaped to Nagalapur was talking to that Brahmin Bhadrinatha. I climbed a tree close by and slithered on my stomach up an overhanging branch, the better to hear them. I listened carefully. They have fixed it so that when he returns from Gooty, which he is scheduled to next month, Achyuta Deva Maharaya will be surrounded and captured. He is to be imprisoned in Bhadri's palace, until he is taken away somewhere else. I waited till they stopped and got down. At the first chance to take leave, I came here. What shall we do?"

"Poor King, his crown is in danger yet again. Barely a year ago, he was imprisoned and escaped. That Bhàdri! His ambition overflows boundaries like the Pampa River in spate! I hope the swirling waters carry away only Bhadri and leave everything else untouched," he said viciously. "Achale must be told immediately. Wait here; there may be work for you to do."

Bhima went in to find Achale in the courtyard near the kitchen, rolling the *sandige* mixture of beaten rice mixed with spices and buttermilk into small balls and then flattening them with the heel of her hand. These she was laying out on a long white sheet. She did not pause, but said, "I cannot stop now as it has to be done when its wet or the grains will all separate. *Amma* suddenly felt that she had not put enough by and the day being so hot, she thought we could safely do this. Anyway, you will have nicely fried *sandige* with your meal tonight. She has gone to see Amalotpava Devi, so Ningi and I had to do this." Ningi who had been laying out to dry the vermicelli she had bought from the Turkish housewives came over muttering, "Pah, so much money and they can't even dry it well!"

Bhima told them the news Chenna had brought. Achale said, "A month hence. Did I not say Bhadri is trying something? It was he who informed against us on that day in Alur, I am sure. Well, we cannot do anything but inform Madhava. Perhaps he can expose Bhadri, but he would have made himself a powerful enemy in Rama Raya."

"Devi, little did I know that you can perform such domestic tasks so well. Your talents are many indeed." Madhava had developed the uncanny knack of appearing just when he was wanted and least expected. Achale and Bhima had soon clued him into the discussion. Bhima said, "We should use every opportunity which offers itself. Achare, do you know how Tenali Rama became a court jester?"

"No tell us, brother."

"As you know, going to court and not being noticed by the King is no use. Then he got his chance. A powerful foreign magician challenged the nobles to a competition. Tenali Rama challenged the magician to do the trick he was about to demonstrate, without closing his eyes. The magician agreed. Tenali Rama then put a teaspoon of chilli powder on his closed lids and after a few minutes washed it off. The whole court laughed when the magician walked off home without a word. Tenali Rama was appointed court jester on the spot." They all laughed heartily, glad of a chance to diffuse the tension of the last few minutes.

"This humble poet cannot hope to aspire to those great heights. But I must think deeply about this. We have a month and anything may happen in that time—we may even be able to find who killed Thulasi and save Betappa's lands. "

"The first thing is for us to find out something about Narayana. Why don't you follow him Bhima? That may tell us what he has to hide."

"Chenna is waiting out. He is a monkey's cousin in that he can climb and hide his own shadow. So, it is better that he follows the Brahmin. Even within the village, he has just to pretend to sleep off a drunken stupor or be a wayfarer, resting."

The Queen's Bath was quite far from Nagalapur. Puttalakshmi had started early with the unguent in a special flask of glass from the itinerant vendor who swore they had come all the way from Venice and insisted that they were worth four costly silk shawls. She had put it by and guarded it zealously from clumsy hands for just such an occasion. However, one could not be mean when it came to a gift for a queen. Who knows what one could get in return? At the least would be information, important in itself or maybe, a purse of *varahas*. One could also be sure of a chance to enjoy the bath and be perfumed and massaged by attendants, a luxury a busy housewife did not get everyday.

At last, they passed the mosque and reached the well where one fork went onwards to the palace and the other towards the Queen's Bath. Puttalakshmi alighted from the cart and asking them to wait went towards the enclosure, where the eunuch guards gave a bored shrug and opened the gate. From outside, it was just a plain building surrounded by a narrow moat with window embrasures surmounted by arches, reflecting the Mohammaddan structures in Bijapur. Inside was a different story. The cool water, strewn with rose petals and jasmine lapped at a gallery dissected by arched windows, from which the queen's retinue, those who were not bathing, watched the sport below. A second level ran around, where the queen would go after her bath to dry off in the cool breeze. The queen was sitting in the water, while two attendants rubbed her limbs with unguents and washed her hair. Puttalakshmi waited in the window embrasure overhanging the bath, near enough to be called but hidden so she wouldn't intrude on the Queen's privacy, until the Queen should see her.

It was not a very long wait, probably, the attendants had whispered to the Queen of her arrival. An attendant brought her to the Queen, who sat up, came out of the bath and was dried off.

"What brings you here, Puttalakshmi? All well with the family?" So she had not heard about Achale. True, queens led sheltered lives.

"I got this new recipe for an unguent to prevent and remove sun damage. It immediately put me in mind of your Majesty. Such skin, like swan's golden plumage needs protection to maintain its delicacy."

"Show me. Have you shown it to anyone else?" In the race to be chief Queen, the rivalry was cutthroat.

"As if I would! Please take it. The unguent should be honoured to adorn skin of such delicate texture, rivaling the jasmine."

She applied a little on her skin and took a whiff. "It smells of saffron and sandalwood."

"Yes your Majesty has discovered the main ingredients with your usual needle-sharp discernment. This recipe was given to me by Thulasi, the mother of the boy-saint of Alur near Anegondi."

"We have heard tell of that incident. Did not the mother die? There was talk of some suspicion regarding the death. Far away as we are, talk has reached our ears."

"Yes your Majesty. Suspicion must naturally fall on the relative of the husband who succeeded to the husband's estate."

"Why, was there not talk of the woman being an outcaste, a widow who bore a son well after her husband died? He would have succeeded then, would he not?"

Yes, you know something about the case. Is it because of your close relationship with Narayana or because you know he killed her? Puttalakshmi wanted to ask, but she made haste not to offend the woman further, "You Majesty is well versed in the law. I know only what people say."

"You must say this then, if you hear talk. It would not do to get an innocent man accused."

"Yes your Majesty." Even if the woman knew something, she would not tell. It would be best to leave. So much for her dreams of a relaxing bath! Making an excuse that she had promised to give a patient a massage in the afternoon, she hurried out.

When Puttalakshmi got back, she reported that Queen Amalotpava Devi may or may not know something about the murder, it was hard to tell. Chenna left on his mission to follow Narayana. Narayana emerged late in the evening, dressed in coarse clothes, his head covered with a coarse shawl. His head looked undressed without a *kulayi*. He proceeded on foot for some miles outside the village until he reached the settlement of sweepers. A light was burning in one house and a man went out the door just as Narayana entered. Chenna understood. It was often so. Brahmin men sometimes found their wives—who did not receive the education that he had heard high-born women and *devadasis* received in pleasing men, and hampered by constant reminders of chastity and piety from their elders—coy and unresponsive in bed. The husband of the sweeper woman surely knew all about it. Probably, the reward was sufficient. Narayana was now a rich man. He could afford to be generous. There was no need for Chenna to linger here.

On his way back, he heard a familiar voice and struggled to make out the words. The *dasa* was singing of rich men puffing themselves off, drunk with avarice. One never knew. When a man had taken to singing instead of talking, every word may be significant. If his poor, untutored brain couldn't make out the words, he could at least repeat it to Bhima would surely know the meaning.

It was now Ningi's turn. She had been given her instructions by Achale. She had to go to the house of the mistress and find out the truth. Was it just the usual liason or something else? Ningi went back to Achale's house, early in the morning. She spent the day there, so she could say with a clear conscience that she was living there. It was all part of the plan. As soon as Achale had heard that Narayana was having an affair with a married woman, she had reasoned that he must have some ulterior motive. He was not merely following his instincts; Narayana was born without instincts and had even sucked his mother's breast calculatedly. She insisted that Amalotpava Devi's pretend pregnancy had something to do with this affair, so Ningi was sent off.

Late that evening saw Ningi wending her way to Alur and the sweeper colony. Chenna had told her there was a toddy and arrack still where the villagers gathered. She felt sure the mistress would be found there. Chenna had not seen the woman, but Bhima had found out from Betappa that she was known as Thimmi. Ningi had dressed up specially with flowers in her hair and around her throat. She took the liberty of arraying herself in Achale's bodice and one of her diaphanous shawls. She could never hope to rival Achale, she doubted if even Kama's wife Rathi, could, but she looked better than she usually did. Now if she could catch the eye of Thimmi's husband, it would be the best way of getting information. The still operator had put out some crude seats made of local casuarina wood. There were also upturned urns and even pot lids as seats. The night was slightly humid, but pleasant. There was even a band of sorts: a village bumpkin was playing the *maddale* and another was playing the flute, while a young girl had been roped in to chime the cymbals. There was a scent of jasmine and roses, probably from the incense smoking in the coal burners.

Terracotta lamps swayed in the breeze casting moving shadows. Ningi sat with pleased anticipation. Immediately, the girl left off the cymbals and ran forward to take her order. They were serving partridge-stuffed pastry and there was a choice of slightly sour toddy, tapped that morning, or arrack. Ningi chose the puffs and toddy, though the girl brought fried gram flour chili fritters along with her pot of toddy and earthenware tumblers.

It felt a little odd to drink on her own; usually Malavva was there with her. A group of young bucks fresh from a day's labour, probably at repairing the temple, were eyeballing her, but she ignored them. There was a man sitting alone. He was older and looked like a trader or perhaps he was an itinerant vendor. Ningi caught his eye and smiled her invitation. He brought his drink over and they sat talking. Her guess had been right. He was an itinerant vendor and he had wound up with the colony, before he went to Nagalapur. She told him the truth about herself. She did not want to bump into him at Nagalpur and be caught out. Besides, the truth sometimes had its uses. You could use a mustard seed to draw out the pungency of a big red chilli. She waited until his eyes began to wander towards her chest, before letting her shawl slip a little as she leaned closer and asked," Your job takes you all over, doesn't it? You must hear so much news!"

"Ha, much good it does me!" the man muttered. Not very promising; this man looked like a morose type. Such people were not much good. He would take his pleasure too quickly to give his partner any. But Achale must be obeyed, so she persisted, leaning even closer as she persisted, "Do you go to the palace often?"

"The palace? You think that traders such as I are allowed there? But I do serve the households of lesser queens. I just sold Queen Amalotpava Devi a rush basket today."

"Really? Sounds as if a baby is expected!"

"I don't know. I sold a basket to a household here as well. They say that Kondayya's wife Thimmi tis expecting. It's her time. There he is, her husband. I expected him to be here before this."

A man came in, a labourer from the look of him and Ningi was glad she need not entice this man; he looked most unattractive, short and bent. The vendor looked much better. However, there was no time for pleasure tonight. Kondayya seemed to be in a hurry, gulping down his arrack.

Bhima had said he would be waiting for her near the crossroad, so she must hurry. When she reached the crossroad, however, she found it empty. She would have to spend the night at Achale's house and leave for Nagalapur in the morning. She felt the ground slip beneath her feet as a hand was pressed to her mouth and she was pulled up onto an overhanging branch. It was Bhima. His hand still on her mouth he whispered into her ear, "Not a word. Something's happening. I saw that Kondayya running towards the village. My guess is he's gone to get Narayana."

They sat quietly for some time. Despite the strange sensations Bhima's closeness was producing Ningi began to slide off into sleep and had to slap herself to stay awake and astride that branch. Suddenly, she felt Bhima stiffen next to her and knew that he must have heard something. Neither her eyes nor her ears were as keen as his. She recognized the bent form of Kondayya and another shawl-covered figure in the faint light of the moon. Then they both disappeared into the colony. It seemed like seconds, but at least a quarter of an hour must have passed, when the shawl-covered one hove into view and this time, he carried a bundle which could be a child in swaddling. As the figure, passed from view down the road, a wailing like someone had died arose in the colony. Ningi and Bhima looked at each other. They should lose no time in contacting Achale. Bhima fixed his eyes on the overhanging branch as he spoke, but Ningi saw with a little thrill that his eyes had a twinkle and they had rested on hers before traveling upwards.

Once again, they were all grouped together, this time in the inner courtyard. Achale was just digesting the news that Bhima and Ningi had brought. "One lady pretended to be pregnant, another was pregnant. Two rush baskets were delivered. Someone died, a child was born, a bundle was carried away. What does it all add up to?"

"A queen who will now have a baby and a Brahmin's mistress who died giving birth. The Brahmin's son will be prince. The father gets untold power. The queen will always be in his debt and for some more time, he will be in her bed." Bhima spat into a spittoon.

"What a succinct summary of such deep skullduggery!" Achale applauded. "Where is Chenna? We can only trust him to deliver the message to Madhava. Now he need not expose Bhadri to the King, but may tell Vajrabahu of this. He may expose Narayana and get his *nayak*dom. He will surely be grateful enough to mention the poet to the king."

"If my ears don't deceive me, this is he," said Bhima as a sound of scraping feet was heard from outside.

Bhima went out and came in again. "*Chikkamma*, Chenna has just come back from Virabhadra's meeting with the Kalabhras. It was difficult but he convinced them that Vajrabahu would make a poor choice as candidate for usurper. "

"I wonder how he convinced them of that."

"Apparently they were much struck by his assertion that a person who could not make an impression even on a *devadasi*, was unlikely to be accepted as King by the populace."

Achale raised her eyebrows at this clever argument. In the meantime, Chenna was dispatched to apprise Madhava of the new developments.

CHAPTER XXIII

SEPTEMBER-OCTOBER, 1536

Bhima was at Betappa's house. They sat on his string cot and chewed betel leaves.

"Soon, I may not have this house." At his words, his wife set up a loud caterwauling. "Go inside, woman! Let me not hear you. We have important things to discuss," Betappa snapped at her.

"Betappa, think hard. Is there anything about the case which puzzles you?"

"Bhima, one thing I never understood. Her hand held fast to a piece of string. I could not make the corpse let go of it."

Bhima raised his eyebrows. He could not imagine how that could be important. He got up. "Come, on brother. Give up these melancholy thoughts. Let us go and water out throats a little at your local tavern."

"Come on, brother. I can promise you good toddy and the arrack that Munianna distils is not so bad either. He puts in a lizard; gives it a rare kick I can tell you."

"Thank you brother for telling me. I think I will stick with the toddy," Bhima said, dryly. They went to the same tavern that Ningi had patronized the other day. This time, the entertainment was much better. There were dancing girls, wearing short lower garments barely covering their ankles and only a strip of cloth as upper coverings. One of them gave Bhima a cheeky grin and stuck out her pert little breasts. He grinned back but decided not to encourage her.

Betappa exercised his privilege as village watchman to call the other one over, whereupon, the first one pouted. Feeling a little sorry for her, Bhima called her over and she came bouncing like an eager little puppy. Soon they were both pouring out the wine, playfully offering the betel with their teeth, cupping their hands for the wine and Betappa's girl became a little bolder, pouring it on her breast, until Betappa, embarrassed, dragged her off to the privacy of the fields. Somehow, Bhima was unwilling to go the length with this girl. She seemed too young. He looked around for something to distract the girl with and pointed her in the direction of another man who seemed enamored enough to keep staring at them. She went with a pout and he sat back with relief. He called for some snacks and tossed the peanuts one by one into his mouth, leaning against the crude stone supports of the thatch-roofed shack.

A man who had been sitting a little away now began to sing raucously, a folk song which involved a long story of a sister and some brothers. He seemed far gone, because he broke off in the middle and began to sob, ugly tearing sounds. This was no maudlin sobbing but real grief. Curious, Bhima looked over. Seeing his interest, the tavern proprietor came over with another platter of snacks and began to talk. It seemed that the drunken singer was a goat herd named Boriah and Bhima wondered where he had heard the name before.Then he remembered—this was the person whom Ningi had reported as showing an unusual love for Manju. He went over to sit next to the man. Sympathetically, he patted his shoulder. "Lost her, lost her," the man kept muttering.

"Whom do you speak of, brother? "Bhima asked gently.

"No one sir, no one. You did not hear me, did you?" He had slipped to the floor and clasped Bhima's legs.

"No, I did not." Bhima raised him and made him sit down but he was half-lolling onto Bhima's lap. Bhima heard singing behind him:

Life is just a play and, the human race, mere puppets....

Then, strangely enough, Acharyulu sat down near them. From where did he come? thought Bhima in amazement. He had not seen him earlier. Acharyulu began to sing the story of Satyakama. Satyakama's mother, Jabala, knew not his father as she had begotten him when she was a young housemaid, wandering from employer to employer. When his guru Gautama asked him for his lineage, Satyakama told him the truth. Admiring his courage, Gautama admitted him in his ashram. Bhima knew Acharyulu was telling him something.

Boriah's mutterings which had stopped when Acharyulu was singing the story, began afresh, this time beating his chest and repeating over and over, "My son, my son!"

Bhima said, "Brother, who is your son?"

"No, no, my son, my son," the mutterings continued.

Bhima never knew what inspired him. "Manju is alright. Madhava Shastry the poet will take care of him," he said. Boriah went limp and still and Bhima knew the arrow had found its mark.

Suddenly, there was a sound of drumming hoofs. Pots and cups went flying, as people scattered in fear, rushing into the fields in reflex. Betappa came running up, hastily retying his loin-cloth and they stood their ground, the serenity of Acharyulu's visage offering some comfort in the melee. Soldiers had ridden up. "You there, where is the dwelling of one Narayana?" one inquired of Bhima, roughly. Betappa spoke up, "I will direct you, sirs, follow me!"

He went with them, running in front, in the direction of the Brahmin quarters.

Acharyulu continued to hum under his breath. Bhima was so struck by the recent turn of events that he simply sat there until the soldiers and Betappa returned. Narayana was trussed up behind one soldier, the other held his chain and the cavalcade went off in the direction of Hampi. Betappa came back and they went their ways, Bhima having indicated that he knew about the reason for the arrest with his raised hand.

CHAPTER XXIV
JULY 1996

Maya woke up, drenched in sweat, as though she had been running. She had just found out that Boriah could have been Manju's father and then she had slept off, the book in her hands.

Kamala came in bright and early, but Maya was even earlier. Since she had hardly slept the previous night, that wasn't surprising. "Madam, I got the documents and the pleadings photocopied. I spoke to the bench clerk. It seems the *matha* wants to sell the lands. They have a buyer. So they have filed a suit for permission to sell."

"You can talk your way to anything Kamala," said Maya with a salutary squeeze. Really, at that moment she adored Kamala.

"Madam, the clerk said that the trustees are always fighting."

"Didn't the HR& CE Board come into it?"

Kamala looked confused. "HRC? No madam. The trustees and the buyer were parties, that's all. It was really difficult to finish the case, but finally, they have reached the arguments stage. There is another case, against the tenants, but that has been decreed in favour of the *matha*."

Maya glanced at the pleadings and saw that the real estate company was called Madhava Perumal Realty. Kamala had done really good work.

"Kamala, you'll have a more difficult job today. You'll have to go to the *tahsildar's* office and the sub registrar's office at Ponmudi and get information about the owner of land going back as far as the records. I'll go to the library and look through the gazetteer. Tell the juniors to take care of the calling work and to ask for adjournments in all the trials and appearance cases. We have to get this done today."

"OK madam." Her enthusiasm had ebbed. It was going to be a long day for her.

When she and Kamala met in the evening, they compared notes. Kamala could find only the *matha* on record, but she had, on her own initiative, applied for an encumbrance certificate going back a hundred years and there you had it, a record for one Yellamma mortgaging the land. After that, there was one more transaction only, the cancellation of the mortgage. All other records showed the *matha* as owner. Her research had yielded nothing. What was the key to this mystery?

"Madam, phone!" announced the typist, just then. This was the outside line, at the reception, so Maya answered it from there.

"Maya!" It was Pat's mother. "I'm so glad I got a hold of you. What are you lawyers doing? There is this big slum, Ponmudi. It's very old, mentioned in all the surveys. They are all going to be evicted. Didn't Tulsi tell you?"

Maya was taken aback. Here was the Ponmudi connection with Tulsi again! "How did you know Tulsi?"

"She had contacted me some time last year about Ponmudi. She had wanted me to do something about the eviction. That's how we started working with the slum. After that we lost contact and then I heard about her death from Pat. So tragic! I thought she may have told you about Ponmudi herself."

Maya remembered the peanut-seller, but did not want to get into all the details. "Actually, I heard someone else talking about it. I'm sorry I can't come, aunty. But I'll ask Pat or Meena if they are free and ask them to call you. I'm tied up all this week."

"Please do that. Thanks."

They spoke a while longer and then rang off.

Maya realized that she had completely forgotten Surilee. The young woman was eaten up with jealousy about Thomas and had an eye on Harsha who seemed quite willing to spread his charms among the women. No one knew her whereabouts on the day of Tulsi's fall.

She had to find out. Who better to ask than Thomas? Even though she was cooling things off with him, it was fine to meet as friends, Maya reasoned with herself. She rang him up that evening. "Thomas, why don't we go somewhere for dinner? I feel like *chaat*. You know this Madras Bhelpuri guy who had a hand-cart opposite Holy Angel's convent? He's moved into a small shop close by. Let's go. *Chaat* with a Madrasi touch. Just right for this heat." He might have been jealous, but better sense prevailed as he seemed only too happy to oblige. Not only did the *chaat* taste heavenly, but Maya also had the dubious satisfaction of finding out that Surilee had not come in at all that day. So where did it leave her?

She didn't know why she felt compelled to ask, but some inner voice was prompting her and for once, she decided to pay it attention. "Tell me something, did Tulsi ever mention Ponmudi, or a *matha* there?" Thomas looked perplexed as he well might, "Ponmudi? No but you better ask Harsha. He was mentioning something about plots coming up there."

"Oh, I went to this club some time ago. He was there."

"Went to a club with Harsha and too busy with work to see me, is it?" said Thomas, narrowing his eyes.

Maya was surprised at his nasty tone. "I went with Toni, a long time back, before I got busy. We bumped into Harsha there."

He looked chastened. "So?"

"Harsha was reeking of money. What does he do?"

"His father owns Madhava Perumal Realty. He doesn't need to do anything. Just has to find plots for them. He makes a cool commission, that's why he is so carefree."

"They sell plots all over Greater Madras, don't they?"

"Yes and the East Coast Road—farmhouses to the yuppies."

"That explains the money."

"Tulsi asked me the same thing about Harsha. He used to drop her home sometimes. I told her to be careful." Thomas was looking at Maya curiously, so she changed the subject. In her mind, however, a clearer picture of Tulsi's murder mystery was starting to take shape.

CHAPTER XXV

SEPTEMBER-OCTOBER, 1536

Bhima was very tired the next day. It seemed as if the weight of the world had descended upon him. The agony in Boriah's voice and the terror on Narayana's face would remain before his eyes until his dying breath. He remained in Achale's house till daybreak, so it was nearly afternoon before he reached Nagalapur.

Achale had sent Ningi out a dozen times since the morning, to watch out for Bhima. She seemed to sense that something would break that day. The truth was that her forced confinement was driving her a little mad. At last, they went out onto the balcony that ran the length of the house on one side, and loosening their hair, enjoyed the balmy breeze. They could see the approach road from there and have some fun while doing it.

At last, the cart carrying Bhima appeared and Ningi was sent down to bring him up. They could talk there without fear of interruption. Bhima had had a hasty breakfast so he begged Ningi to get him some food before they went up because Achale, in this mood, semed insatiable and would keep them up all afternoon. Ningi agreed and hurried him into the kitchen, where she quickly served him some *idlis* left over from the morning with a little tamarind chutney which Bhima washed down with buttermilk.

Achale was in a towering rage by this time, but her rages always made her incoherent, so she merely smouldered, reminding them of Durga's third eye. Bhima begged pardon for being late; he had eaten, as he was hungry. This made Achale smile and she said, "So now you want to add slave-driver to my iniquities?" Having lightened her mood slightly, Bhima launched into an account of the previous night and if his voice broke while he spoke about Boriah, no one found it strange as their eyes were wet as well.

Characteristically, it was Ningi, who broke the silence after he spoke, "*Chikkamma,* Thulasi was pregnant before Bhadri gifted her land, after she was cast out. This was more than nine months after her husband died, which is why they suspected her. Even Bhadri would not trouble a pregnant woman, nor would he have taken her under his wing unless there was something between them. Thulasi might have been meeting Boriah in the forest, but she must have had some relationship with Bhadri in the same period, or else, why would he do so much for her?"

"Ningi, you are right. The cowri and the top knot do not shake without reason," Achale said.

"Boriah believed Manju was his. Bhadri believed Manju was his. That is why he saw to his education and gave Thulasi hand-outs. Acharyulu sang the story of Satyakama Jabala last evening as Boriah was speaking. I did not understand till now. Thulasi herself probably did not know. She must have encountered both during the riots after Krishnadeva Maharaya died. They must have thought the widow was easy prey. She decided that Bhadri was likely to be a better father for the boy as he had more to give and also to lose, if it came out. Betappa told me a strange thing yesterday. It seems Thulasi had a piece of string in her hand when she died. He seemed to think it may be significant. What do you think?" Bhima interjected.

"I can't imagine how that will help us find the murderer," Achaled said ruefully.

"*Chikkamma*," Ningi said excitedly, "All we have to do is see if there is a place which has strings hanging from it."

"Have you ever seen anything like that, anywhere? Manju said on that night that she went to the Madhavaswamy temple, don't you remember?"

"Yes *Chikkamma*. What poison could have been used to kill her? Manju said she vomited and she was burning up—she must have meant inside, in her stomach. He went out to call Rangi but she had disappeared."

Bhima said, "I have heard that dhatura produces such symptoms. She must have thought going to the river would cool her off, but instead she died."

"She may have died by drowning. Sometimes, small children die if left near a small pot of water, because they stick their heads in and can't remove it. We'll never know. But datura seeds must have been crushed by some villain and given to her," Achale mused.

There was the sound of hurrying footsteps. Bhima was reminded of the soldiers' hoofbeats the day before. They all relaxed when they discovered that it was Madhava. Chenna would have given him the news the day before and he had come to tell them the ending.

"Oh well met, *Acharare*! Narayana's arrest means that Vajrabahu acted quickly. True, they say, even nectar becomes poison after being kept out for too long. Our King, having just returned from a victorious campaign against the rebels at Gooty, must be in a mood to reward the loyal and punish traitors."

"Yes, I had a meeting with a courtier, Vajrabahu's well wisher, who has promised to stand my friend. But I came to tell you all what I heard today. It seems Bhadri has accused Narayana of killing Thulasi."

"The person who remains in a ruined village is its headman! How clever of Bhadri. He can rest in peace, since Narayana's head is already in the noose, what does it matter if it rolls for one or two crimes? It will also divert suspicion from him."

"Suspicion? Who suspects Bhadri of my sister's death?"

Achale, Bhima and Ningi vied with each othet to tell him of their conjectures in the past hour. "We have not been able to connect him definitely to the murder."

"*Chikkamma*, the corpse smelt of camphor. Do you think that is important?"

They heard cymbals and bells, from downstairs and realized that Acharyulu must be passing by. He was singing.

"Camphor and salt look alike,

As you taste and observe,

You realize they have different characteristics,

So is the essence of the virtuous unique,

Viswathabhirama listen to Vema."

As if in a dream, Achale said, "He mixed the dhatura seeds in holy water, masked it with tulsi and camphor, to hide the bitter taste. He met her at the temple. She must have told him that she had a doubt about whose son he was. Remember, the women at Alur laughed that she was not happy about making her son a saint. She must have wanted him to lead an ordinary life. A Sri Vaishnava priest is allowed to have a family and becomes a *sannyasi*, a hermit, only at the *vanaprastha* stage. But being head of a *matha* is still a responsibility and she must have feared that he would become a *sannyasi* young, since he is already full of spiritual power. She would not have trusted Bhadri. He only wanted a *matha* to be created at the temple."

"Would exposure have injured Bhadri's cause? People already know he is a widow's son. The miracle has already happened."

"But a lower caste person's son elevated as *matha* head? Look at the problems the Madhava *matha* is having with Kanakdasa of the Kuruba clan, a feudal chief no less. Boriah is a humble Bedar, employed with his clan, in looking after the sacred grove of Bilva trees on the edge of the forest and the boundary. His son would hardly be the bait to attract such big fish as the founding of a *matha* and rich grants."

"On account of this I am sorry for Boriah," said Bhima.

"Sorry for Boriah! Next you will be sorry for Bhadri. Boriah took advantage of her, took her by force and you say you are sorry for him!" exclaimed Ningi.

"Whatever he did, he has paid for it long since with his remorse. I have been thinking, the string…Bhadri's sacred thread was knotted. I saw it myself, at the Mahashivarathri celebrations and later."

"She must have pulled it in anger against what he proposed for Manju."

"But the body has been cremated. That is the only clue tying Bhadri to the incident. That and Betappa's word. Who would believe it against that of a Brahmin and a powerful one at that?"

Madhava shook his head. He gave a great sigh. "There is only one thing to do. We cannot let out Thulasi's secret and harm Manju. I have to speak to Bhadri. Let him acknowledge his deed to me and I will try to get him to settle something about the boy."

The group broke up. Madhava let himself out of the house.

Madhava was walking towards Virupakshapura and thence to Alur by boat to visit Bhadri's house when he heard himself hailed. The courtier Somanatha, who was passing by on his horse, came to a grinding halt.

"I was just sending a messenger to your house. I have spoken to the royal chamberlain. He has agreed to get you an audience with the King. You better get ready with your best poem in his praise. Such poems are a bit thin on the ground right now, except of course, for that great epic that Rajnatha keeps talking about, *Achyutabhyuda*. Yours is bound to be a refreshing change after the King has listened to that for the fiftieth time at least!"

"I bow to you, great benefactor," Madhava saluted him with folded hands. "How much time do I have for my debut?"

"I have asked for a week's time."

"Thank you. I will begin straight away."

Bhadri certainly thought well of himself, thought Madhava, as he was ushered into an exceedingly ostentatious hall, the walls hung with paintings, the floors of marble inset with semi-precious stones, and wood carvings from Tirupati and Thanjavur hanging from cornices. The seats were covered with copper foil. No wonder such a man coveted wealth and power. He liked to live in royal style! It was surprising he had not made a bid for the throne. Madhava was a skilled chess, or *chatrunga* player. He knew the value of each move. He decided to attack.

"My cousin sister went to the temple on the night she died. Some people have told me that you went there."

"Going to the temple at the same time as a woman who later dies, elsewhere, I may add, is hardly a crime. Especially as it is well known I have been exceedingly kind to an outcaste's son."

"Some may say too kind, as if there was a reason."

Bhadri's smile grew wider. "People always speak ill-natured gossip if one is rich and powerful. It would well behove a young man, on his way to preferment by the king, of such a precarious post as court poet, to have a care what he repeats."

"It would not be idle gossip to say that Thulasi told another that she was forced on the day of the riots and a very powerful man, childless, thus far, has been atoning for his evil deed ever since."

"While that may be a sin, it would not be considered a punishable crime, if one has atoned."

"There is also the fact of a doubt about his fatherhood."

"An uncle, well-disposed towards an infant, would not want such filth to be street talk." Bhadri had stopped smiling.

"Your house is beautiful. Your clothes are rich, yet your sacred thread was knotted in one place. You would have changed it during *avani avittam*, but I have seen it. Others have seen and remarked on it and it is well known that Thulasi's corpse had a piece of string in her hand. If I lay my evidence before the King, I think he would want a full account. Better still, Manju would want to lay it before the King."

Bhadri bit his lip and Madhava knew he had drawn blood. Manju was the one weak link in his armour and he would not want to do anything to hurt the boy. "I have to think. I need time."

Before Madhava could speak, he raised his hand for silence. "You have my word. You already know I will do nothing to harm *my* son. Yes, my son. If the gods had not decreed, would he have received the sacred thread?" Madhava marveled at his certainty. So, the miracle had not been a stunt engineered by him with a minion and a reed to breathe with. But the boy was too innocent to lie; he must remember that, even though Thulasi had never revealed the truth about his birth to anyone but Bhadri. Madhava left him sitting at his desk, writing something on what looked like a sheet of palm leaf.

CHAPTER XXVI

AUGUST 1996

The phone was ringing as Maya let herself into her flat again. Surprise, surprise, she thought. Another caller with an urgent message. Last time it had been Srinivasa Shastry with his tid-bit about Ponmudi. Who could it be this time? It was Dr. Gopalakrishnan. He wanted to see her urgently. He was leaving town and wanted to give her something he had found. She heard a sound in the background; another ringing sound. "Ah, that's my other line. I must go, it's a long distance call. Don't forget, Maya. See you!" He rang off.

Maya went to meet him the next day and caught him just as he was leaving hurriedly for Bombay. He got right to the point.

"I found something...." He drummed his fingers for a moment, then got up and went over to a steel bureau in the corner. From the locker inside, he took something out which Maya couldn't see from where she was sitting. When he came back to his seat, he showed her a small faded piece of very old looking palm leaf, the writing on it was curly old Telugu, which Maya couldn't read.

"I don't understand..." Maya was totally bewildered.

"It's an old fragment of a grant. Your client had left it with me, so I could try to find the missing bit. But I'm afraid I never could."

He reached into his desk's drawer and came up with a magnifying glass. "This says, *matadhipati* Manjunatha, then that sentence is missing, next word is Boriah, the Bedar, Alur, the rest is missing. Next words are Ponmudi… forever. Makes no sense, without more of the document." But to Maya, the lawyer, it did. These were the words she read everyday. The legal language in transfer documents, title deeds. This seemed to be a transfer of some land, probably, in Ponmudi to Boriah from Manjunatha. Where was the rest of the document? It would give the limits of the land, its identifying boundaries, though if it was so old, everything would have changed. Even so, it was valuable, just as a historical record.

Where Tulsi had got the ancient document from was a mystery, but that it was a fragment of a land grant was unmistakable She rang up Meena as soon as she could. "What if I had a grant, centuries old, before British rule, from a temple which, during British times, was registered as a trust. And what if, some time during the beginning of this century, the grantees line dies out completely—could the temple resume the land?"

"I should think the ordinary rules of succession would apply and if the line dies out, it belongs to the government by escheat."

"So a tenant would have an arguable case against the *matha* that they were not the owners and they can't carry out the eviction, right?"

"I suppose so. At least there would be a delay of a few years until it was decided one way or the other. What have you found, Maya?"

"I'll tell you tomorrow."

Whether because he somehow divined it, or because he had found out, the boy who became a *jeeyar* was granted a *matha* in Tamil country. He, in turn gave Boriah, whom he knew to be his father, a piece of land, far away from Alur so as not to cause unwanted comment. This land had been handed down through the generations in Boriah's family. The *matha* had simply resumed it instead of it going to the government by escheat. The scheme suit to allow the land to be sold had reached a critical stage and if the opposing party knew this detail, it could have scuttled the sale. If the tenants had found out, they could have appealed and blocked their eviction which could have made it hard to find a buyer for such prime land. And because she knew this, Tulsi had died.

The next day, at the dance class, she would know, for sure. She debated whether she should tell Thomas. Suppose some old sense of loyalty prompted him to sound a warning? The best form of attack is to surprise the quarry. She did not doubt Thomas' innocence anymore but she'd better not take any chance. She had to play a lone hand.

However, she needed backup, if only to clear up any mess there might be later, especially getting police help. She'd better alert Meena. But Meena was a worrier. How to get her help without revealing too much? Never would she let Maya do this alone and to have her presence looming over the class would alert the quarry. In the end, she called Meena and invited her home for dinner, saying she wanted to discuss something. She asked her to meet her after class and told her to come in a little early so she could watch their rehearsal. Meena was mystified but put down Maya's reluctance to reveal details of what she wanted to discuss as something to do with her relationship with Thomas. She agreed to come as soon as she could get away and Maya was satisfied.

Maya chose Harsha as her partner. He looked quizzically at her but seemed happy enough. They danced a while.

They were in the second movement, when she said, "Madhava Perumal Realty is your father's company isn't it?"

"I am one of the partners. Why, is a client interested in one of our properties?"

"No, I just found it funny that you are going after a property when the title is weak."

His body stiffened as they did a turn and he did not pull her smoothly through, so the next step was delayed. "Which one are you talking about?"

"That Ponmudi property does not belong to the *matha*. It never did. The first *jeeyar* gave it to one Boriah. His family died out so it belongs to the government."

"What rubbish are you talking?" He was pulling and pushing her with barely concealed anger and she had to fight to keep her balance.

"The *matha*'s case against the tenants has been decreed. But they can always go on appeal. The scheme suit is pending, so the field is still wide open. I wonder if the opposing faction of trustees knows this. Do *any* of them know it?" The dance had come to an end. As they walked off the floor, he muttered for her to stay back after class.

For the next dance, she had a different partner. Throughout the dance, Maya felt Harsha's eyes on her most of the time, brooding, angry. When it was time for the third dance, Harsha quickly cut in, before Sunny who had just turned to claim her and they were partnered again.

"I know you're a lawyer, but I thought you only handled divorce cases. Why are you representing the tenants? Perhaps we can talk about it. How much do they want? We could include your fee." He looked down at her smiling, but his eyes were watchful. The loud music was the best muffler, so no could hear them. She thought she saw Thomas glance at them a couple of times, but could not be sure. It was time, Maya decided. Another few steps and the class would end. She had to force a resolution in this class, one way or another. Here, with Meena on the way and Thomas watching, she would have a better chance, than if she revealed enough to make him suspect she knew the truth and the showdown did not happen. He could be a serious threat, if he caught her alone outside.

"I was Tulsi's lawyer."

"I know that, but Tulsi is dead. Why do you care about the property?"

"Didn't Tulsi tell you why she cared?"

"Tulsi was a nut! She wanted me to give up crores worth of property for some strange dead claim to an old shepherd's family. Our lawyers checked all that. No one inherits the claim and we have already won against the tenants."

"Well the tenants can appeal based on this information."

"We can't afford that. We have already accepted deposits from prospective buyers and we have invested those funds. Why should you care?"

"I care because Tulsi cared."

He twirled her around, then caught her close, so the watching class could think, they were merely dancing a little intimately.

"How do you know about the grant? What did Tulsi tell you?" Harsha said menacingly. "The tenants are bound to lose the appeal. We have ways to get the government to transfer the land to us."

"The question is, how do *you* know about the grant? What did Tulsi tell you and when? You could only have got the information from her. When did you leave the class on that day?"

"I left with all the others, as I told the police."

"No one saw you go."

Harsha did not reply as the dance ended there, but she felt his grip tighten, and heard the intake of breath and knew she had hit home. How would she follow it up, keep him talking, till Meena arrived? Damn her, she *had* to be late this day of all days! Finally, the stretches were completed and the class was free to go.The students started streaming out and Thomas after a few glances in her direction, went off to his usual place, near the outer door.

To her surprise, Harsha found her, touched her on the shoulder and dragged her none too gently towards a changing room. She glanced around, but she could see through the glass doors that Meena had not yet arrived. She had to keep him talking until Meena came in. Where *was* she?

"You knew I was Tulsi's lawyer at the party. Have you been trying to get close to me just to find out if I knew anything?

"There is nothing to know, Maya. Come on, we can work something out, I'm sure. Why don't I set up a meeting with my father?"

Maya ignored this. "Were you and Tulsi an item? Everyone seems to think so."

"There was nothing between us. Tulsi wanted to talk about the case. She wanted to convince me to let the tenants stay on. She felt that would be more in keeping with the spirit of the grant, you know: poor people living there. Crazy!" He shook his head.

In the small cupboard-like space, there was barely room to stand and Maya suddenly felt the menace of Harsha's presence, especially as they were now standing close, though Maya retreated as far back as she could. She couldn't see the main door, so she didn't know whether Meena had arrived. She decided to up the ante a bit. She had to get out of this space.

"You wanted to know where she lived, didn't you? That's why you suggested dropping her off. I know you killed Tulsi. You can't get away with it.The police did not find a key among her belongings. You took that key didn't you? You wanted that grant. You couldn't take chances that she would show the tenants or someone in the government, slow up things, make things hot for you. As you said, there are crores riding on the property. I'm going to be filing a case in the High Court to reopen the investigation and I have the fragment of the grant that Tulsi found." Maya felt out of breath.

"Damn! I took her key and searched in her apartment, but could not find it. You had it all along? I should have got you at the party! Shot up, you could have OD'ed and no one would have been the wiser. Have you told anyone else?" Harshe seemed manic.

"My partners know and so does the tenants' counsel," Maya lied.

"Where is it?"

"In a place you'll never find." Harsha opened the room door a crack and welcome fresh air rushed in. The smell of sweat and fear had been too strong and Maya had felt like passing out.

"Come on, they've all gone. Thomas will come in any minute to lock up. He usually spends some time outside, going over the books, seeing off the dancers." With a sinking sensation, Maya saw that the outer office was empty. Not even Thomas was there. There was still no sign of Meena.

He caught hold of her arm and pulled her with him to the big window.

Now Maya began to panic. She tried to resist, but he was much stronger and he put his arm around her waist and half-lifted, half-carried her to the window. With one arm, he pushed it open. Air rushed in, cool and crisp, with a hint of rain. It was dark outside, just the street lamp in the distance, cutting through. Maya was getting frantic. "My partner Meena said she'd come by."

"You'd better not try anything." He shook her hard. The room was soundproof, so screaming for help would be of no use. She struggled but nothing she did seemed to bother him. Better to keep him talking. "Was this how you killed Tulsi?" she yelled. Harsha hauled her up on to the sill with surprising strength. His silent purpose was somehow more frightening than anything else. He was well built and tall, and years of dancing had given him brute strength; he looked unfazed at having to handle a tall woman like Maya. He pushed her legs over the sill. Maya struggled, but there was little she could do, one false move and she'd be over. His grip was like a vice and his hands were now locking her head against his chest. This is how Tulsi died and for the same reason. Why hadn't she told Pat and Meena her suspicions? Or Toni?

"I've given it to my partner who put it in a locker. There is no way you'll get it even if I die. And you can't escape. They all know."

Harsha hesitated.

"Help! Thomas!" she tried to shout but it came out like a strangled gasp, before his hand came over her mouth.

"I could have really fallen for you. We would have made such a good team! What a waste!" There seemed to be genuine regret in his voice.

He dropped her body over the ledge, until it was dangling, her hands beating uselessly in the air. "One word and I'll drop you. Where is it? Don't lie." He uncovered her mouth.

With all her might, she screamed and at the same time, launched herself, twisting from his grasp and flying towards the ledge. His grip had slackened in surprise and the time was enough for her to grip the ledge. Her fingers were sweaty; she did not know how much longer she could hold on.

Harsha began to prise her fingers away, leaning forward to grip her waistband to jerk, when it happened: one moment he was reaching to shove her, the other he was flying through the air, to land like a rag doll on the ground below. Maya was screaming and dangling from the air. She tried to twist her body and jackknife it to grip the wall with her knees, but her body had given up on her and she could only cling to the ledge and shout.

She looked up and Thomas was there, looking shocked, "Maya, what happened?" He hauled her up and she had never felt so good in his embrace as she did at that moment. Her knees gave way, when she was finally in the room and she had to lie down on the floor for some time. Her brain was on overdrive however, so she asked, "Thomas, how did Harsha get there?"

"Harsha? Wha…where?" Thomas leaned over her and looked down and clapped his hand on his mouth. "Oh my God! What happened? I was just outside, near the lift, talking to Surilee about the show." Thomas looked totally bewildered.

"Careful!" She cautioned him. The last thing they wanted was another accident. "How did he get there? One minute I was dangling and he was trying to push me off and the next minute, I swear he went down like he was thrown." Maya was shaking badly. How had Harsha fallen as if he had been pushed when no one was there? Was her mind playing tricks or was that Tulsi's perfume she could smell?

"I thought you were having an argument or something. I wanted to butt in. You've been acting so strange over the last few days, I didn't know what to do. I thought I'd wait for you outside. I never suspected this! What happened?" He held her tightly.

Maya'st hroat hurt and her voice came out in a hoarse whisper, "Thomas, if you knew Harsha and I were having an argument, you could have butted in, whatever the state of our relationship. Anyway, we were OK, that day when we had *chaat*. You wanted him to finish me off, so you could throw him over. Two birds..."

He had turned to get her water so she could only see his back. When he turned, there was a bewildered look on his face. Hand outstretched, he advanced. As she backed away, she continued, "It was always Surilee for you but you had to pretend, first with Tulsi and then with me. You pushed him over just now didn't you? Why, Thomas, why?" Her voice rose and cracked. Tears were pouring down her cheeks but she didn't stop to wipe them.

"The show would cost a lot. Harsha was financing it, wasn't he? You needed him. Did the both of you push Tulsi? Was he blackmailing you because you knew and were silent? Did you sleep with me because he told you to?" She stopped, as sobs tore through her.

"Maya!" Thomas yelled. "Calm down! You are just overwrought. I *never* threw Harsha down. Why would I save you if I wanted him dead? I know nothing about Tulsi and him. Less than you, in fact. All I know is I come in to check out what is happening and next thing I see, Harsha is down there!" Thomas seemed genuinely distraught.

Clever, her paranoid brain screamed. So that's the way he was going to play it: make out that he was a witness so she would need his evidence to prove she did not kill Harsha. What proof did she have anyway, to tie him to this murder or the previous one? Nothing. Perhaps there would never be a way to find out the real truth.

Maya wiped her eyes, wearily, "I'm sorry. Could you please get my address book from my bag? Call Meena. She said she would come. She'll know what to do. I'll tell you everything, when she gets here."

"When who gets here?"

"My partner," she said and closed her eyes. Thomas came over after he had made the call and put his arm around her. She didn't resist. What was the point? He had won and they both knew it.

It was going to be a long night, but hopefully after that, she could sleep.

After the formalities with the police, Meena and Pat waited with Maya to be seen by the doctor. It had been a gruelling evening, but Pat and Meena still had questions.

"What I don't understand is why Tulsi interfered at all. How could she have gotten so involved with a book?" asked Meena.

"You wouldn't ask that question if you had been the one reading *Middle Time,*" said Maya. "It was all real to her. She was dreaming it and so many centuries later, to see the grant unrecognized must have gone against the grain. We will never know. Maybe she never thought he would kill her. She could have genuinely wanted to warn him against making a bad deal. They were friends."

Characteristically, Pat said, "What's a little murder between friends?" Maya turned away, but Meena grinned weakly.

When Pat turned back to Meena, however, she was serious. "Why were you late that day Meena? Poor Maya need not have gone through all that horror."

"Oh God, the dog threw up just as I was running out. I couldn't have just left him!" Meena's voice rose defensively.

"Never mind, Pat, what came later more than made up for it. I don't know how she made the police realize Harsha's death was an accident. Thank God for Meena!" Maya hugged her.

"The moral of the story is, Maya, you never keep secrets from your friends...ever!" admonished Pat.

"Never again!" Maya shuddered.

A strange look passed over Meena's face for a moment. "You know, when I came in, I distinctly smelled that patchouli scent Tulsi used to wear. Have you started using it Maya?"

"I didn't even know what it was. I smelled it too, but only after Harsha slipped and fell." She couldn't tell them her doubts about whether he fell or was pushed; not yet, anyway. She could tell no one. She tried to swallow the sick feeling it gave her.

Pat looked at her and shivered, but said nothing.

"When did you begin to suspect Harsha, Maya? You said on the phone you would tell me everything, remember, when you called to ask about the relevance of the grant to the case, but we never had that conversation," Meena wanted to know.

"I think it was when I saw him flinging money around at the club. I remembered Thomas telling me that Harsha once locked up another dancer to prevent him auditioning for a role they were both interested in. I realized then that he was ruthless and liked money. I also heard that he used to spend time with Tulsi. At first I thought they were seeing each other."

"You told us, remember?" interrupted Pat and Maya nodded.

"Then," Maya went on, "Anees and Toni told me that he was more interested in me! That's when I realized that something else was going on between Tulsi and him. When we had collected all the information about the Ponmudi land, and I had read the fragment, I was sure."

"Fragment? You never told us about this!" Pat exclaimed.

"Oh, yeah! Remember the box in which the book was? I think she kept a bit of a grant in Telugu script. It said that land had been donated to Boriah by Manjuantha, the *matha* head. Dr. Gopalakrishnan had it. Tulsi gave it to him for translation or maybe for safekeeping. That would have given the tenants some ammunition, no? It was a precious document. They could have dragged on the case. Harsha didn't want that, he had collected deposits for the construction, etc.".

"Already?" Meena was amazed.

"You must have been terrified, no?" Pat stroked Maya's back. "That's why she called you with all your criminal law experience and of course your dog had to fall ill just that day." She smiled wryly at Meena.

Meena smiled sheepishly.

"Where was Thomas when all this was happening?" asked Pat, an eyebrow raised.

"Outside, seeing off the students."

"Didn't he hear *anything*?"

"The class is soundproof. That's how Harsha murdered Tulsi."

"Never mind, I'm sure he must have been very sympathetic afterwards, eh? When's the wedding, Maya?" teased Pat.

"Not for a long while, if ever. I don't know, Pat. I can't make up my mind...I need to see if things will still be good between us. After what happened..." Maya trailed off, at a loss for words.

Meena patted her sympathetically. "Let's take it one day at a time, OK?" But over her head, her eyes met Pat's and she grimaced. It looked like that was all the requiem the relationship was going to get.

Pat was stil not done with the mystery, however. "Do you think Manju was a saint after all? That it was a miracle?"

"We don't know otherwise, do we?"

"All I know is that Achale and Thulasi were qualified for sainthood but you can bet they didn't get any recognition!" Maya shrugged.

"Hmmm. Women saints were few and far between and only if they were great poets!" said Meena.

"What about you, Saint Maya?" teased Pat.

"Saint? Not me. Too much *kama*. I've still to go through *dharma* and *artha*. The only *nirvana* for me is in bed."

"Whose bed?" instantly asked Meena. And so, in their shared laughter, Maya was able to forget the horror for a brief while.

Then she remembered. She still needed to know what happened to Achale.

Chapter XXVII

September-October, 1536

The first inkling they had of it was when a man rushed through the streets, shouting, "The Mohammedans are coming, they have reached the town gates, run for your lives!" Achale, Bhima and Ningi went in search of Puttalakshmi. Her father had gone to the palace. He would be safer there than anywhere else.

If the enemy had reached the city gates, there was no time to lose. If she could get everyone to the Jambunatha Konda, they would be safe. They set off by cart, and were soon within sight of the hill with its small shrines to Hanumanta and Anantasayana half way up and Jambunatha on the top. They reached the hill and began to climb. Soon they had reached the Hanumantha shrine and Achale settled her mother and her servants there with instructions to hide behind the rocks if they should see anything. Achale looked at Bhima and Ningi and without a word, they slipped back down the hill and took the cart towards the town. When they reached the centre of Nagalapur, they alighted.

The sounds of fighting were deafening. Huge battering rams like ugly *rakshasas* hurled boulders into the city. The dust from crumbling buildings was everywhere. Elephants ran amok, knocking down buildings and people. O Raya Krishnudu, you built a beautiful city for your queen who was a *devadasi* and see where it is now, thought Ningi. She stepped on something soft and jumped aside when she realized it was the severed arm of a child. A fountain lay on its side, like a drunken lout. Tall palaces lay gaping in astonishment, their crowns about their feet. People were everywhere, mothers and children fled in terror, some with bones protruding from broken limbs. The trumpeting of elephants, the screams of people, the wails of the bereft, the cries of pain, the whinnying of horses and the shouts of *Death to the infidel!* were deafening. One could not even think. The invaders were chasing people through the streets and slaughtering them, but they were still a few streets away and the damage at the centre was from the battering rams. Blood flowed from a destroyed house, where numerous inhabitants lay dying and mingled with a puddle on the street. Achale noticed a flash of white. She picked up a whimpering child, too shocked to even wail, and began to walk towards the figure. Could it be *Ajji* Jakkini? Bhima had taken two scythes and gone to join the citizens resisting the invasion. The air was thick with dust, blood, and something else, perhaps fear.

Ningi was tearing strips of her scarf, uncaring that her upper body was completely uncovered. This was no time to worry about trifles such as modesty. If the soldiers saw them, they would be raped anyway, clothed or not. For what seemed like days but was probably only a few hours, they worked silently, offering water to victims, tying up wounds, moving among the dying, offering comfort. "Look into my eyes, beautiful lady," whispered a young boy, with cracked lips. The glaze of death was already in his eyes, so Achale lifted him up and held his head against her breast, until his head dropped and he was still. Death had frozen the smile on his lips. An old man searched for his son among the wounded and dead. A man who had come on a visit to his sister had lost nine members of his family. Three women, labourers from the look of them, who had come to work on a merchant's house from over the border, near the Nizam's territories, searched for their children, "Boya! Malamma!" they shouted, but no one would be able to hear over the shouts, the screams and explosions. The Mohammeddans had even brought the new-fangled fire sticks of the Portuguese.

The horses' snorts and whinnies came closer. "Quick! Achale, Ningi," Bhima thrust them up a building's stairs, which ended in nothing but provided temporary shelter. They waited until the hoofs had gone on and went back on the street. The horse had dragged its wounded rider and then bolted. "Vajrabahu," breathed Achale, breath leaving her body in horror.

"I have got my kingdom," he smiled, "They are waiting for me. Devi, one token, just one, of your esteem, will speed me on my way." Tears streaming down her face, Achale bent and placed her lips against his bloody mouth. She cradled his head in her lap, until he died. Bhima stood respectfully; head bowed and now took the body, gently lowered it on to the step of a nearby house and closing the eyes, arranged the hand on his chest. There was only one arm.

"Achale, Ningi, we have to go back to Jambunatha Konda. Remaining here will not serve." Bhima did not want to tell them, but the invaders were naturally gaining ground, there was no army to meet them, only a rabble of citizens and nobles. Hordes of people were on the road from Nagalapur. Some were going towards Kadirampuram and some towards Jambunatha Konda. They joined the latter stream. For some time, Achale put one foot forward, then another. Her soul was weary. Poor Vajrabahu, his dreams of kingship mingled in the dust with the boy and the labourer's children. The man who had lost nine family members, how would he rebuild his life?

When they were half-way to the hill, a battalion of soldiers from Hampi passed through the crowd. Weary, battle-scarred as they were, the crowd raised a cheer. When the cavalcade had passed, they resumed their march, but Bhima and Ningi had either fallen back in the confusion caused by the cavalcade's slicing through the crowd, or they had gone on ahead. Achale decided to press on with the crowd. There was some safety in numbers. After they had walked some distance and the hill was clearly visible, she felt a tug on her scarf and saw that Virabhadra was grinning at her. Relief at a familiar face and his remembered strength surged through Achale. She reached into his embrace and for a time they stood thus, while the impatient crowd surged around them. Then, hand in hand, they continued their walk up to the hill.

Bhadrinatha watched Hampi from Malyanta Parvatha. That was the best vantage point for someone who wanted to see the city. He had wanted his goodbye to be like this: with the city he loved spread before him, his beloved Alur visible in the distance and the Pampa River flowing through it all beguiling in the sunlight. The sun was glinting on something else, could that be armour and shields, swords, spears? He was afraid so. This was not a military review but an invasion. Bhadri forced himself to calm his mind. What did such things matter to him now? He had a different purpose. He had decided on *atmaghata*, suicide, to preserve the prosperity and traditions of the temple—to preserve the secret of Manju's birth. Manju would be protected in this world as well as the next, as he had left him all his wordly goods. If the world believed him to be the fruit of an illicit liason, it was still better than the other. The scriptures permitted suicide for *srikarya* or the service of Perumal. The sword glinted in the sunlight, like those below. Sitting in the yogic *padmasana* posture, his palms joined, he meditated on the Lord. Fixing his thoughts on the Lord, he took the sword. One clean sweep, the trunk fell lifeless, the sword no longer glinting.

They sat on the rocks near the temple of Jambunatha, but at the back. There was a breeze, which blew away the stench of battle. She tried to tell Virabhadra what she had seen, down below, but the words died in her mouth. Virabhadra was also silent, reliving the battle, which for him, had been pitched; he and some youths hurled stones, pots, ladles, bricks, even chili powder, at the soldiers below. It had halted abruptly, when the soldiers had found them too irksome and had begun to let off their fire sticks. Then they had joined the crowd going south west.

Achale knew that soon she would have to come up with an answer to his proposal, though that felt as if it had happened in another age. Her body and mind were too involved in the horror below. The old Achale had questioned how free she would be if she married. But attachment with or without marriage created bonds. She realized with a jolt that she did not know how Bhadri had taken the news when Madhava confronted him. It seemed unimportant in the here and now. New images, new urgency filled her being. It was as if the Achale who had investigated Thulasi's death was gone. The scale of the massacre they had just witnessed made even a murder commonplace. Her soul was burdened with the pain of the hundreds of people dying and those they had left behind to mourn. *Ajji* Jakkini was still there, quietly providing succour to those in need. While she, Achale sat here, safe, because of attachment to others.

Long ago, in another life, she had gone down the Pampa with Ningi and had asked why she could not be left alone to love God. She could now look back and laugh at that innocent self who had known nothing of the depth of pain the heart was capable of. But if she had to make sense at all of this senseless life, if she had to continue to live in this topsy-turvy world of power hungry nobles and men of false learning, she would have to walk with God. Kunti's children, born to her as the gifts of the Gods, finally, after much strife, inherited a ghost kingdom. What use ultimately is a house, youth, beauty, fame, even husbands and children? They could be gone in a flash and you would not even have the solace of God, as you had lost the habit of belief, diverting that love to wordly pursuits and attachment to your family. Better to let it all go, before it was too late and she was completely immersed in *samsara*. It was good she had not married or had children. It made easier and less burdensome the path she was choosing now. She would not have to add the pain of regret to her already overburdened soul. Only in serving others could she hope to lessen the burden.

She stood up. "Bhadra, would you give me your loin-cloth and take my sari?" Virabhadra was mystified by this strange request. But if Achale wanted this, she would get it. He took off his *panche* and Achale for a brief moment let herself enjoy the splendid specimen of manhood who stood before her, naked except for a small strip of cloth covering his loins. Achale then removed her garments and it was Virabhadra's turn to gaze awe struck. They exchanged garments and Achale took up his shawl as upper covering. As a blessed respite, it began to drizzle, and then rain. Taking off her jewels, one by one, she laid it on a rock. Achale turned to Virabhadra. "I am going. I have decided to range the world until I find peace like *Ajji* Jakkini and Acharyulu. I am sorry, but I can no longer live the life of a householder of any kind. Please tell Bhima and Ningi to look after my mother and *Ajji* Roopavathi. They will always have a home in my house."

The breath left his body. Virabhadra found himself begging, "Achale, you need not marry me, please let us continue as before!" Achale merely smiled, raised her hands in a salute and continued down the hill.

The upper garment that she had discarded, picked up by the wind, began to fly down with her, until it came to rest on the shoulders of Madhava, who was hurrying up the hill. "Achale, my brave girl! Everyone is talking about your service to the ill and dying. The King has entered into talks with Ibrahim Adil Shah. Anyway, with the rain, they have stopped fighting. I think it is safe to go home and in a few days; time, I have an audience with the King. I would like your views on my poem in his praise."

Achale smiled and began to sing, as with a bemused face, he took in her attire, "Seek Govinda...*Bhaja Govindam...*"

She continued down the hill while Madhava looked on, dumbstruck. "Achale?" it came out as a hoarse whimper but it was loud enough to bring Virabhadra, whose legs had turned to stone till then. Tears mingling, the two men clung together, as love walked out of their world. Halfway down, Achale remembered that she was still wearing earrings. She took them off and searching for a loose rock, placed them in the opening and covered them again. Then she continued on her way, still singing.

Epilogue

October, 1996

October had come, bringing with it the rains. Meena and Pat had jumped at Maya's idea that they visit Hampi. They had spent a wonderful few days exploring the magnificent surroundings. Achale's house was not there, nor was Alur or Jogahalli. There was no Madhavaswamy temple. Perhaps it had all been destroyed later when Hampi was razed to the ground in the battle of Talikota. But the Soolai bazaar was there as was the Queen's Bath. Virupaksheshwara Temple still functioned and they had taken a coracle to trail down the Tungabhadra, tracing Achale's route to work. Now finally, they were on the Sandur hill that housed the temple complex of Jambavateshwara. The shrines of Hanumanta and Anatasayana were long gone.

As they were climbing, Maya was searching for the ruined steps of Achale's time. It was difficult as she had to negotiate large rocks, but somehow, she made it to a niche at one side of the hill. If she was right, it had to be here. It was almost too much to hope for. Perhaps someone else had got to it earlier. She began to work loose the stone, which was wedged in, covering the hole, using her fingers and nails.

Pat and Meena came to investigate, and Meena found a flat stone which Maya could use to pry loose the stone. At last, the stone was loosened. Maya put her hand into the aperture. In the book, Achale had put the earrings here and if Tulsi's dreams could be called real, then she would find them. She put her hand in. Maya's excitement had conveyed itself to Meena and Pat and they were quivering with hope and dread because the whole idea was so strange.

She put her hand in quite far and groped about for some time before she felt something hard. It was just a pebble, and she was about to throw it away when Pat stopped her. She rubbed it with the edge of her shirt and a small gold screw was revealed. Excited and recharged, Maya reached inside again. When she passed her hands over the side, she found them, tucked away under a stone. She took them out, small gold hoops, with little fish dangling from them. At that same moment, the sun came out, and a ray of light shot down on the fish. For a moment, it was as if they had moved.

AUTHOR'S NOTE

Part of the fun of writing historical fiction is the research and the rest, of course, is the recreation. Which parts of the story are based on fact? Achale, her family and friends are made up. But the background is real. The Madras (now Chennai) part of the novel is entirely fictitional, except where physical environs are described, and any reference to a living person is merely coincidental. As far this author knows, there is no *matha* at Ponmudi, which is not a suburb of Chennai. Also, there is no *matha* head called Manjunatha, at least of the Sri Vaishnava persuasion.

I have tried to describe Vijayanagara and its physical environs as accurately as possible. The official Hampi website and the wonderful book, *Hampi Ruins* by A.H. Longhurst, were of great help in siting the various events in the story. I had a fascinating time researching the background to the Achale story. While *The New Cambridge History of India South Asia* special edition on Vijayanagara by Burton Stein formed a sort of ready reference, I read as many different accounts of Vijayangara history as I could get, including K.A. Nilkanta Shastri's *History of South India* and *Forgotten Empire* by Robert Sewell, which gives translated eyewitness accounts by Fernão Nuniz and Domingo Paes, medieval

Portuguese travellers. Legend had firmly established Hampi's claim to fame as the site of certain events from the *Ramayana* as well as the *Mahabharata* and such legendary 'hotspots' are mentioned by Longhurst. Hence the several allusions to Sita and the name Bhima, used for both man and elephant.

The Vijayanagara kings recreated the glory of the old sixth century A.D. Chalukyan kingdoms at Badami and Aihole (in modern Bijapur) at Hampi near modern Hospet, in Karnataka, in medieval times. After the fall of the Hoysalas and Kaktiya kingdoms in their wars with the Delhi Sultanate, notably, Mohammad-bin-Tughlaq, there was a brief interregnum with the rule of the Kampilis at Anegondi, across the river from Hampi. Then, Harihara and Bukka established the first Vijayanagara dynasty, after Kampili Deva Raya fell to the marauding armies of Mohammad-bin-Tughlaq. There were a number of Vijaynagara dynasties: the first were the Sangamas or Yadavas, who ruled from about 1340 till about the late fifteenth century, when Saluva Narasimha, a general, usurped the throne. Within a short time, the third dynasty of the Tuluvas, to which Krishna Deva Raya and Achyuta Deva Raya belonged, came into power at around 1505 and ruled till 1542, when Aliya Rama Raya of the Arividu line established their dynasty and ruled with diminishing authority until the late seventeenth century.

Rama Raya did challenge Krishna Deva Raya's chosen successor, Achyuta Deva Raya's authority in 1529 and again in 1535, as mentioned in the novel. The invasion by the Bahmani Ibrahim Adil Shah of Bijapur is mentioned by several historians, including Sewell. The idol of Vishnu in the Chidamabaram temple was taken to Tirupati for safekeeping and there is a grant recorded in the temple for its restoration in Achyuta Raya's time, but it is not till later and a further grant that the actual restoration took place. Legend has it that Ranga Sani was a courtesan of Simhapuri and did lock horns with Tenali Rama. Kai Dala was a famous sculptor of Hoysala times and the Lepakshi temple was built by the brothers Veeranna and Virapanna. However, Virabhadra is a fictional character.

There was never a poet called Madhava Shastry but Dindima was the court poet and Tenali Rama is a real historical character. Purandara *dasa*, Vyasa *tirtha* and Kanaka *dasa* were contemporaries of Krishna Deva and Achyuta Raya. Annanamacharya pre-dated them. Their songs are popular even today, so this did not present any great difficulty. Acharyulu and *Ajji* Jakkini exist in my mind. I have attempted to quote classical poets like Harsha, Kalidasa and Bhavabhuti by giving the general meaning of their lines.

The story of a widow's son who entered a temple tank and came out wearing a sacred thread is mentioned in the colonial gazetteer, but this happened in Virinchipuram in the eighteenth century. I took the bare bones of that story and transposed Manjunatha and Thulasi's story in Alur onto them.

Acknowledgements

In writing this book, I have been helped by many people. I can get by in Tamil and Kannada, though I cannot read the latter, and I know only a smattering of Telugu. Luckily for me, my husband, S.S. Vasudevan, my sister-in-law Usha Narasimhan and brother-in-law T.M. Narasimhan were very patient with my questions and translated the proverbs as well as the songs.

My agent Mita Kapur of Siyahi read the many different versions of the manuscript and helped a lot with the editing and of course plugged the book successfully in a short while. Many thanks are due to her. Thanks are also due to the team at Niyogi books, who were very responsive and my editor Nandita, whose comments were inspired and illuminating. My nephew T. M. Narendran helped me untangle the philosophy and the Sanskrit poems, for which I am grateful.

This book is therefore a team effort and I thank all those who have helped.